THE SHADOWS OF DOOM

ALSO BY JENNIFER BELL

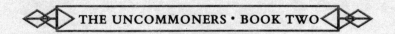

THE UNCOMMONERS · BOOK TWO

THE SHADOWS OF DOOM

JENNIFER BELL

illustrated by

KARL JAMES MOUNTFORD

A Yearling Book

This is a work of fiction. Names, characters, places, and incidents either are the product of the author's imagination or are used fictitiously. Any resemblance to actual persons, living or dead, events, or locales is entirely coincidental.

Text copyright © 2019 by Jennifer Rose Bell
Interior illustrations copyright © 2019 by Karl James Mountford
Cover art copyright © 2019 by Kirbi Fagan

All rights reserved. Published in the United States by Yearling, an imprint of Random House Children's Books, a division of Penguin Random House LLC, New York. Originally published in hardcover in the United States by Crown Books for Young Readers, an imprint of Random House Children's Books, a division of Penguin Random House LLC, New York, in 2019. Originally published as *The Smoking Hourglass* by Penguin Random House U.K., London, in 2017.

Yearling and the jumping horse design are registered trademarks of Penguin Random House LLC.

Visit us on the Web! rhcbooks.com

Educators and librarians, for a variety of teaching tools, visit us at RHTeachersLibrarians.com

Library of Congress Cataloging-in-Publication Data is available upon request.
ISBN 978-0-553-49847-9 (trade) — ISBN 978-0-553-49848-6 (lib. bdg.) —
ISBN 978-0-553-49849-3 (ebook) — ISBN 978-0-553-49850-9 (pbk.)

Printed in the United States of America

10 9 8 7 6 5 4 3 2 1

First Yearling Edition 2020

Random House Children's Books supports the First Amendment and celebrates the right to read.

For Beks, Nichol and Tara.
Uncommon friends.

CHAPTER ONE

Ivy hurtled headfirst through the darkness. Her brown curls blew into her face as the bag walls flapped noisily around her. "Seb!" she shouted. "Are you still there?"

A crack of light appeared in the distance.

About time.

She slowed as the crack grew into an opening, and then squeezed her way out of the burlap bag, her body expanding back to normal size like a balloon filling with water.

She found herself in a small, lavishly furnished room. Moonlight streamed through a single porthole window, illuminating a polished oak desk, leather armchair and deep-pile rug. Leaning against one wall was a boy with pale skin, green eyes just like hers and messy blond hair.

"Seb, where are we?"

Her brother's cheeks bulged. "Can't speak . . . trying not to hurl."

"We're on a ship," answered a shaky voice behind her. "And we're not alone."

Ivy turned to find their friend Valian with an expression of distress on his tan angled face. He was kneeling beside the body of a man wearing a black uniform. The man lay sprawled across the floor, one arm above his head, the other squashed under his side. He looked about the same age as Ivy and Seb's parents—midforties—with a curly blond beard and a white streak of hair through his left eyebrow.

"Is he sleeping?" Ivy asked, crawling closer. The man's eyes were closed. She nudged his shoulder, but he was unresponsive.

Valian lowered his ear to the man's lips, and then felt his neck. "He's not breathing."

"We've got to help him!"

"I don't think we can." Valian lifted his fingers away, swallowing. "He hasn't got a pulse."

Ivy went still. "You mean . . . ?"

"He's dead," Valian said somberly. "He's still warm. It must've happened only recently."

There was a loud bang as Seb bolted through a door, hand clamped over his mouth. Through the gap Ivy glimpsed a white marble bathroom. "Maybe he tripped over the rug and fell," she suggested. As she stood up, the floor swayed. On a tray in the corner a set of whiskey glasses rattled.

Valian frowned. "I don't think so; there's no bump on his head and no blood from a wound." He got to his feet and studied the cabin. Amidst the jeweled lamps and gilt mirrors, his straggly dark hair, slashed skinny jeans and muddy red basketball shoes looked completely out of place. "We need to find out what vessel we're on."

"There's a badge on the man's jacket," Ivy observed. Beneath a logo were some words. *"Chief Officer,"* she read aloud. *"MV* Outlander."

A toilet flushed and the door to the bathroom swung open. Seb wiped his mouth on the sleeve of his hoodie. "Sorry—I couldn't hold it in any longer."

Ivy crinkled her nose as he tramped into the center of the cabin and slipped his cell phone out of his jeans pocket. "Can you just do something helpful?" she asked. "You're the one who made us rush into this whole thing without a proper plan."

Seb glared down at her. "It's an experiment—I was using my initiative. I didn't know there'd be a dead person here." He was broad-shouldered and tall, with the muscular arms of someone who—unfortunately for Ivy—did an hour's drum practice every evening. She didn't know how they were siblings; she was so slight.

Valian peered over Seb's shoulder. "Can that device tell you where we are?"

Ivy still found it odd that Valian knew next to nothing about common technology.

"Hmmm." Seb slid his finger across the phone a few times. "GPS is working, but I'm on a different network operator, so we must be somewhere outside the U.K." His eyes widened. "Whoa. By the looks of this, we're just off the coast of Norway!"

"Norway?" Valian grabbed the burlap bag that Ivy had just crawled out of and snatched at the paper luggage tag tied to the top. He read it twice. "I definitely wrote the label correctly—it says *Selena Grimes*—but what would she be up to in Norway?"

Seb jerked his head. "Er, parent-napping? Blackmail? Torture? The Dirge probably do bad-guy stuff all over the world."

A chill ran through Ivy's body. The Dirge was an organization that was so evil, just hearing their name left her cold. "We don't know for sure that she's here yet. The label might not have worked." Secretly she was hoping it hadn't. Selena Grimes was dangerous. The last time their paths had crossed, Ivy had almost been eaten by Selena's pet wolf. "Perhaps the bag can't take us directly to a person, only to a certain place, like all other uncommon bags?"

"This bag is *different*," Valian insisted. "You know that. The Great Uncommon Good are the five most powerful uncommon objects in existence—I'm telling you, this thing is capable of more than we know."

Ivy considered the shabby old potato sack. It was strange to think that something so ordinary-looking had the power to transport you thousands of miles in only a few seconds. But that was the thing about all uncommon objects—even the most normal, everyday item could be hiding an extraordinary ability.

Seb squinted at the chief officer. "What's that in his hand?"

Ivy turned her attention back to the body. There was something glinting in the man's grasp. Grateful that she was wearing gloves, she gently pried his fingers apart to reveal a tiny silver coin. It was bent in the middle and there was writing around the edge.

"A crooked sixpence," she blurted, scrambling away. She'd recognize the coin anywhere—it was the Dirge's calling card.

"One of the Dirge murdered him," Valian said with a scowl. "The label on the bag *must* have worked; it's too much of a coincidence otherwise. Selena did this."

Seb cast a sidelong glance at the door that led out into the rest of the ship. "Selena must have left the cabin only moments before we arrived. Which means she's on board somewhere, possibly with other members of the Dirge." He grabbed the Great Uncommon Bag off the floor. "You were right; we didn't think this through. Let's get out of here."

Ivy was about to raise an alarm to warn the crew, when the bitter whiff of chemicals wafted into her face, making her blink. "Yuck—where's that smell coming from?"

Valian sniffed and turned his gaze to the crooked sixpence in the chief officer's hand. "Tongueweed," he growled. "I'd know the stench anywhere—the Dirge used it on my parents. It's a poison that makes you speak the truth right before you die. The coin's been coated in it; it must have penetrated the man's skin."

Guilt tugged at Ivy's heart as she thought of Valian's mum and dad. "We can't leave yet," she told Seb. "If we can find out why Selena killed this man and what she's doing here, it could help us understand what the Dirge are planning—and stop them."

"Ivy, it's too dangerous!" Seb protested. "Selena's already killed this guy; if she sees us here, she'll kill us too."

Ivy wanted to tell her brother that he should have thought of that before he started all this, but there wasn't time to argue. "We don't know how long Selena will be on board; we've got to take the opportunity now."

"I've got something that'll help us," Valian said. "I mean,

with the not-being-seen part. Can you find the layout of this ship on your device, Seb? It's called the MV *Outlander*."

With a grunt of disapproval, Seb stuffed the Great Uncommon Bag inside his hoodie pocket and got out his phone. "MV *Outlander*—here we go. It's a cargo ship that sails between Norway and London. There's three levels plus the engine room, and a big crane on the deck where the containers are stored."

Ivy wondered why the Dirge would be interested in a common ship like the MV *Outlander*. "Let's go up on deck," she suggested. "We can examine the containers. Perhaps the cargo will give us clues as to why the Dirge are here."

"Good plan." Valian stuffed a hand inside his leather jacket and brought out a small crystal perfume bottle. It was fitted with an ornate brass atomizer and filled with a small measure of dark liquid. "A ship this big will be teeming with crew. We'll need to use this to keep ourselves hidden." He shook the bottle, checking that there was liquid left in the bottom.

"What *is* that stuff?" Ivy asked, drawing closer.

Valian aimed the brass nozzle at her head. "Technically it's just fountain water inside an uncommon perfume bottle, but most uncommoners call it liquid shadow. It enables the wearer to blend into any shadow they're touching. It won't make us totally invisible, but people tend to notice shadows a whole lot less than they notice actual humans."

Ivy sniffed as the dark liquid fell in droplets on the shoulders of her navy duffle coat and into her hair. It smelled a bit like smoke.

"We'll have an hour before it evaporates and the effect wears off," Valian warned, squirting the stuff over Seb before turning the spray on himself. "Let's go."

They shut the cabin door, leaving the chief officer's body where it lay. The passageway outside, with its curved metal walls covered in rivet heads and gray gloss paint, was like a futuristic tunnel. The unnatural lighting cast shadows everywhere. Ivy stepped into the first one she came upon.

"No way!" Seb whispered, staring right at her. "Ivy, you've disappeared."

She reached forward but couldn't see her hand. She examined her body. There was no skirt, bobbly wool tights or scuffed white sneakers to be seen. They seemed to have dissolved into the gloom. As an experiment, she extended her foot into the light, and a toe-shaped shadow appeared on the floor.

Valian signaled at them both to hurry up. "Come on."

They hastened along the corridor toward the stairs. The hull interior was stark and cramped, and echoed with strange noises. Ivy tried not to dwell on the warning signs everywhere—*fire valve (main section), explosive hazard, life buoy, emergency door.*

She had only just grasped the handrail at the base of the stairwell when the stamp of heavy boots sounded overhead. Valian nosedived into the darkness under the steps, taking Ivy and Seb with him. Ivy flattened herself against the wall, breathing heavily, as a group of sailors in navy uniforms came clattering down.

Incredible. The liquid shadow had worked.

Crewmen shouted orders in another language as they hurried through a heavy door into the next passage. When they were out of sight, Ivy, Seb and Valian left the shadows and scuttled up the steps.

Outside, the night air was filled with the crash and rumble of the ocean. Ivy stood with her legs apart as the ship swayed, her skin prickling in the cold. A string of electric lights rattled in the wind, illuminating the giant metal containers spread out across the deck. They were arranged in rows, with space for people to pass between, but the place seemed eerily empty. Valian pointed to the top of a large crane standing in the middle of them, and they headed toward it.

As they moved into the shadows, Valian and Seb disappeared. Ivy knew they were there somewhere but, unable to see them, she felt alone.

The huge containers were painted in bright colors, with thick steel bars securing the doors and serial numbers stamped on the front. Ivy examined each one carefully as she passed, but there was no clue to what they might hold.

Creeping by a red container, she heard a loud clang and froze. It sounded like something was moving *inside* it. Ivy jumped back as two dark shapes came gliding *through* the corrugated wall. She clamped a hand over her mouth to stop herself from gasping. Only one kind of people could move through solid matter like that: *races of the dead*.

There wasn't enough light to see the pair clearly, but one was very tall with an odd-shaped head, and the other wore a long hooded cloak trimmed with white fur. Checking that she still had the appearance of a shadow, Ivy kept still. The cloaked figure drifted into a patch of moonlight and slid back her hood. A glossy dark braid fell to her waist.

Selena Grimes.

Ivy flinched. The ghoul had the same movie-star good looks as she remembered: glowing skin, angular cheekbones and bright red lips. Selena's dark hair framed her delicate face, making her piercing blue eyes look all the more intense.

"Even with the tongueweed, that fool told us nothing," she snapped. Her steely voice made Ivy shudder. "I should've killed him sooner. Are you certain the Jar of Shadows is on board?"

"The tracing serum I have been using to track it is highly accurate," whistled Selena's companion. The voice sounded as if the owner was talking through a set of panpipes. "The jar is definitely on this ship; I would not have contacted you otherwise."

The speaker stepped out of the darkness. He looked like a human-sized praying mantis, with smooth green skin and a flat, triangular head mounted with two glowing yellow eyes the size of salad bowls. Sharp mandibles hung from his jaw, and Ivy counted a total of six stick-thin limbs protruding from his tailored emerald wool suit: two that he was using as legs; another four that were adapted into arms with thorny, clawed hands. The arches of silky green wings poked above his shoulder blades.

Ivy recoiled in horror. She wasn't sure what race of the dead he was; he certainly wasn't a ghoul like Selena.

"I will continue searching the cargo until the vessel docks," he pledged. "The ship is scheduled to arrive in London in the early hours."

"London?" Selena's eyebrows rose in surprise. "But that's perfect. Lundinor opens for spring Trade tomorrow; someone must be taking the jar there." She smirked. "They have no idea that the object has Pandora's power. Wait till the ship unloads, then hunt for the jar in Lundinor. And do it quickly."

Mantis Man lowered his head. "As you wish, Wolfsbane."

Ivy shivered. Wolfsbane was Selena's code name. The other members of the Dirge—Ragwort, Blackclaw, Nightshade, Hemlock and Monkshood—were named after poisons too.

"And contact me again with any news," Selena continued. "It is imperative that I get hold of the jar as soon as possible. There is no time to waste." She removed one of her black satin gloves and examined her fingers. The skin on her hand was scabbed and rotting, oozing with yellow pus. Ivy looked away in disgust. "The Dirge's age in the light is coming." Selena flicked a maggot off her knuckles. "Soon it is the muckers who will understand what it's like to live in darkness."

Ivy wasn't sure what Selena Grimes meant, but it couldn't be good. *Mucker* came from the expression "common as muck." It was the horrible slang term for commoners—people who, by blood, weren't entitled to know anything about the uncommon world.

All of a sudden something hit her on the arm and she squeaked in shock. Seb was standing beside her, Valian a little way behind him. An angry hiss filled the air, making the hairs on the back of Ivy's neck stand on end.

"Spies," Mantis Man growled, his antennae clicking.

The liquid shadow had worn off.

Selena shouted, *"Get them!"*

With a great *whoosh,* Mantis Man extended his wings and rose into the air as Selena shot in Ivy's direction.

Ivy ran, her feet hammering across the deck. Sprinting

ahead, Valian turned down the next aisle. Ivy raced after him and almost collided with Seb.

"Keep going!" he cried, pumping his arms. "The bug guy is right behind us."

They could hear the ominous beat of wings overhead. Seb snatched the Great Uncommon Bag out of his hoodie and whispered something into the opening.

"Throw it here," Valian yelled.

Seb lobbed the bag, and Valian caught it in one hand before skidding to a halt by the ship's rail. The sea beyond was black. "We have to jump," he told them, panting. "Trust me." Using one hand for support, he hurdled the bar and leaped over the edge.

Seb shoved Ivy forward. "Ivy—go!"

Scrambling up onto the rails, she snuck a look over her shoulder. Selena Grimes and Mantis Man were almost upon them. Inhaling a great lungful of air, she jumped into the waves.

Her limbs flailed. She spied the Great Uncommon Bag fluttering just out of reach, the heels of Valian's red basketball shoes disappearing inside.

"I-veeeeeeee!" Seb called, falling behind her.

Wind screamed in her ears as she forced her arms down and aimed her head at the opening, diving into the bag.

CHAPTER TWO

I vy adjusted the desk lamp to see the wound on Seb's forehead more clearly. The scratch wasn't very deep, but the skin around the edge was puckered and red. "That Mantis Man must have caught you in midair before you got inside the bag," she said, patting the graze with a damp cotton ball. "Do you think he's Selena's new henchman?"

Seb gripped the edge of the table, wincing. "Got to be; I didn't see her pet grim-wolf with her." His voice echoed up to the high ceiling of their dad's office at the Victoria and Albert Museum. The room was stuffed with more reading material than a small library: string-tied bundles of academic journals packed the windowsills and never-ending volumes of encyclopedias filled the shelves. In one corner an old microscope sat on a desk, and on a table in the center, a brass desk plate gleamed with the words EMMET SPARROW, RESEARCH DEPARTMENT.

"Make sure the wound's clean," Valian advised, standing guard by the door. The hallway beyond was dark. "I've never seen a race of the dead like that before, so I don't know if that guy had venomous skin or not."

Seb's face fell. "Sorry . . . venomous skin?"

Ivy stuck a Band-Aid over his wound, threw the used cotton ball into a wastepaper bin and closed the first-aid kit. As she returned the box to the window ledge, a lone black cab rumbled past on the puddled road outside. Only an hour and a half had passed since eleven p.m., when they'd left in the Great Uncommon Bag; London was quiet.

She sat down on her dad's chair; his sweater was slung over the back. An image of the chief officer's dead body crept into her mind and she pulled the sweater onto her lap and squeezed it tightly, wishing her dad was there.

Valian hurried away from the door. "Quick—get down!"

Light flickered out in the hallway. Seb rolled onto the floor and Ivy slid under the table as a flashlight beam illuminated the room. It moved slowly across the walls and then, after a few seconds, disappeared—along with the sound of fading footsteps.

"We can't stay here," Ivy whispered, wriggling back into the chair. "If a security guard sees us, we won't be able to explain how we got in."

Seb poked his head up. "The only reason I told the bag to bring us here is because Dad's books might help us understand what Selena Grimes was saying. You know—about that *Jar of Shadows*." He asked Valian, "Does the name mean anything to you?"

"No, but I've got an idea what it might be." Valian's

expression darkened. "A name like the Jar of Shadows suggests it's a one-of-a-kind object; and we already know five one-of-a-kind objects that the Dirge are interested in."

A bead of sweat ran down Seb's forehead as he pushed the tatty Great Uncommon Bag into the center of the table. "You mean, you think the Jar of Shadows is like this, one of the Great Uncommon Good?"

Ivy shifted in her seat. If the Dirge ever got hold of one of the Great Uncommon Good, everyone—uncommoner or not—would be in danger. "What do uncommon jars do?" she asked Valian.

"They store *fears*," he told her with a tremble in his voice. "If you cry into an uncommon jar, your greatest fear leaves you and remains in the jar until it is opened again. Uncommoners use them as a way of dealing with phobias. The more powerful the jar, the greater the number of fears it can hold."

"Right . . . so why would the Dirge want one?" Seb asked. "They don't exactly seem the scared type."

"Maybe not," Valian replied. "But I once saw a commoner break a jar by accident. It must have contained a fear of falling because after it shattered, a gigantic chasm appeared in the ground and the man dropped right into it."

Ivy had a hollow feeling in the pit of her stomach. "So you're saying that maybe the Dirge don't want to *store* a fear at all; they want to *release* one. . . ." She drummed her fingers on the table. "Maybe not *just* one . . . If the Jar of Shadows really *is* one of the Great Uncommon Good, there must be a huge number of fears inside it. Didn't Selena say something about the jar having *Pandora's power*?"

"Yeah, but I've only heard of one Pandora before," Seb said, "and she had a *box*."

Ivy vaguely recalled her dad telling her the story of Pandora; it was from Greek mythology. She scanned the bookshelves until she spotted a volume titled *The Greek Myths*. Opening the book on the table, she skimmed the contents before turning to the right chapter. "Here we go—Zeus created the first woman on Earth and named her Pandora. He gave her a box that, when she opened it, released all evil into the world."

"Great gift, Zeus," Seb muttered drily. "Does it mention anything about Pandora's power?"

As Ivy read ahead, a cold sensation swept over her. "No, but according to this, over thousands of years the myth has been mistranslated. In the original story, Pandora isn't given a box at all. . . ." Her hand started to shake. She looked up at Seb and Valian. "She's given a *jar*. The Jar of Shadows and Pandora's box are the same thing!" She traced her finger across the text. "When Pandora opened the jar, it released *sickness that brings death to men and myriad other pains*."

Seb smiled thinly. "Fun times, then."

"Sounds like the Jar of Shadows contains all the fears of the world," Valian said. "We've got to stop the Dirge from getting hold of it."

"Great," Seb huffed. "It's just our luck that we're heading back to Lundinor at the same time as the jar. What's the plan?"

The name *Lundinor* drifted through Ivy's head like a secret password. It felt like only yesterday that she and Seb were wandering the cobbled streets of the gigantic underground market, staring wide-eyed at all the uncommon objects for sale. "Valian, shall we meet you there?"

He nodded. "I'll see what I can discover beforehand. If I can find out who is importing the jar, we can narrow our search in Lundinor. There can't be many traders that use the MV *Outlander*. I'll take the Great Uncommon Bag to the Scouts' Union in Edinburgh—it's where scouts from all over the U.K. meet; it'll be the best place to find out. In the meantime, make sure you keep out of Selena's way."

Ivy could feel the cold hands of danger on her shoulders. "I wonder why she hasn't followed us here already."

"Too much of a risk," Valian said with certainty. "Seb, you remember what you told me a few days ago?"

For the past few months, while they'd been at school, Seb and Ivy had been communicating with Valian using uncommon feathers.

"What, that the Ripz have just released their new album?"

Valian's expression went blank. "No. The other thing— about seeing an underguard on the way to school."

"Oh." Seb smiled awkwardly. "Yeah—I thought it looked like an underguard uniform. I tried to follow him, but he disappeared."

Ivy had seen one too. Or so she thought. If underguards showed up in the common world, it was usually bad news.

"Well, since you left Lundinor last winter, I think the underguards have been monitoring you," Valian explained. "It makes sense that they'd want to check up on you, what with your family history . . . No offense."

Seb sighed. "None taken. Our great-grandfather was in the Dirge; we can't ignore it."

"*And* our great-uncle," Ivy added in a small voice. She wished they *could* ignore it or, even better, that it wasn't true. Living with the knowledge that Blackclaw and Ragwort were her relatives was so painful.

"Thing is," Valian continued, "Selena won't risk coming after you herself, not with the underguard likely to spot her and ask questions."

"So what do we do when we get to Lundinor?" Seb asked. "I mean, apart from trying not to be killed by Selena Grimes and her giant bug servant."

"Keep your eyes open," Valian replied, "and listen for anything that might be useful. We need to locate that jar."

"If we find it, we can't destroy it," Ivy told them. "That'll just release the fears inside. We'll have to think of something else."

"Great," Seb moaned. "Low chance of success, high risk of mortal danger. What's not to love about this plan?"

"There's one small trip I need to make first," Valian said, his dark eyes shining. "Now that we know that the bag can take us to an actual person, I figured . . ."

Rosie, Ivy thought. Valian was going to see whether the bag could find his missing little sister in the same way it had found Selena Grimes. "Good luck," she offered with a hopeful smile.

"Thanks." Valian pulled a few short brown feathers out of his jacket pocket. "Here—take some of these in case you need to contact me. When you get to Lundinor, keep to the busy areas and don't go anywhere on your own. Selena will be waiting for you to slip up. Don't give her a chance."

CHAPTER THREE

"Are you sure about this, Granma?" Seb asked, tugging on the straps of his rucksack. "It doesn't look like there'd be an entrance to Lundinor hidden around here."

Ivy peered up and down the quiet residential street that Granma Sylvie had led them to, only a ten-minute train ride from their London home. It seemed totally ordinary: a row of brick houses with gravel driveways and, on the opposite side, a long wooden fence. As there were no buildings peeping over the top, Ivy assumed that this backed onto railway tracks or undeveloped land.

Granma Sylvie's heels clicked along the pavement. "I agree it seems unlikely." Her long silvery hair had been swept back into a neat bun and she was wearing a fitted velvet jacket and wide-leg palazzo trousers. She looked smarter than usual, as if she was on her way to a job interview. "However, I asked Ethel to repeat the instructions three times and we're definitely in the right place. There should be a gate farther along."

Hearing that Ethel Dread had been involved, Ivy felt more at ease. Granma Sylvie's long-lost best friend was the proprietor of the House of Bells in Lundinor, and more steely-eyed and streetwise than any other trader Ivy had met. "Did Ethel say why we're not using bag travel like last time?"

Granma Sylvie stiffened. "Apparently there are restrictions on gaining access to Lundinor this season. You need a special permit to travel via uncommon bag; otherwise you have to pass through an entrance like this."

Restrictions . . . ? Ivy studied her granma's expression to see if she knew more than she was letting on, but Granma Sylvie's hard mouth and twitchy eyes only showed that she was nervous. Ivy didn't blame her. Returning to Lundinor in the shadow of their dark family history would never be easy.

Granma Sylvie stopped by an unlocked gate in the fence. "This must be the one." She inched the gate open and the three of them slipped through. On the other side was a huge over-grown field of gardens, dewy and flattened after last night's rain. Plots of freshly turned earth sat alongside beds of bushy green cauliflowers and red cabbages. Wild bluebells swayed among the weeds at its edge.

Seb dodged an overturned plant pot. "Maybe the entrance is disguised to stop commoners from discovering it."

Ivy rubbed her nose—the air stank of compost, making it twitch. She searched into the distance. There were a few people tending to plants or digging soil, but the place seemed very quiet. "Either that or underguards are continuously stripping commoners' memories to make them forget what they've seen," she suggested. She had an unpleasant flashback of her parents having their minds wiped by uncommon whistles, and shook her head clear. Thank goodness they were on holiday this week, celebrating their wedding anniversary. At least they'd be safe.

"Why *have* the underguard summoned you back, anyway?" Seb asked Granma Sylvie.

She squared her shoulders. "It appears that as I'm the only member of the Wrench family known to be alive, I have inherited the entire family estate. The underguard told me I must be present while they catalog everything, before I can formally claim it."

"Sounds boring," he commented, flashing Ivy a sidelong glance. "Will we get to see you much while we're there, or will you be too busy sorting that out?"

Granma Sylvie adjusted her handbag shakily. "I don't know. I haven't met any of these . . . *underguards,* but the tone of their communications hasn't exactly been friendly. Can either of you see this entrance? Ethel said we'd spot it easily."

As they tramped farther in, Ivy searched for anything that might be out of place, but the gardens seemed quite ordinary.

"I must have known about this entrance when I was younger," Granma Sylvie said. "I'm sure Ethel feels strange having to explain it all to me again; thank goodness I have her to help."

"We're still learning too," Ivy said, offering her a sympathetic smile.

Granma Sylvie ran a hand through Ivy's messy hair. "I

know. It would just be a whole lot less frustrating if my memories returned in one go. Instead, moments of my old life trickle back without warning."

Ivy studied her closely. "Have you had any other memories return?"

Granma Sylvie's expression darkened. For a second Ivy thought she wasn't going to say anything, but eventually she sighed and admitted, "Something came back to me a few days ago. . . . It's complicated."

Ivy shot Seb a nervous look. The last time Granma Sylvie remembered something from her time in Lundinor, it had proved to be so significant, it had helped Ivy and Seb to rescue their parents.

"The details are still hazy," Granma Sylvie continued, "but I recall a large black door. I'm not quite sure where it is, or what's around it, but it felt very familiar, as if I'd seen it many, many times."

A door . . . Ivy ran through the possibilities in her head. Lundinor was the size of a city; this door could be anywhere.

"Painted across the front of the door was a symbol." Granma Sylvie rummaged through her handbag for a notepad and pen, scribbled something down and held it up. "There. It's like a figure eight, with a flat base and a flat top."

Ivy considered the drawing carefully. "Like an hourglass." Her mum used a timer that shape when boiling eggs.

"I thought so too," Granma Sylvie agreed. "But there was something really odd about the symbol; it appeared to be *smoking*—as if it had been drawn on with acid that was burning through the door." Her voice hardened. "And when the door opened, Selena Grimes was standing on the other side."

"Do you have any idea what it means?" Seb asked. "What Selena's doing there?"

Granma Sylvie fiddled nervously with the scrap of paper. "Something to do with the Dirge, maybe. We know my father was a member; I suppose I can't dismiss the possibility that I too was involved somehow."

Ivy's eyes widened as she heard the doubt in Granma Sylvie's voice. There was no way *she* had ever been complicit in her father's horrific crimes!

A black door. A smoking hourglass. If Ivy could find out how they were connected to Selena Grimes, she might be able to put her granma's mind at rest *and* learn more about their enemy. They had to try everything to stop Selena from finding the Jar of Shadows.

"Why do you think it's come back to you now?" Seb questioned.

"The night before the memory returned I received a featherlight from the underguard, summoning me back to Lundinor," Granma Sylvie replied. "When I woke the next morning, that black door was in my head."

Seb took the piece of paper from her to examine the hourglass symbol. "Do you think Valian'll recognize this?"

"I've got a better idea." Ivy opened her satchel and pulled out a stainless-steel bicycle bell. There was a deep groove cut into the top, as if it had been damaged in a nasty cycling accident. She smiled as she flicked the lever on its side.

"Mornings to Ivy!" the bell declared in a ting-a-ling voice. It sounded high-pitched and breathless, like an excited child.

"Scratch!" Ivy hugged him close. Sometimes it was easy to forget that Scratch was an uncommon bell and not her best friend. "Do you know anything about a black door painted with a smoking hourglass?" She didn't add a question about the Jar of Shadows; Scratch had been with her on the MV *Outlander*—if he knew something, he would have said.

Scratch trilled. "If the black door smokings, know hourglass not," he told her sadly. "But Lundinor to be goings and there are of investigations. Askings you can at the Timbermeal."

Seb raised his hands. "All right, Yoda. Slow down. What's the *Timbermeal*?"

Ivy patted Scratch sympathetically. Like all other uncommon bells, he could speak, but the damage to his surface caused him to talk in a strange order—"back to fronted," he called it.

"Always what is with a *Yoda*?" Scratch asked, frustrated.

Seb smirked and shook his head. "Scratch, when we get back from Lundinor I'll tell you all about Yoda—promise."

Granma Sylvie put a finger to her lips. "You know, Ethel mentioned this *Timbermeal*. It's some sort of traditional celebration at the opening of spring Trade. All uncommoners have to attend at one time during the day."

All uncommoners . . .

Ivy thought of Selena Grimes. If everyone was going to be at the Timbermeal, it could provide an opportunity to spy on her; she might lead them to the Jar of Shadows or the black door. Whispering thank you to Scratch, she stashed him back in her satchel and fastened it tight. "Have you talked to Ethel about what this new memory could mean?"

Granma Sylvie sighed as she stuffed the hourglass drawing into her jacket pocket. "Not yet. We're still getting to know each other; I don't want to worry her."

Ivy didn't press it any further. She guessed it must be a

tricky situation for them both: Ethel's best friend had returned after more than forty years, only to have no memory of their friendship.

Granma Sylvie came to a halt by a trellis covered in sweet peas. Ivy peered around it and saw a small orange potting shed. The shed itself looked ordinary, but the long line of people waiting outside didn't. A muscular man in frilly breeches and samurai armor stood in front of a scrawny boy in a cravat and Hawaiian shorts. Behind them were a couple of women in gold-edged pink saris, narrow-cut trousers and espadrilles. Ivy counted one firefighter's uniform, four pom-pom hats, two pairs of intricately embroidered lederhosen and at least three clown outfits on display.

"Ladies and gentlemen, we have a winner," Seb said drily. "There's only one kind of people who dress like that."

"Uncommoners," Ivy breathed.

The door to the potting shed swung open and, as the three of them watched, a blond lady in a yellow beret, chef's jacket and tennis skirt strutted in, and shut the door behind her. There was a series of loud noises—a rattle, some shouting and what sounded like a small explosion—and then the door reopened and the next person in line went in.

Granma Sylvie, Ivy and Seb looked at one another nervously as they shuffled to the end of the line. The other traders, who were chatting quietly among themselves, took no notice.

"I guess I'd better put these on now," Granma Sylvie said, withdrawing a pair of long lace gloves from her handbag as they reached the front of the line. *"Like all uncommoners, you must wear your uncommon gloves inside the Great Gates of Lundinor,"* she recited in a tight voice. "Officer Smokehart sent me six featherlights this week explaining the rules of GUT law. He thinks I'm either a criminal or an idiot!"

Ivy grimaced. If any single member of the underguard had it in for their family, it was Smokehart. After a moment's thought she took out the short white dress gloves folded inside her satchel.

As she pulled them on, she admired the neat pin-tuck creases ironed into the knuckles. She wasn't quite sure how to be an uncommoner just yet, but at least the gloves made her feel more like one on the outside. Seb hadn't yet "taken the glove," as it was called. He was old enough, but he still needed the permission of a quartermaster. On their last visit she had seen children in Lundinor without gloves; at least Seb wasn't the only one.

"If you wear those gloves the whole time we're in Lundinor, won't your whispering abilities drive you crazy?" he asked.

Ivy flexed her gloved fingers and felt a familiar prickly heat spread through her skin. She had the same reaction when she touched any uncommon object. She was a *whisperer*—a person with the rare gift to sense the very thing that made uncommon objects special: the sliver of human soul trapped inside them. "I thought so too at first," she told him, "but the warm sensation will fade in a minute or so. I've tested the gloves before."

She raised one glove to her ear and listened for the sounds coming from inside. The voices of trapped souls were too indistinct for her to hear what they were actually saying, but she could normally sense their presence.

"You all right?" Seb asked, watching her.

Ivy pursed her lips. Her capabilities had been changing recently. . . . "Can you hold these for a sec?" She took off her gloves and handed them over, then closed her eyes and tried to concentrate on the noises around her—the drone of insects whizzing through the gardens, the twitter of birds in the bordering trees, the rumble of distant traffic . . .

But at the very edge of her hearing she could discern something else: a shrill voice, like a marble rattling around in a jar. Ivy focused on it carefully. It was coming from the fragment of soul trapped inside the gloves.

She opened her eyes. "That settles it," she decided, taking the gloves back. "There's definitely something new going on with my whispering. Normally I have to be touching an uncommon object to hear the noises inside it, but recently I've been able to hear them without having any contact at all."

Seb's brow furrowed. "Could it be getting stronger?"

"I don't know. Maybe there's someone in Lundinor I can ask." It would be risky. Whispering was a dangerous gift, especially now that the Dirge had returned: in the past they had kidnapped people like her and made them sort through mountains of rubbish, searching for uncommon objects.

The potting shed door sprang open with a crash. Granma Sylvie flinched. "We're next."

A man in polished boots and a black uniform was standing to attention inside. He wore a purple visor, and there were silver braid epaulettes on his shoulders; on the lapels of his dark jacket were embroidered the letters *SB*.

Special Branch. These were members of the underguard whose job it was to prevent commoners from discovering the existence of the uncommon world.

The underguard took one look at Ivy and sniffed. "Gloved traders must shake my hand."

Ivy blinked. She hadn't expected to have to use her gloves so soon. Seb twiddled his bare thumbs while she and Granma Sylvie obliged. The underguard had such a firm grip, Ivy considered whether he might be a race of the dead. Some looked so much like the living.

"Very well," he announced. "You may take a sack each."

A sack? Ivy cast her eyes around the shed. In the corner lay a pile of plastic garden-waste sacks, and at least ten green hoses were looped over hooks on the wall. As she headed toward the pile, something stopped her in her tracks. Pinned to the back of the shed door was a poster:

WANTED
—Jack-in-the-Green—
Uncommon assassin (dead: a gobble)
guilty of murder on six continents.

Master of disguise. **Extremely dangerous.**

Reward for information as to his whereabouts:
objects to the value of **1,000 grade**

An artist's drawing showed a tall creature with a hard green body, huge yellow eyes and razor-sharp clawed hands.

Selena's henchman. Not all the details in the drawing were accurate—but it was definitely the same person. Ivy had never heard of a gobble before. She went cold.

Seb tripped as he caught sight of the drawing. "Ah—who is . . . ? I mean, what's that doing there?"

"Just a precaution." The underguard sounded like he'd had to explain the poster more than once already that morning. "There have been several recent sightings of Jack-in-the-Green in other undermarts. We're on high alert to prevent him from entering Lundinor. That's why it's important you attend the Timbermeal as soon as you arrive. We need to register you there too."

Jack-in-the-Green . . . That explained the restrictions, then.

Granma Sylvie held a hand to her chest. "I'm sorry—high alert?" She stepped closer to the poster, reading it in more detail.

Ivy tried to think quickly. They couldn't give Granma Sylvie the chance to reconsider—she and Seb *had* to go to Lundinor to find the Jar of Shadows.

"I don't have all day," the underguard said, nodding toward the pile. "Sack. Now."

Ivy hastily bent down and picked up a sack. She half expected it to be uncommon, but when it grazed her arm, her skin remained cool.

The underguard went over to one of the hoses and began to pull it loose. The shed trembled as a rattling sound filled the air. Ivy soon understood why: there weren't several hoses hanging up; there was just one *very, very long* hose.

As the underguard tugged it down, the rubber uncoiled like a huge snake dragging its belly around every hook on the walls.

"Stand back," the man warned, pulling down his visor. He pointed the end of the hose toward the wooden floor and bent his knees, bracing himself. With a tiny click, he twisted the nozzle at the end—

The hose shot through the shed floor like a bullet, splintering the wood with a startlingly loud crack and burying itself deep in the earth. Ivy steadied herself against the wall as more and more of the hose disappeared underground. After a few moments the Special Branch underguard got out a penknife and leaped onto the remaining coil, wrestling with it till he was able to slice through it. The severed end flew out of his hand, stretched to the size of a toy hula hoop and lay down on the floor, forming the entrance to a dark hole.

"Off you go, then," the underguard said, pushing up his visor and wiping his brow. "Put the sack down first before you get inside."

Granma Sylvie stared first at the hole and then back at the WANTED poster. Seb looked confused.

"Come on, keep it moving," the underguard groaned, putting away his penknife. "For security reasons, the hose will disappear once the three of you are down."

Ivy studied the dark circle in the floor. It looked a bit like the entrance to a waterslide.

I wonder . . .

She ventured forward, swinging her satchel around to her back. "I'll go first," she said. If Seb wasn't going to volunteer, then it was up to her.

"Ivy, be careful," Granma Sylvie warned, stumbling forward. "I'm not sure if . . ."

Ivy laid her sack on the edge of the dark hole and tucked her legs inside. "I'll be fine," she said in as confident a voice as she could muster. "I'll see you at the other end."

It's just a slide, she told herself. *I used to love slides when I was little.*

She looked over her shoulder and gave Seb and Granma Sylvie a wobbly smile before pushing off with her hands. She slipped forward, the sack gliding easily over the rubber, and then plunged into darkness.

"Whoooooooa!" The hose spiraled left and right, throwing Ivy's body from side to side. She fumbled for the edge of the sack, desperately trying to keep her balance. The air hummed as she slid faster and faster.

The wind forced tears from her eyes as a smile broke across her face. She hadn't felt this exhilarated since the time she'd used an uncommon belt to fly up an old elevator shaft.

Soon, there was a glow of light ahead of her, and a rumble of voices grew louder—until the rubber walls fell away and Ivy found herself gliding down a polished wooden slide that spiraled around a white tower. Below her, she recognized the main arrivals chamber in Lundinor, with its toppling stacks of luggage and busy unloading areas. She got a warm feeling inside as she spied the details from her last visit: the ceiling dripping with glittering stalactites, the traders buzzing with a thousand different conversations as they arrived from all over the world.

She slowed as she reached the bottom of the slide, where another underguard from Special Branch was waiting to collect her sack. She hit the ground with a dull thud, her bottom taking most of the impact, then struggled to her feet.

"Hurry up," the man said. "The next one'll be along soon."

Ivy staggered forward, trying to get her bearings. Those last few turns had left her feeling dizzy. She turned to study the slide. The white tower she had descended was shaped like an upside-down ice cream cone and painted with red stripes like a lighthouse. Ivy thought she'd seen something like it at the end of Brighton Pier—an old-fashioned fairground ride called a helter skelter.

Odd. She could swear it hadn't been in the arrivals chamber before.

She scanned the crowd. Traders greeted one another while smoothing lapels, fluffing out skirts and adjusting hats, making sure their Hobsmatch was looking its best. Dark patches of underguard uniform were dotted around like blackspot on a rosebush. Ivy assumed they were checking for Jack-in-the-Green.

In the distance, she recognized the Great Gates that marked the entrance to Lundinor. Their hinges were mounted into two stone figures who represented the founding traders of Lundinor—Lady Citron, a woman with a wide-skirted dress patterned with lemons, and Sir Clement, a stately gentleman wearing a garland of oranges around his neck.

Ivy squinted at the statue of Sir Clement. Before, she had been able to see his face clearly, but now a series of tiny dark cracks ran over it. She looked at his hand, which rested on a cane covered with . . .

Hang on.

Ivy rubbed her eyes, worried she was seeing things.

They're not cracks.

The statue was now covered by a climbing plant. Thick, glossy green leaves sprouted off the branches as they looped their way around Sir Clement's body.

Ivy didn't understand how it was possible. She'd never seen any plants in Lundinor before; it was underground—there was no sunlight for anything to grow. Her eyes followed the plant as it coiled down Sir Clement's cane and crawled over his feet and along the stone floor into the tunnel between the Great Gates.

Oh my . . .

A dazzlingly green lawn spread across the tunnel floor, and the walls and ceiling were almost obscured by branches that were heavy with purple blossoms. Ivy's jaw dropped. The last time she had seen the tunnel it had been dusty and bare.

Spring had come to Lundinor.

CHAPTER FOUR

I vy clutched her satchel to her chest as she squeezed through the crowd. The heat was stifling, and the roar of conversation made it hard to hear Seb and Granma Sylvie behind her.

"'Scuse me, ladies and gents, coming through!" called a voice.

Ivy turned. A man wearing a bicycle helmet, flowery board shorts and a red kimono was maneuvering his way toward her, holding one arm above his head. "Can't let go of these or chaos will break loose."

When Ivy looked up, she saw a cluster of transparent balloons bobbing from the ribbons in his hand. Inside each one was a swirling rainbow-colored gas. She spotted a price tag hanging from one of the necks: *2.2 grade*. They couldn't be that powerful, then. The scale for uncommon objects went up to ten, and Ivy knew there were only five objects with that value:

the Great Uncommon Good. She tingled to think that she had used one of them—the Great Uncommon Bag.

Granma Sylvie gave the balloon trader a wary look and leaned closer to Ivy's ear. "Was it this busy last time?"

"No, but Seb and I weren't here on the first day of Trade before." Ivy shuffled forward. Even for someone as small as her, it was difficult to move.

"This might be rush hour in the Great Cavern," Seb suggested from behind. "We should head for the Market Cross; there's always loads of space there."

Ivy lifted an eyebrow. *Sometimes* her brother actually had good ideas. The Market Cross was the meeting point of the four main roads through Lundinor, each one leading to a particular quarter of the undermart. On her last visit, Ivy had seen the East End and the Great Cavern; the West End and the Dead End she had yet to explore, though she knew that each quarter was very different.

She stepped up onto a crate beside the road and peered out at the river of people trudging down the Gauntlet, the main road through the Great Cavern. It was busy, as usual, with traders frantically unpacking goods and setting up shop, ready for the start of Trade at midday . . . but it looked nothing like the Lundinor that Ivy remembered.

Smart gray-brick houses and shadowy cobbled streets had been replaced by lush green fields scattered with crocuses, tents and wooden stalls. The Gauntlet—now a muddy, tree-lined avenue—was flanked by thatched-cottage shops with picket fences and antique vans selling fast food. Everywhere Ivy turned she saw bobbing lanterns and colored flags waving to get her attention. It was like they'd walked into a massive

34

underground festival. The air even smelled of a combination of fried onions and freshly cut grass.

"I don't understand how they've made it so sunny when we're miles underground," Granma Sylvie said as Ivy stepped down.

"Beach towels," Seb said, pointing above his head. "See?"

During their last visit the cave ceiling had been veiled in shadow. Now a canopy of neon-colored towels were suspended between the jagged brown stalactites, glittering like scales on the belly of a fish. Each one radiated light.

As they plodded on, Ivy eyed the various objects cradled in people's arms or poking from the tops of their carts and bags. The Jar of Shadows could easily be among them.

She spied with interest several handwritten signs hanging in shop windows:

Entry by Appointment Only

THIS SHOP IS GUARDED AT NIGHT

Ivy had no recollection of seeing anything like that before. She studied the nearby stalls and carts. The phrase *Beware: this vendor station is alarmed* appeared on several chalkboards.

"Seems a bit less friendly than last time," Seb commented. "Like everyone's nervous about something."

Ivy tuned in to the buzz of gossip, hoping it might reveal more.

"Four grade 'e's trying to flog 'em for! Good luck. I know a lot of folks 'oo won't even be coming this season."

"Come on, quick! The Timbermeal will 'ave started by now."

"I 'eard it almost got canceled. You know, because of Jack-in-the-Green. If 'e's been seen, it can only mean one thing."

Ivy only caught fragments of conversation, but the trader's mention of Jack-in-the-Green made her shiver.

At the Market Cross, the stone courtyard had been transformed into a vast village green, complete with bandstand. An area in the center of the grass was sectioned off by a wicker fence, and a group of underguards with tricorne hats were stationed outside, checking off the names of those lining up to get in.

"*Alexander!*" a voice boomed.

Ivy stumbled aside as a burly, broad-chested man with a thick beard plodded past her.

"Slow down or you'll make fools of us both." There was an American twang in the man's deep voice. "I don't see anyone else here running. Do you?"

A skinny boy in smart gray trousers, antique leather gym shoes and a colorful tasseled waistcoat was hurrying ahead of him. They both had the same fiery orange hair.

"Sorry, Pa," the boy said with a similar accent, slowing immediately.

"You *will* be sorry if you ruin this for us," the man warned, yanking on the sleeve of his son's shirt. "One look at you and everyone here will think we don't do things properly where we come from."

Poor kid. Ivy watched as the man lumbered into a line, dragging his somber-faced son behind him.

"That must be the Timbermeal," Seb said.

Ivy felt Scratch whirring excitedly in her satchel.

"We'd better get it over with," Granma Sylvie decided nervously. "Stay close to me."

As they headed over, Ivy heard music coming from the bandstand. An underguard with a toilet brush in his belt stopped them on their way in.

"Name?" he asked, making a note in the air with a feather.

Granma Sylvie hesitated. "Sparrow."

The officer paused, making a second assessment of Ivy and Seb. "I see."

"We're Sparrows too," Ivy said.

The officer's mouth twitched. "Oh, I know who you two are."

Ivy pursed her lips and tried her best not to scowl. Perhaps the officer had been one of those assigned to monitor her and Seb over the past few months.

The guard allowed them through and Ivy saw that, beyond the fence, a gigantic tea party was taking place. Traders in elaborate Hobsmatch sat at circular white tables, each seating four or five on a range of different chairs. She spied a moth-eaten armchair, an executive leather recliner, a wooden milk stool and a striped deck chair, among others. Gleaming silver trays of finger food surrounded the centerpiece of each table: a wooden sculpture of either Sir Clement or Lady Citron.

Ivy noticed Granma Sylvie tapping her fingers against her hip as they navigated their way between the tables, trying to find a seat.

Seb lowered his mouth to her ear. "That Jack-in-the-Green guy could be here already, looking for the jar."

Ivy had to hope that the heightened security had slowed down Jack-in-the-Green a little. They needed all the help they could get if they were going to find that jar before he did.

In the distance, at the edge of the green, she spotted a familiar face. "Ethel's over there, Granma."

Ethel Dread was sitting on a velvet chaise longue beside Violet Eyelet, a button trader, and Mr. Littlefair, the innkeeper of the Cabbage Moon, who was perched on a barstool.

"'Ere, quick—nab a seat before they go," Ethel told them when they were close enough. She was wearing her normal outfit—well, normal for Hobsmatch: long dark pilot's overalls, fingerless gloves and a brightly colored silk headscarf, under which sprouted tufts of spiky black hair.

"Delighted to have you staying at the Cabbage Moon again," Mr. Littlefair said with a cheery smile. "Your things arrived yesterday via bag travel."

Ivy beamed at him. It was good to see them all again. She took a plastic egg-shaped chair; Seb plonked himself down on a metal patio seat beside her. Ivy noticed a price tag hanging from the arm. It had been stamped with the logo of a shop, François Filigree's Furniture Jamboree.

"Well"—Violet nudged her thick spectacles higher on her nose—"I must say, it's lovely to see you two again." Her lenses were foggy. As always, Ivy doubted whether she could see them at all. "And good to find *you* safe and well too," Violet added, reaching for Granma Sylvie's hand. "It's been a long time."

Granma Sylvie gave a forced smile. "Very long." She sat with her back ruler-straight, her hands cupping her knees, as if she was under inspection. Ivy wondered if that was how it felt to meet friends you didn't remember.

"I only wish it was under better circumstances," Ethel said, pursing her lips. "News that Jack-in-the-Green 'as been sighted 'as sent shockwaves through Lundinor. Nasty piece of work, 'e is."

"What do you know about him?" Ivy tried to sound casual. "Has he been in Lundinor before?"

Ethel folded her arms. " 'E used to work for the Dirge; and since Ragwort's arrest last season, their name's on everyone's lips. People 'ave started to believe they'll return." She lowered her voice. "A possibility the six of us know is all too real."

"Is it a surprise everyone's terrified?" Violet asked. "These Fallen Guild rumors have got people spooked." She looked over her shoulder at a table of dead diners. "If you'll pardon the expression in present company."

Ivy could understand the traders' paranoia. For all they knew, there were four Dirge members still unaccounted for—Nightshade, Blackclaw, Hemlock *and* Wolfsbane. And they could be anyone—your friend, your neighbor, your employer . . . No wonder people were suspicious of one another.

"Apparently Selena Grimes 'as issued the underguard with a new set of powers to combat the Dirge." Ethel snorted.

"I wish you wouldn't use that word so much," Violet said, looking around. "Can't you just say Fallen Guild, like everyone else?" She pushed her glasses back up her nose with a shudder.

Ivy appreciated why people preferred not to use *Dirge:* the word seemed to turn the air cold whenever anyone said it.

"Let's not think about all that just now." Ethel glanced sympathetically at Granma Sylvie, who was shifting in her seat. "Why don't we 'ave a toast, eh?" She raised her glass toward Ivy, Seb and Granma Sylvie, who each grabbed one of their own. Violet and Mr. Littlefair copied her. "To friends old and new!"

After they'd taken a sip, Ethel nodded at Ivy and Seb. "Bet

you two've been lookin' forward to getting to know Lundinor more this season. You must be itching to go off and explore."

Ivy gave Seb a meaningful look. They needed to begin their search for the Jar of Shadows as soon as possible.

"Are you sure it's safe for them to be exploring with this Jack-in-the-Green around?" Granma Sylvie asked. "I was thinking Ivy and Seb could work with you in the House of Bells."

Ethel batted a glove through the air. "Nonsense. The very essence of being an uncommoner is the pursuit of the unexplored, the spirit of adventure. For thousands of years, our kind have been hunting uncommon objects and discovering what they can do." Her eyes softened. "They'll be fine, Sylv, I promise."

"We won't go far," Ivy assured her granma. "We can stay in touch via featherlight."

"Yeah," Seb agreed. "Please?"

Granma Sylvie stared at them for a long moment. Finally, she sighed. "OK, but any more sightings of this Jack-in-the-Green and you stay inside at the Cabbage Moon. Understood?"

They both nodded.

Seb assessed the spread of food on the table. "Now, what to have, what to have . . ."

There were bowls of fresh raspberries and glistening melon balls, plates of miniature Victoria sponges, tiny Scotch eggs, cucumber sandwiches . . . And among the regular food, Ivy spotted the occasional *uncommon* dish—a tier of fighting scones that kept turning one another to crumbs and a bubbling jar of lemon curd that made a sound like a trumpet every time it popped.

Seb reached for a miniature pork pie and took a large bite.

Ivy nudged him in the ribs. "There's no time for this; we've got to get going."

He scowled at her, his cheeks bulging, then gulped.

Ethel was nibbling on a chicken drumstick. "So what do you think of Lundinor in the spring, then?"

"It's *different*," Ivy said.

Ethel pointed her drumstick toward the bandstand in the center of the green, where a single table of diners was being served by waiters in black-and-white Hobsmatch. "Got Mr. Punch to thank for that. Not sure how he does it, though. He's over there at the quartermasters' table."

Ivy spotted Mr. Punch deep in conversation under the bandstand. His wiry cinnamon beard fell over the lapels of a long scarlet ringmaster's coat, and a black top hat sat proudly on his head. There were two other diners at the table who, Ivy deduced, were the quartermasters of the West End and the East End: a plump blond woman wearing a rust-colored dress and medieval veil, and a scrawny gentleman in a shabby brown suit, fedora and sunglasses. Between them a chair stood empty, where Selena Grimes should be sitting. Ivy wondered where she was.

A tiny white plate appeared on the table in front of Ivy. Seb frowned at the identical saucer that had materialized before him. "That's a bit small, isn't it? For all this food . . ."

Ivy regarded the other diners. Perhaps you were supposed to eat very little at the Timbermeal; all the portions looked small and no one had filled their plates.

All of a sudden her chair vibrated. "What in the—?" She grabbed hold of the seat as, of its own accord, it rose and began moving to the left.

She looked up. Everywhere, the chairs had started changing places. Heavy armchairs were lumbering on to the next table, while dainty barstools did pirouettes and ornate dining chairs waltzed their way forward. It looked like a strange, awkward dance, but the diners were eager to see where their chair might be taking them.

"Ivy, what's happening?" Seb shouted, dropping his pork pie into his lap and grabbing the arms of his chair.

"I don't know!" She saw that all the other diners had put down their empty plates before taking a firm hold of their seats. "This must be what uncommon chairs do."

Granma Sylvie dug her fingernails into the seat of the chaise longue as it started to move, her face flushing. "Ivy! Seb?"

"It's OK!" Ivy called. "We'll meet you back at the House of Bells later! We'll stay out of trouble!" She saw Granma Sylvie's

 fretful expression, but Ethel gave her a firm smile and Granma Sylvie's shoulders relaxed.

"Way to give you indigestion," Seb complained as his chair tap-danced off.

Ivy's chair strutted over to another table, this one laden with poached pears and tea cakes and . . .

"Fondant fancy?" a lady asked, offering Ivy a plate of tiny square cakes. "They're awfully light."

"Oh, er . . . No thanks."

She reached for the table edge to steady herself, but her fingers met the grubby digits of another. "Sorry," she mumbled, turning to the diner at her side, "I didn't mea—" Her words died in her throat.

On her left, lounging in a straw beach chair, was a pale man in a tatty waistcoat, ripped jeans and sneakers. He smiled, showing broken teeth. "Pleasure to see you again, Ivy Sparrow." He removed a wobbling jester's hat from his head and offered her a little bow of greeting.

Ivy smiled awkwardly. *Johnny Hands.* He was a ghoul like Selena Grimes, and over five hundred years old, if she remembered correctly.

"What ever happened to that yo-yo I gave you?" he asked. "Make good use of it?"

Ivy tried to swallow her shock at seeing him again. Johnny Hands was one of Valian's Trade contacts—a scout who dealt in weapons. Remembering her previous dealings with him, she knew he could be trusted only so far. "I don't have it anymore. I lost it in the basement of the Wrench Mansion," she told him.

Johnny Hands shrugged. "Things are rarely lost forever in Lundinor." He picked up a tea cake and two segments of poached pear and put them on his plate. He looked at the fondant fancies, but the dish was out of reach.

Ivy's mind started turning. The last time she'd wanted information about something uncommon, Johnny Hands had given her a good lead. He was devious, though; she'd need to ask carefully if she wanted help this time.

"Mr. Hands," she began, idly stroking the edge of her plate. "There are a lot of doors in Lundinor that lead to all kinds of places. Have you ever seen a black door?"

Johnny Hands took a bite of his tea cake. "There are many black doors, dear girl."

"Right," Ivy said. "But what about a black door with a symbol painted on it? Say, a smoking hourglass."

Johnny Hands's eyes glinted. "A smoking hourglass?" He fingered his chin. "I've got a hazy memory of a black door covered in smoke, but"—he stretched his neck toward the distant fondant fancies—"I'm not sure I have the strength to remember."

Ivy took the hint. She grabbed the plate of little cakes and slid them across. Johnny Hands grinned before selecting one, pinkie extended.

"Yes, now I recall exactly where I saw it: there's a black door in the middle of the carousel in Hangman's Square, in the Dead End. I've seen smoke coming from it quite often." He winced. "Smoke's a bad omen in Lundinor."

"A carousel?" Ivy repeated. "Why would—?"

"Any further answers I'm afraid you'll have to pay for." He eyed the fondant fancy. "Properly." He reached into his trouser pocket and brought out a small black card, handing it to Ivy. There was gold text on one side that read:

Jonathan Edward Hands, Esq.
Procurer of Uncommon Arms
Member of the Guild of Tidemongers

"Do you like it? I've had them printed with this new forwarding ink. You only have to hold the card and say, 'I desire to inquire,' and then I get the message. You can contact me with this if you want to make a deal."

Before Ivy could respond, she felt her chair rising off the ground again.

Johnny Hands snatched up his plate and put it in his lap, grumbling. "They never give you enough time to try everything." He lifted his fondant fancy into the air as if it was a sword and he was about to ride into battle. "Onward!"

Ivy's chair quickstepped with a garden bench on its way to the next table. Seb turned up opposite, his face flushed. "At least now we know why the plates are so small," he said. "And I think the chairs move to allow everyone to meet each other."

Ivy smiled weakly, her mind churning after what Johnny Hands had said. Ensuring the other diners weren't listening in, she told Seb what she'd learned.

"I know Hands." Seb nodded. "Dead guy, weird jester's hat." He allowed the end of one of his uncommon drumsticks to poke out of his sleeve. "Gave me these."

"But a door on a carousel in the Dead End . . ." Ivy had experienced uncommon doors before: they led to a different place each time they were opened. It could be one of those. "In Granma's memory, Selena Grimes was behind the door. If this is the same door, it might lead us to the Jar of Shadows. We have to investigate it."

Seb sighed and nudged his plate away. "Guess I'm done here, then."

Ivy's chair reared back on its hind legs and began to tango off toward another table.

Not again . . .

"I'll meet you outside!" she called, gripping the underside of her seat.

CHAPTER FIVE

"OK, OK, fine. I'll ask." Seb reached up and rang the nearest street bell. "Which way to the Well at the World's End?" He looked at Ivy to check he'd said it right.

The bell jangled. *"Take the third left off the Gauntlet, go to the end of Rhubarb Lane and it's in the square opposite."*

Ivy thanked the bell before flashing Seb a smug smile. She had discovered on their last visit that the Dead End was entered via the well; Seb should learn to believe her.

They walked on, hearing laughs and groans from the revelers—both living and dead—as they left the Market Cross and stumbled back to their shops and tents. Ivy thought of Scratch tucked away in her satchel. It seemed odd that her little friend was connected to the races of the dead, but all uncommon objects got their powers from the same thing—fragments of a broken soul. Somewhere out there,

Ivy reflected, was a dead creature made of the other part of the soul inside Scratch.

A little way down the Gauntlet they came upon a crowd gathering at the base of a white obelisk in the middle of the road.

"The Great Cavern Memorial," Ivy whispered to Seb. "Why are there so many people here?" She knew that the memorial had been erected in memory of those who lost their lives on Twelfth Night 1969, when the Dirge had led an army of the dead onto the streets. Ivy liked that it had remained unchanged after Lundinor's grand spring transformation; it seemed more respectful.

As she drew closer, she saw that the trad-ers were in great distress. Some had tears running down their cheeks; others were clutching a hand to their chest, gasping and shaking their heads.

Grabbing Seb's arm, Ivy squeezed her way toward the front: a symbol had been sprayed across the immacu-late alabaster in garish purple paint. It fizzed, giving off plumes of vapor. As Ivy identified the design, goose pim-ples rippled across her arms.

A figure eight with a flat top and bottom; *and* it was smok-ing, just like in Granma Sylvie's memory. It was unmistakable:

The smoking hourglass.

Seb's eyebrows jumped halfway up his forehead. This couldn't be a coincidence.

As Ivy shuffled forward, trying to get a closer look, she heard a shrill scream, which silenced the traders. It was followed by a deep, gruff voice, pleading.

"That's my Freddy!" cried an elderly woman. "It's his voice—I'd know it anywhere. It's coming from beyond the grave!" She pointed a shaky finger at the memorial plaque.

Ivy scanned the list of names engraved on the brass. FRED FAIRWEATHER was the third one.

"The paint!" someone shouted. "It's doing something to the memorial so that we can hear the voices of those who perished on Twelfth Night!"

Seb signaled toward the opposite side of the memorial. "That's not all it's done," he told Ivy in a grave voice.

Lying on the grass there, she saw the lifeless bodies of two underguards, their black capes spread out beneath them. Their necks were coated in a crusty purple fungus—the same color as the graffiti.

". . . and it's got to be them," Ivy heard someone uttering. "Who else would be behind such a thing?"

"Poor blighters. 'Eard they tried to get it off the memorial . . . The paint poisoned 'em, apparently."

"Yes, but what does it mean? Has anyone seen that symbol before?"

"I'll bet you five grade it's got something to do with the Fallen Guild."

"Poisoned," Ivy said softly. *Again.* With a heavy heart, she wondered what Valian would make of it all. She hoped he'd had some success at the Scouts' Union and was on his way to meet them; they could use his help.

She stared at the hourglass, at the purple vapor fizzing off it. The symbol was dangerous, and no one seemed to know what it meant.

All at once several figures in black underguard uniforms pushed their way through the crowd. With a sinking feeling, Ivy recognized the milk-white skin and dark glasses of one of them.

Officer Smokehart. His long black cape twitched as he came to a halt at the foot of the memorial. There was something new about his uniform, Ivy noticed: a red trim on his shoulders.

"Your attention!" he roared, and everyone fell silent. Smokehart had the kind of voice that made nails down a blackboard sound pleasant. Ivy wondered if it was public knowledge that he was one of the Eyre Folk, a race of the dead. She knew that behind those glasses of his were two empty sockets of swirling darkness.

"This is the scene of a very serious crime," Smokehart announced. "There may be vital evidence beneath your feet; be careful when you disperse. We will be questioning everyone in due course."

Behind the memorial, a trio of underguards covered their colleagues' bodies with black sheets.

Smokehart examined the graffiti, being sure to stay a safe distance away. It was still smoking and emitting anguished cries. "It appears that our culprit has no respect for the Departed." Ivy saw his studded gloves curl into fists. "I can assure you all that whoever is responsible for this will be hunted down and punished using the full power of GUT law."

There were a few claps and shouts of support, though most people simply muttered quietly to one another. Ivy touched her wrist, remembering how sore it had been when Smokehart gripped it. She knew he'd stop at nothing to uphold the law, no matter what methods he needed to use.

"Inspector Smokehart!" cried a voice.

The traders parted—and suddenly Ivy's skin turned to ice. She gripped Seb's arm as Selena Grimes glided up to the memorial, tossing her sleek dark braid over her shoulder. She was wearing a purple silk dress that floated over the grass.

"What's she doing here?" Seb hissed.

Ivy ground her teeth, suspicious of Selena's swift arrival. "I'm not sure, but she's still quartermaster of the Dead End. That means she's in charge of the underguard."

Selena Grimes laid a gloved hand on the memorial and lowered her head. Ivy noticed several underguards pointing something at her. Catching a glint of silver between their thumbs and forefingers, she racked her brain. Uncommon needles—she'd once learned they were used as video cameras. Perhaps this scene was being broadcast around Lundinor.

When Selena looked up, her blue eyes were brimming with tears. She skimmed the faces in the audience. "My thoughts are with the families of the two honorable underguards who have lost their lives here today," she said in a honeyed voice. "This is an unspeakably evil crime."

Liar! Ivy wanted to shout, but she knew it wouldn't do any good. Selena had held too much power for too long: the uncommoners of Lundinor wouldn't question her position.

Selena glided around the edge of the crowd. "I'm sure Inspector Smokehart and his team will do everything they can to remove this vile substance as soon as possible. We *will* find the culprit."

Someone shouted something about the Fallen Guild, but

Selena silenced them by raising her glove. "I do not think it is wise to draw hasty conclusions. We must wait until the investigation concludes."

People began to mutter again. Ivy watched their nodding heads; clearly, they believed everything Selena said.

"For extra security," Selena continued, "I have granted the underguard a number of additional powers. Not only has underguard equipment been improved but, from today, Inspector Smokehart and his team will be able to send convicted criminals directly to the Skaptikon. I believe reopening the facility will act as a strong deterrent against committing crimes like this."

The crowd was growing restless. As Ivy tried to make out what they were saying, she felt Scratch stirring in her satchel. The mention of this Skaptikon—whatever it was—had made him agitated.

Smokehart's lips curled into a thin smile. "Thank you, Lady Grimes. I'm sure I speak on behalf of all uncommoners when I say that Lundinor is a safer undermart when someone with your foresight is in place to lead us."

There was a spontaneous murmur of agreement, then a man at the front shook a fist in Smokehart's direction. "What about Jack-in-the-Green?" he demanded. "He's still on the loose!"

Smokehart stiffened. "Regarding the sightings of a certain infamous criminal in other undermarts, I can assure you that, in Lundinor, we have everything under control."

Selena hovered toward the bystander. "Do not doubt, sir, that I will use every resource in my power to protect the traders of Lundinor from *all* criminals." She scanned the gathered faces.

Ivy tried to hide, but her movement attracted attention. Selena Grimes's dazzling eyes fixed on her and then flicked to Seb. Her expression faltered.

Ivy's heart was in her mouth. All she could hope was that, with so many people present, Selena wouldn't try to harm them.

Very slowly, the tips of Selena's needlelike teeth slid out from under her lip. "I promise you this," she told her audience—though she was staring directly at Ivy. "I will not rest until I have put an end to everything."

CHAPTER SIX

"Come on," Seb urged, tugging on Ivy's sleeve.

Ivy's legs were trembling as she wove her way through the traders walking along the gravel path. All she could think about was how much danger they were in. Selena and her henchman had eyes everywhere and they had no way of knowing how she was planning to neutralize them.

The track opened out into a leafy orchard, and Seb headed in among the people milling around under the branches. He dumped his rucksack by the base of a tree and slumped down beside it, panting.

Ivy took a seat on the grass, trying to catch her breath. There were so many questions whirring through her brain. She squeezed Scratch, looking for support.

"Underguards no signing," he said. Ivy had never been able to fathom how he could see without eyes, but she trusted him: they were safe, for now.

Seb scuffed his sneakers in the dirt. "She's definitely onto us! *Put an end to everything,* she said—she was talking about me and you."

"She must have some plan to stop us from revealing her identity," Ivy said with a painful swallow. She rubbed her hands down her thighs, not wanting to think about it.

"Do you think the graffiti was her doing?" Seb asked. "We already know she's connected to the smoking hourglass because of Granma's memory; she must have something to do with it."

Ivy followed Seb's train of thought, but something didn't quite add up. "Why would the Dirge use a smoking hourglass, though? Their coat of arms is a crooked sixpence—everyone knows that." She shook her head. "We need to find out more about the smoking hourglass. Hopefully this black door in the Dead End will give us some answers."

They got to their feet and went on, stopping at a quiet T-junction north of the Gauntlet. In one direction the road meandered through a shadowy copse of cedar trees, while in the other it opened out onto a field where a group of semitransparent uncommoners were playing cricket. Black marquees decorated with dead flowers stood at the edge, with skulls on poles marking each opening. "I think we must be close to the entrance," Ivy said.

Seb observed a group of ghosts bobbing by. "Yeah, I'm definitely getting that dead feeling, all right."

A silky voice drifted into Ivy's ear and she turned to see where it had come from—before realizing that it wasn't the kind of sound anyone else would have heard. It took no effort on her part to sense the quiet babble of uncommon objects all around her.

She caught the voice again. There was something different about it. The voices of uncommon objects usually emanated from fixed points, but this one was moving. . . .

"Hey," Seb said. "Do you think *that's* it?"

He was pointing to the roadside, where a small well was set into the foot of a grassy hill. It reminded Ivy of a wishing well from a fairy tale—a round structure made of weathered gray stone bricks, with a tiled roof and a rope dangling from a rusty winch. A carpet of dark moss, glistening with moisture, hung over the well.

Ivy assessed the nearby traders, but nobody seemed to be paying the well any special attention. "Pass me the guide."

Seb fished a battered, tea-stained pamphlet out of his jeans pocket and handed it over. The front read LUNDINOR: FARROW'S GUIDE FOR THE TRAVELING TRADESMAN.

"Is there anything else in there about the well?" she asked Scratch, fishing him out of her satchel.

The little bell jangled as she laid him on top of the first page. "Six page to turn."

Ivy found page six and he vibrated softly on the page as he read: *"The Well at the World's End was designed by the sootsprite Bartholomew Gumble, a renowned uncommon engineer from Serbia."*

Ivy smiled proudly. The only time Scratch didn't sound "back to fronted" was when he was deciphering the coded words of *Farrow's Guide.*

"Traders must answer a riddle before the well will allow them passage to the Dead End," he continued merrily, *"a design component often attributed to Gumble's natural mischievousness. The well came under scrutiny on several occasions, most notably after the visit of Lady Saltwater—a quartermaster from Lochlily undermart in*

Edinburgh—who disappeared down it in 1773 and has never been seen again. The IUC has now declared the well a World Uncommon Heritage Site."

Ivy and Seb shared a wary glance as Ivy tucked Scratch and the guide back into her satchel. "We need to remember that not all the dead are bad," she said, trying to convince herself.

"No, no," Seb mumbled. "Just the ones that work for the Dirge, and the ones that tried to kill our parents, and the ones that tried to kill us . . ."

They attracted no attention as they approached the well. A trio of specters hovered outside the nearest tent, chatting quietly. On her last visit to Lundinor, Ivy had seen a choir of them; up close, even their speaking voices sounded melodic.

Seb reached into his rucksack and took out his wallet. Ivy frowned.

"There," he said, pointing to the well by way of explanation. Etched into the stone bricks was a message:

> *Throw a coin to meet the three,*
> *Answer our query and you will see.*

Between his fingers Seb held a shiny copper two-penny piece. "Well then?"

Ivy laid her hands on the moss at the side and peered over the edge. There was only darkness below, and a putrid smell crept into her nostrils. She withdrew quickly. "Yuck, it smells like something's died down there."

Seb tensed. "I bet it does. Let's just get this over with."

He held his hand over the well and let the coin slip into

the shadows below. The stones quaked and, deep inside, there was a sound of rushing water. Ivy shuffled backward as voices erupted from within.

"Well, I never!"

"Never have I seen such a pair."

"Pair of newbies, that's for sure."

There were three different speakers, their voices croaky and sharp, like bickering old granddads.

"Sure you two want to go to the Dead End?"

"End up losing your mind in there, some do."

"Do you really want to go in?"

Seb dared a glance into the well. "H-h-heads," he stuttered, hitting Ivy's arm. "Look!"

Ivy inched her face over the edge. Tar-black water had risen to within a foot of the top—and bobbing in it were . . .

"Three heads," Seb said again, pointing.

Ivy tried to suppress a gasp. The heads were severed at the neck; they had greenish-purple skin and patchy hair. They had been horribly mutilated—one was bleeding from a cut on its forehead, while the others sported scars across eyes and chin. They only had four ears and five eyes between them.

Seb turned away. "What are we even *doing* here, Ivy? Seriously—let's go back to the dancing-chairs party. Dancing chairs: yes. Talking zombie heads: no."

Ivy gave the floating heads a second look; they weren't going away. "Seb, with the smoking hourglass on the memorial, I'm even more convinced that we need to make sense of this new memory of Granma Sylvie's. If we can find the connection between Selena and the smoking hourglass, it could give us an advantage—we could even stop her from finding the Jar of Shadows."

With a grimace, Seb regarded the severed heads once more. He opened his mouth, but then closed it.

Ivy wasn't exactly overjoyed herself about venturing into the Dead End. She pulled out one of the uncommon feathers Valian had given her earlier. "If it makes you feel better, I'll send a message to Valian to let him know where we're going."

She angled the feather between thumb and forefinger, and wrote in the air as if it was a pen.

Valian,
Seb and I are off to a carousel in the Dead End to
try to find a black door with a smoking hourglass on it.
See you later,
Ivy x

She watched the feather disappear with a little puff and, when she looked up, found Seb glaring at her, his arms folded. "I want it on the record that I'm not OK with this."

"Whatever. It's on the record." Ivy leaned over the edge of the well. "Er . . . hello?" she called. She tried not to wince as she caught sight of the mutilated heads again; she didn't want them to think she was rude. "Would it be OK if my brother and I came into the Dead End?"

The three heads turned to one another, sending ripples through the water.

One of them blinked. "Into the Dead End, you say?"

"Say, can you find us an answer?" the second asked.

"Answer us this and you shall pass."

Ivy listened carefully. The three heads opened their rotting mouths to speak as one. It sounded like a strange wireless recording.

> *"I am the dawn, the endless race,*
> *Save me or mark me, but please don't waste.*
> *I have no wings and yet I fly.*
> *If you master me, you will never die.*
> *What am I?"*

"*I am the dawn, the endless race . . .*" Seb shook his head. "Ivy, any thoughts?"

Ivy bit her lip. She'd never been good at riddles. She hated the way they tried to trick you. *No wings . . . but it can fly . . .* She remembered the balloon trader earlier and considered whether *balloon* might be the answer. *But then, mastering balloons doesn't allow you to conquer death. . . .*

She started from the beginning: *the dawn, the endless race . . .* As her mind whirred through the possibilities, she recalled that the last time she'd raced against anything, it had been to save her parents' lives: the Dirge had sent her an uncommon alarm clock counting down to the moment of their deaths. . . .

"Time!" she declared. "The answer is *time*." She rushed through the clues. *The dawn of time, time flies, save time, mark time, waste time . . .*

The water in the Well at the World's End began to froth, and the three floating heads vanished in a flurry of bubbles. Ivy heard a loud crack.

"Is that the well?" Seb asked, stepping back to look at the stones. "Maybe it opens into the entrance."

"Entering Dead End below!" Scratch warned frantically. "Is dead always under living!"

Too late, Ivy felt the ground shudder. A deep crevice had formed in a circle around her feet.

"Seb?!" She looked over, but his arms had already lifted into the air as he dropped through the ground, shouting.

Ivy lost her balance and plummeted after him.

CHAPTER SEVEN

She landed with a soft thud on a pile of multicolored bean-bags. Seb was beside her.

"What the—!" he complained, scrambling off them. "Are they trying to give us a heart attack?"

"Now, now," said a voice. A chubby man in a tiara and a wrestling costume was standing on the muddy grass in front of them. "At least you've got a working heart. Most people in these parts don't." He gestured over his shoulder.

Behind him was another huge cavern. Ivy scrambled to her feet, staring.

Seb was already up. "Er . . . ," he started.

Ivy couldn't blame him for being unable to find the right words.

The Dead End looked *just* like the Great Cavern—if the Great Cavern had been through a war, or an apocalypse . . . or both.

Plaster crumbled from the scorched walls of cottage shops, their thatched roofs emitting sooty fumes. Frayed tents and dilapidated huts filled the brown fields between swamps and blazing tar pits, and the charred remains of trees stood like bare flagpoles on the distant hills. Ivy couldn't see a single patch of green anywhere.

The main street was teeming with the dead. Some of them glided along like ghouls, while others slunk from shadow to shadow or appeared out of thin air and then disappeared again with little *pfft* noises. Ivy even noticed traders with scaly skin and webbed feet diving in and out of marshes.

The man in the tiara ushered them forward. "Off you go, then, you two. Good luck with your business—whatever that might be."

Ivy covered her nose with her sweater sleeve; the air stank of sulfur and burning. Seb straightened his shoulders, trying to appear more confident. "So . . . ," he said in a high-pitched voice. "Where is this black door, again?"

Ivy stepped cautiously onto what she presumed was the main road. "Johnny Hands said it was in a carousel."

Unlike the straight Gauntlet, this path wound its way around shadowy corners and mysterious mounds. The gnarled branches of dead trees hung over the route like giant claws trying to pick up pedestrians.

Seb rubbed his arms. "Is it me or is it cold down here?"

The temperature had definitely dropped. Maybe it was something to do with the lack of body heat. "Let's ask a bell," Ivy suggested, veering off to the corner of a tent. "We don't want to be here any longer than we have to."

The bell in question was tarnished and hanging from an

old piece of string. "We need to find a carousel," Ivy said in a hushed voice. She could have spoken louder, only there was a pale wispy creature snoozing in a rocking chair outside the tent and she didn't want to wake it.

The bell swung slowly. "Carou-sellll," it slurred. "Third right off Undertaker's Lane till you reach Hangman's Square."

Ivy shivered. Even the bells here gave her the creeps.

Sticking close together, they followed the bell's directions. Despite the disaster-zone scenery, the dead traders seemed cheery—laughing and chatting to one another, bartering at stalls and haggling over prices. A woman with tentacles for legs slithered past.

"What makes them look different?" Seb asked, trying not to stare.

"According to *Farrow's Guide,* it has to do with the way someone dies," Ivy said, "but I'm not sure. After the Dirge started doing research on the subject, it was made illegal." She frowned. "Did you hear Smokehart talking about the Departed earlier?"

Seb nodded. "Departed must be *properly* dead—you know, gone for good. But what makes someone become Departed rather than dead?"

Ivy considered the question carefully. With a sense of unease, she wondered whether the Dirge had found the answers.

A voice buzzed in her ear, making her twitch. It had an echo—like someone speaking in a cave. It was strange; there seemed to be more fragments of soul in the Dead End than in the Great Cavern. Perhaps, Ivy thought, her whispering also allowed her to sense the fragments of souls that had transformed into a race of the dead.

They arrived at Hangman's Square within minutes. It was a large brown field flanked by derelict cottages with festering swamps for gardens.

"Well, spring in the Dead End is cheerful," Seb muttered, staring at some kids who were playing catch with a skull.

In the center of the field stood a rusty silver carousel. The pewter-skinned figures mounted upon it moved up and down very slowly, dancing an old-fashioned waltz. Their outlandish dresses, jackets and hats made Ivy think they might be wearing Hobsmatch, but she wasn't sure. As the carousel turned, tiny squares of light spread out across the grass, like the reflections of a mirrored ball.

"Seb, that's got to be it." Ivy tugged him across the field. The carousel was busy: traders with sad faces massed at the

foot of the steps as they waited for their turn. She wondered why they looked so forlorn.

"I can't see a black door," Seb noted. "Can you?"

Ivy squinted. She could hear the structure creaking and moaning as it spun, but the flashing reflections of the pewter dancers made her eyes ache.

She felt a hand on her shoulder. "On you get, then—no need to wait!" A dark-eyed man with a shepherd's crook gave her a gentle push up the steps.

"Oh no, I—" Ivy's legs started moving before she had finished her sentence. She tried to stop herself, but it was like she'd lost control of her body. As she climbed onto the carousel, she could see Seb having the same problem.

"Seb!" Ivy attempted to get his attention, but as she stepped onto the revolving platform she became so light-headed she couldn't speak. The glare from the dancing figures flooded her vision. She grabbed on to the nearest pole to steady herself. "Seb?" she croaked. She couldn't see him anymore; everything outside the carousel was spinning, and all she could make out were the blurred faces of the pewter-skinned dancers, smiling eerily as they twirled.

I've got to get off.

She zigzagged her way through the silvery figures, shouting Seb's name. Just as she thought she'd finally discovered an exit, she found herself back at the same spot she'd started from.

She rubbed her eyes, trying to keep a grip on reality. She wasn't trapped; the carousel didn't have bars on it; there *must* be an exit.

Suddenly one of the dancers broke ranks and came lumbering toward her, swaying from side to side like a possessed statue. It stretched a metallic hand toward her throat, its eyes solid white like marble.

"Get off me!" Ivy screamed, stumbling backward. "Oomph!" Her body slammed into something hard . . . and her mind cleared.

She found herself on a fixed platform in the middle of the carousel. "Seb!" she shouted again. She could see traders stumbling helplessly among the dancers, their expressions dreamy.

Ivy knew she couldn't risk going back to find her brother; she might never get off again. *There must be a different way out.* She did an about-face and came to a knocker with a tall black door. There were intricate designs carved into the ebony frame—ghoulish faces and swirly patterns—but no hourglass symbol painted anywhere. Smoke rolled from under the doorframe, making Ivy cough.

"Seb!" she cried one more time. "I've found the door Johnny Hands was talking about!"

As before, there was no reply. Ivy hesitated for a moment, wondering if she should wait there for Seb or go through the door without him. The only way to see if it was the door from Granma Sylvie's memory was to learn what was behind it. Ivy put a gloved hand on the doorknob. She'd just take a peek. . . .

The door opened easily, but all Ivy could see on the other side was thick, sooty smoke. Covering her mouth, she shuffled forward over the threshold, squinting through the fog.

Just one step farther . . .

The smoke started to thin, and gradually Ivy could see a small room beyond.

Maybe one more . . .

Emerging on the other side of the smoke, she found herself standing in a circular room. The wood-paneled walls were adorned with antlers, animal skins and mirrored cabinets gleaming with trophies and satin rosettes.

There was a white chalk circle drawn on the floor, and in the middle stood a high square table with a chopping board on it. The smoke was coming from the base of a large crystal chandelier suspended from the middle of the ceiling. It spread out to the walls and over the door, forming a misty curtain.

Ivy ventured in slowly; she was still buzzing with adrenaline. There was no one else there; the room was empty. She stepped over the chalk line and approached the table, wondering if she might find anything important. She batted smoke out of her eyes as she inspected the chopping board. It had a black band painted around the outside, with a bright red square in the center. She pulled back her glove and touched it; it felt tingly and warm. *Uncommon.*

Just then, someone came stumbling into the room behind her. Her nerves jangled as she spun around.

"Ivy!" Seb cried, falling toward her.

Ivy was overcome with relief. "Seb?" He looked like he'd been in a fight. His lip was bleeding, his skin pale. "What happened? Are you OK?"

"It's those silver figures on the carousel," Seb explained hastily. "They're alive! Well, I mean, they're dead, but . . ." He flapped his hands. "You know what I mean. They are *not* friendly! One of them winded me when I tried to get through to the door." He leaned against the table, panting. "Just let me get my breath back. Then we'll go and tell that idiot who pushed us on here where he can shove his carousel." He rested his hands on the chopping board.

"That's uncommon," she told him. "I don't know why it's here."

Seb looked at all the trophy cabinets. "Is there anything else? Have you seen the smoking hourglass anywhere, or anything Dirge-related?"

Ivy was about to say that she hadn't yet explored the place, when she heard voices outside. Seb shot a look over her shoulder. He scanned the room and then, without explanation, grabbed Ivy by the elbow and shoved her behind a white bearskin rug hanging on the wall. There was just enough room for her to fit without making a noticeable bulge, but Seb was left in plain view.

All at once Ivy heard footsteps in the room.

"Well, look at this: the grimp's turned up early," a sly voice announced.

"Must be keen to lose," a second voice slurred.

The first speaker laughed menacingly. "He's new. Perhaps he's never heard of us."

Ivy needed to see what was going on. She spotted a mirrored cabinet against the wall to her left. By tilting her head, in one surface she could see a reflection of the whole room. She saw two figures emerge through the smoke and knew that they were dead. One was the size and build of a grizzly bear—except that instead of fur it had slimy yellow skin and a drooling mouth, like one of those jelly aliens she'd played with when she was younger. It was wearing thick black rubber gloves with tight elasticized cuffs that dug into its gelatinous skin. The other looked more human, with raggedy orange hair on its head and chin, and freckles on its nose . . . and it also had *three* arms. Tucked under one was a metal box with a hinged lid.

Seb ran a hand through his hair while covertly wiping the sweat off his forehead, trying to appear relaxed. He glanced surreptitiously in Ivy's direction, his eyes flashing with panic. Hurriedly he slid off his rucksack and lobbed it toward the rug. Ivy flinched as it landed with a thud on her feet. She looked down, not realizing they'd been sticking out.

"If I've said it once," the sly voice continued, "I've said it a hundred times." The three-armed man was speaking. "I'll never be beaten at Grivens by a blasted grimp."

Three Arms thinks Seb is a grimp . . . ? Ivy had come up against grimps before—they were shape-shifters; they ate the body parts of living humans in order to resemble them. Three Arms and his slimy friend must think that Seb had assumed the appearance of a living boy.

"Er . . . hi," Seb said in a deeper voice than normal.

The slimy guy lowered his head in greeting, goo dripping onto the floor.

Three Arms grinned. "I hope the silver security didn't give you too hard a time on the way in—they might look like harmless dancers, but they can be fierce." He rubbed his hands together as he stared at the chopping board. "You know what it's like—can't have any law-abiding folk getting in to see the game. They'd snitch."

"Talking of which," the slimy guy began with a snigger, "better take these off so the Ugs don't know where we are." He pulled off his rubber gloves and flexed his greasy fingers, sighing happily.

Three Arms removed his own bobbly black wool gloves before noticing Seb's bare hands. "Where are yours, then?"

Seb rolled his eyes, searching for an explanation. "Took them off earlier," he muttered. "Had some, er . . . business to take care of."

The two dead creatures took up positions opposite each other, next to Seb. Ivy wished she was closer to her brother so that she could reassure him; instead she had to just watch him try to keep up the pretense.

"Jack's bringing the snacks," Three Arms said, opening his metal box. "You'll probably just want toenails. That's all right—eh, grimp?"

Seb nodded quickly as Three Arms offered the box to him. "Choose your pieces. No cheating, now," Three Arms said. "Just pick one of each and put 'em on the board."

Seb stared hard into the box and eventually drew out three carved wooden objects, each small enough to fit in his hand—a suitcase with catches, a ship's bell and a single glove with a buttoned cuff.

Next Slimy Guy selected a different-looking bell, suitcase and glove from the box. "What's your name?" He was addressing Seb.

Three Arms placed his bell, suitcase and glove on the board in front of him. Set out on three sides of the board, the models looked a bit like chess pieces.

Seb cleared his throat. "My name?" His voice wobbled. Ivy hoped the two dead guys couldn't read his face as well as she could; to her it was obvious that he was about to lie.

"Aye," Three Arms said. "Don't much fancy calling you 'grimp' all evening. I'm Mick the Stretch, and this here is Squasher."

Ivy had no idea what Seb was going to say. His legs were trembling.

"Ripz?" he answered, almost like it was a question.

Ivy's heart sank. *Ripz*. Really? That was all he could come up with—the name of his favorite band?

The other two laughed. Squasher drooled. "Sounds bloodthirsty."

"Indeed," Mick the Stretch added. "I hope you're as tough a Grivens opponent as your name suggests—then we might have some real fun."

Ivy didn't like the sound of this.

There was a creak and the sound of odd, scratchy footsteps outside. Then the black door swung inward.

No.

Emerging through the smoke came the tall thin shape of Selena's henchman, Jack-in-the-Green. He was wearing the same emerald-green wool suit she had seen on the MV *Outlander,* this time teamed with a pale fedora that had holes cut out for his antennae to poke through. His mandibles clicked in greeting. "Gentlemen."

Ivy pressed herself back against the wall, remembering Jack-in-the-Green's WANTED poster: *Assassin guilty of murder on six continents . . . Master of disguise.* It couldn't get much worse.

Or could it . . . ?

With a cold trickle of horror, Ivy realized that Jack-in-the-Green might recognize Seb from the ship.

"There you are, Jack. Got the snacks?"

The assassin's gaze moved slowly around the table, but he didn't react. Instead he held up a gray drawstring gym bag, jabbed a claw into the opening and retrieved two crinkly transparent packets. Their contents shuffled noisily as he dumped them onto the table.

Ivy's chest deflated with relief. She could only suppose that, in the darkness, Jack-in-the-Green hadn't got a clear look at Seb's face.

He also tugged a thick leather-covered notebook out of his bag and tapped it. "You were right about the formulas written in here," he said in his strange, tuneful voice. "There was a tracing serum that was particularly useful. We should do business again." He stuffed the notebook back into his bag and scanned the room with his headlight eyes.

Ivy held her breath as his gaze lingered on the bearskin rug. That WANTED poster hadn't mentioned anything about X-ray vision. . . .

He lowered his head toward Seb's rucksack and chucked his drawstring bag in the same direction. Ivy flinched as it hit her feet, but her body flooded with relief.

Jack-in-the-Green scuttled into the only remaining position at the table—opposite Seb. Ivy could see the outline of the black door in the smoke behind him.

As far as she knew, it was the only way out.

CHAPTER EIGHT

"Here you go, Ripz," said Mick the Stretch, proffering one of the plastic bags brought by Jack-in-the-Green. A handful of thin yellowish toenail curls shuffled out into a little mound beside Seb's elbow.

Seb stared at them, straining for a smile. "Er, thanks. Every grimp loves toenails." He sounded like he was going to vomit. Ivy began to feel sick herself.

"Well," said Mick the Stretch, "give them a try. Folks don't call me the best Grivens host in Lundinor for nothing, you know." He waited, looking at Seb expectantly.

With a shaking hand, Seb picked up a toenail.

Oh no no. Ivy couldn't watch.

Her brother opened his mouth and forced his fingers onto his tongue. His face went gray as he closed his lips. Ivy was certain he was going to be sick, but instead he chewed once and swallowed.

Ivy's jaw dropped.

Jack-in-the-Green made a buzzing sound with his antennae. "Before we start the game, I need information." He slid a square of paper onto the uncommon chopping board. Mick the Stretch grumbled as some of the pieces were knocked over, but one look at Jack-in-the-Green's razor-edged pincer arms made him think twice about complaining. Seb and Squasher leaned closer to see.

"The tracing serum formula from the notebook isn't working as well in Lundinor. I need you to tell me if you see the jar." Jack-in-the-Green pointed at the paper. "These are the dimensions. It should have arrived here this morning."

Ivy's skin tingled. *The Jar of Shadows.* She glanced at Jack-in-the-Green's bag with the notebook tucked inside.

Seb shrugged. Squasher shook his head, splattering slime across the table. "Haven't heard nothing about a jar," Mick said, stroking his wiry orange beard, "but I'll let you know if I do . . . for a price, obviously."

Jack-in-the-Green tipped his head. "I need it by the evening of May Day."

In two days' time . . . Ivy wondered what the urgency was.

Mick the Stretch smacked his three hands against the table. "Right then, now that's done, let's get this game started." He offered his metal box to Jack-in-the-Green, who picked a suitcase, bell and glove and placed them on the board.

"Here's my rules," Mick the Stretch began. "We play traditional Grivens: you only move one piece per round. Last person still fighting after three rounds wins."

Ivy imagined Grivens must be some kind of board game, but the chopping board had no grid, just an outer black section

74

and an inner red square. Her gaze drifted across the trophy cabinets to a mahogany shield studded with two silver plates. They were engraved with the words:

INTERNATIONAL GRIVENS CHAMPIONSHIP 1979,
MAI MASIMA, THAILAND: RUNNER-UP

INTERNATIONAL GRIVENS CHAMPIONSHIP 1781,
MOSVOK, RUSSIA: WINNER

She bit her lip, growing more and more anxious. Seb looked like he was about to run away at any moment. Ivy could only imagine what was going through his mind. The dead players would turn murderous if they realized he wasn't who he said he was.

"Right, gentlemen," said Mick the Stretch. "Time to select your first weapon and move it into the red."

Using a long green claw, Jack-in-the-Green pushed forward his suitcase piece. Squasher chose his glove, Mick the Stretch his bell. Seb's eyes flicked between the three pieces on his side of the board before he gave the suitcase a panicked nudge.

"See you on the other side!" Mick declared gleefully. He struck the chopping board, sending it spinning with a loud thrum.

The air stirred.

With a sinister hiss, everything within the chalk circle went blurry. Ivy rubbed her eyes, assuming it was some kind of illusion, but as clarity was restored, the hairs on the back of her neck stood on end.

Seb and the three dead players were still standing around

the square table, but their surroundings—up to the edge of the chalk circle—had completely changed. The dark hunting-lodge decor had been replaced by a tarmac helipad, blue skies and a view of a sprawling glass metropolis in brilliant sunlight. It was as if they had been transported to another part of the world entirely.

Seb's chest was going up and down, though Ivy couldn't hear him panting. Everything in the room was silent—but now the Grivens pieces were moving, changing shape.

Jack-in-the-Green's suitcase opened to reveal a miniature samurai sword, which then materialized—much larger—in his claws. He drew away from the table and began swiping it back and forth. Ivy held a hand over her mouth. Mick the Stretch was swinging a rusty ax. She didn't understand. . . . Had the pieces turned into weapons?

Seb looked like a trapped animal as he glanced from one opponent to the other. Ivy wasn't sure what to do to help him. A red and white football helmet appeared in his hands and, after a moment's hesitation, he shoved it on his head.

Jack-in-the-Green aimed his sword at Squasher. There was a flash of silver, and then, with a *whoosh,* sound flooded back and the four players returned to the room, exactly as they had been before. . . .

Except that Squasher had no head. It fell to the floor with a squelchy thud, a dumb grin on its lips.

Seb grabbed the table edge, his knuckles turning white. Ivy had no idea how he was staying in character.

Mick calmly scooped Squasher's head off the floor and placed it back on top of his body. There was a wet crackle, and then . . .

"OK, OK," Squasher groaned, punching a fist on the table. "I admit it: those were some good blade skills."

Ivy couldn't believe it. Grivens wasn't like any board game she'd ever heard of—how could a beheading be part of the rules? Squasher wouldn't be so cheerful if he was a living, human player. . . .

Like Seb. Ivy knew she had to do something to get them both out of there.

Her eyes flicked toward the bag that Jack-in-the-Green had thrown at her feet. Careful not to disturb the bearskin rug, she sank to her knees and folded back the top of the bag. She could sense without touching it that it contained only one uncommon object.

She slid off her gloves and, with her bare fingers, prodded around inside. They grazed what felt like the leather-bound book Jack-in-the-Green had been holding earlier, and she brought it out. She could sense voices emanating from within, though it didn't feel warm to the touch.

As she flipped it over, she started.

The leather cover was embossed with the symbol she had been staring at barely half an hour before: a smoking hourglass. This time, the smoke was drawn on in wiggly lines.

The graffiti . . . Perhaps the Dirge *did* have something to do with it, after all. . . . And if whatever was inside the book had led Jack-in-the-Green to the Jar of Shadows, then the smoking hourglass *must* be connected to the jar. When Mick the Stretch began speaking again, she hurriedly stuffed the notebook into her satchel.

"Well then, you lot." He cracked his three sets of knuckles. "Second round?"

Ivy checked the reflection of the room in the trophy cabinet. Seb was desperately eyeing the bearskin rug.

"Ripz?" Mick the Stretch looked suspiciously at Seb. "You all right?"

"Oh, er . . ." Seb laughed nervously as the room fell quiet.

Ivy was trembling. *Think. Think* . . . She could jump out and shout, "Surprise!" but she was fairly certain she—and Seb—would be killed within seconds if she did that. In her panic, she scuffed the back of the bearskin rug with her hand.

The rug swayed.

Ivy jolted. It was *uncommon*.

"Don't yooo like yoo-urr toenails?" Squasher asked Seb. "Yooo haven't eaten any."

He mumbled something that sounded like "I'm not very hungry."

The table creaked as Jack-in-the-Green leaned forward, resting on his pointy green elbows. "Not *hungry*? I've never met a grimp who wasn't hungry."

Ivy knew by the sound of his voice that she'd run out of time.

She had one idea left, but it was completely crazy. Taking a deep breath, she swung her arms and leaped up toward the top of the bearskin rug, ripping it down off its hooks.

The bear's head roared with glee as its hide fell through the air and stopped, hovering just off the ground. Ivy grabbed Seb's rucksack off the floor and sprang on top, trying to recall the stance people assumed when they were riding uncommon rugs.

Seb gawped. *"Ivy?"* His voice was shrill.

The faces of the three dead players showed first surprise and then anger. Jack-in-the-Green's long arms twitched. . . .

But before any of them could move, there was a sound like a cork popping, and a frayed burlap sack appeared in the middle of the floor. Shaggy dark hair and a brown face poked through the opening.

"*Valian?*" Seb exclaimed, his voice climbing higher still.

In the space of a second Valian seemed to take in the scowling faces of Mick the Stretch and Squasher, Seb's terrified expression and Jack-in-the-Green's glowing yellow eyes. Everyone was still for a moment.

And then all hell broke loose.

"Kill them!" Jack-in-the-Green's wings burst out of his suit as he rose into the air, aiming straight for Ivy.

With a growl, Mick the Stretch climbed onto the Grivens table. Launching himself out of the Great Uncommon Bag, Valian rolled aside just in time to dodge Mick as he thumped down on the floor, attempting to pulverize anything that moved.

Squasher started toward Seb. "Ivy," Seb shouted, "*do* something!"

Ivy took hold of the fur that had once covered the bear's shoulders and tugged it hard, steering the rug toward the ceiling. "Get on!"

With a massive leap, Seb caught hold of the edge and clambered aboard, narrowly avoiding a double blow from Squasher's slimy arms. Valian skidded under the Grivens table, escaping Mick the Stretch. Ivy saw him fishing around in his inside pocket. She caught a glimpse of three gunmetal ball bearings in his hand before he tossed them into the air. . . .

And then everything was *floating*. Ivy's stomach shot into her mouth as she was lifted up toward the ceiling. She was weightless, like an astronaut in space. She clutched the bearskin, trying to pull herself back down, but the rug was wobbling all over the place.

Seb splayed his fingers through the bear's fur, trying to hang on. "What's happening?" His hair was standing on end.

A few feet away, the game table rose into the air, along with a confetti of Grivens pieces.

"The ball bearings are uncommon, from a Newton's cradle!" Valian shouted, his arms flailing as he swam out from underneath it. "They suspend gravity." With an effort, he managed to work his way toward them, pulling himself onto Seb's back.

Mick the Stretch and Squasher bellowed furiously as they hovered up to where Jack-in-the-Green was floundering against the ceiling. "You cannot escape me!" he snarled. Two of his arms darted toward Ivy like long green spears.

Seb kicked one of them away; Ivy ducked to avoid the other.

"We need an exit!" she cried. She hadn't thought that far ahead. She urged the rug toward the wall it had once been covering, but it moved incredibly slowly, as if traveling through molasses.

Seb slipped his uncommon drumsticks out of his sleeves and beat them as hard as he could in the direction of the wall. With an earsplitting crash, the wood paneling smashed and a hole the size of a small car opened onto the carousel. The silver figures stopped dancing and gaped as the bearskin found a turn of speed and zoomed through the gap. Ivy pulled hard on the bear's shoulders so that they swooped up out of the reach of any silver arms and accelerated high over the Dead End.

Angry roars sounded behind them. An orb of green light shot past Ivy's head and landed with a crackle in the stubby branches of a withered black tree below.

"What was that?!" Seb cried, throwing his hands protectively toward his hair.

Ivy heard the thud of wings and looked over her shoulder. Jack-in-the-Green was in hot pursuit, his yellow eyes pointing in their direction.

Valian fumbled with the Great Uncommon Bag, muttering something into it. "Ivy, do you think you can fly us into the bag on the back of this thing?"

"Anytime now would be good!" Seb shouted as he was narrowly missed by another orb.

Ivy tugged the bear's fur with one hand and they banked left, out of the way. "I can try."

"OK, here goes." Valian hurled the bag out in front of them and it billowed open like an old wind sock.

Ivy aimed the bear's head for the dark hole. "Everybody get down and hope this works!"

CHAPTER NINE

The bear gave a roar of surprise as they all whooshed into darkness. Ivy gripped its fur tightly, trying to keep it straight, despite the fact that the Great Uncommon Bag was really in control. She felt the bearskin relax between her fingers, as if it was glad to escape from Jack-in-the-Green. Cool relief flowed through her limbs too—for a moment back there she'd thought they weren't going to make it.

The bag tunnel was unexpectedly short. Ivy, Seb and Valian emerged into a small dusty room that was flooded with light. The rug slipped out from beneath them and landed in a heap against one wall; the bear's tongue lolled from its jaws as it panted.

Climbing to her feet, Ivy looked around.

The Cabbage Moon.

She and Seb had stayed in the inn—in the very same

bedroom, in fact—on their last visit, only it was subtly different now. The view through the window was framed by the dark edge of a thatched roof, and over the empty fireplace the once-plain uncommon wallpaper—which could fold itself into ornaments and furnishings—was patterned with warm sunflowers. Ivy's duffle coat hung over the wardrobe door in the corner and her suitcase was on a chair beside the bunk beds.

Seb got to his feet and raised an arm, grimacing. "Yuck! Get it off. Get it off," he cried, wiping his tongue with his sleeve. "I can't believe I had to eat a toenail to avoid being killed. Being an uncommoner *sucks*."

Ivy frowned. "Are you OK?"

There was a dark ring of sweat around the top of Seb's T-shirt, and his hands were shaking. "What do you *think*?"

Behind her, Valian, still short of breath, got to his feet. "Why were you two playing *Grivens*?" He looked from one to the other disbelievingly. "It's a miracle we weren't all killed."

Ivy averted her eyes, feeling like she'd let everyone down. She should have figured out a way for her and Seb to escape sooner.

"Seriously," Valian continued, stripping off his leather jacket and throwing it over the end of the bunk. *"Explain."*

Seb had an unhinged look, as if he was reliving what had just happened. "What *was* that game? Do you know anything about it? Do you play it?"

"Me?" Valian raised his eyebrows. "Absolutely no way! Even when the game was legal, the only living uncommoners who played it were professionals . . . and *crazy*. Grivens is infamous for causing the deaths of hundreds of competitors over

the years. That's why they banned it in the UK. It's still legal in America and a few other countries in Europe."

Ivy thought back to Squasher's grisly severed head. "The chopping board was uncommon. I felt it."

Valian nodded. "That's how the game works. When a Grivens piece is pushed into the red square, the board imbues it with a unique power—it can turn into a weapon or a shield. The four opponents must stay within the chalk circle to play."

"Yeah, but I wasn't *in* that circle all the time," Seb interrupted. "That's why it was so freaky! When they spun the chopping board, the room changed; it's like we went somewhere new."

Ivy blinked, the scene returning to her. "You *did* go somewhere new—at least, that's what it looked like. I couldn't see you for a while, and then it was as if a portal had opened up in the middle of the room and you were . . . somewhere else."

"It happened instantly, for me. We were on a helipad, really high up." Seb looked at Valian. "How is that even possible?"

"It's all part of the game," he explained. "When the chopping board spins, everything within the chalk circle gets taken to somewhere in the Krigvelt and the game continues there. There's normally a short interval before those on the outside can see what's going on."

"The *Krigvelt*?" Ivy repeated. "What's that?"

"It's a collection of combat arenas located in various places around the world," Valian said. "Every time the chopping board is spun, players get transported to a different battleground. If you die fighting in the Krigvelt, you die when you return to the original location too."

"And people actually *watch* this?" Seb asked, wiping the sweat from his forehead.

"I told you—it's illegal in most countries now," Valian said, "but hundreds of years ago, Grivens was a really popular sport. There's still a huge stadium in the West End of Lundinor."

Ivy considered the silver figures that had tried to attack her and Seb on the carousel. "That's why those dead guys didn't want an audience. They didn't want to be found out."

Valian scoffed. "If those dead guys are associates of Selena's henchman, they're probably some of the most wanted criminals in Lundinor. That's why there was an uncommon chandelier on the ceiling—it releases masquerade vapor, a gas that disguises dark deeds."

"Ivy and I found out who Selena's henchman is," Seb remarked. "An assassin named Jack-in-the-Green."

Valian froze. "Jack-in-the-Green?"

"You've heard of him?" Ivy asked, perching on the bottom bunk.

"Everyone's heard of him—I just didn't know that's what he looked like." Valian sank down and leaned against the wall. "Gobbles like him can change their appearance, and I don't mean in a grimp-eating-toenails way." He smiled apologetically at Seb. "Gobbles can transform into anything—a tree, a brick wall, a glass of water. I heard that Jack-in-the-Green once disguised himself as a chair and waited for weeks until his victim finally sat on him; then he slit his throat."

"Well, one thing's for sure," Seb said. "With a professional assassin at her disposal, Selena is even more powerful than before."

Ivy's spirits sank, but she clenched her fists. "Jack-in-the-Green said that he hadn't found the jar yet; he needs it by May Day. Selena and the Dirge must be planning to use it then."

Valian's eyes flashed with panic. "That's the day after tomorrow! I didn't find out anything useful at the Scouts' Union. Have you guys discovered anything else?"

"Well, I did get a glimpse of that piece of paper Jack-in-the-Green showed at the Grivens table—the one with the measurements for the jar," Seb said. "It's almost as tall as Ivy—it's going to be difficult to hide it."

Ivy bit her lip. "That black door on the carousel can't be the one Granma remembers, but at least we didn't go through all that for nothing." She opened her satchel and pulled out the leather-bound book she'd taken from Jack-in-the-Green's bag. "Jack-in-the-Green said he'd been using a formula inside this to hunt for the jar. It's got a smoking hourglass on the cover—just like the one Granma described and the one on the Great Cavern Memorial."

"I don't recognize the symbol," Valian admitted.

"Nor does anyone else," Ivy said, running her fingers across the cover. "Do you think it's connected to the Dirge? Jack-in-the-Green's working for Selena. Seb's right, they might be behind the graffiti that killed those underguards."

Valian's nostrils flared. "I can't think of anyone else evil enough to commit a murder at a memorial."

Ivy examined the notebook carefully. Inside, the pages were blank except for the top left-hand corner of each sheet, where the letters *AS* had been written in black ink. "The leather feels old, but there's nothing inside except some initials. And *something* about it is uncommon, I'm just not sure what."

"There's obviously more to the notebook than meets the eye," Seb said, pulling his hoodie out of his rucksack and putting it on. "We need to find out what the smoking-hourglass symbol means. If Jack-in-the-Green has been using the notebook to hunt down the Jar of Shadows, we might be able to use it too. It's our only lead."

Ivy shoved the notebook back inside her satchel and laid Scratch on top. "Shout an alarm if anyone goes rummaging through," she instructed.

A knock sounded at the door. "Housekeeping!" announced a silvery voice.

A girl with a sleek black bob and wide hazel eyes glided in, a basket of linen tucked under one arm. She wore a tattered patchwork waistcoat and a pale pink tutu over a striped leotard, with vintage roller skates on her feet. Ivy had seen her working at the Cabbage Moon before. She had thick metallic purple eyeliner drawn across her eyelids, and freckles scattered over her golden skin.

"Oh . . ." The girl blushed. "Sorry, I didn't think anyone was in here." She frowned as she looked back along the corridor. "Wait. How *did* you get in?"

Ivy tensed, realizing that the Great Uncommon Bag was lying open on the floor.

"We only got here a moment ago," Seb said quickly, kicking the bag under the bottom bunk. "Maybe you were . . . facing the other way?"

The girl tilted her head.

"I've seen you around here before, haven't I? Last season." Her gaze moved from Seb's jeans to his baggy hoodie, sussing him out in seconds. "Not in your Hobsmatch yet, then. Everyone's gone crazy for medieval this season; I don't know why—that stuff's so frilly."

"Er . . ." Seb rubbed the back of his head. "Yeah?"

The girl glimpsed the Ripz logo on his hoodie. "No. Way. You like the Ripz? I don't know anyone who's into common bands! Have you listened to their new album?"

Seb's cheeks went pink. "Yeah, of course. Track eight—'Misfits Anonymous'—that's gotta be their best. It's a total return to their old sound."

They smiled at each other, bright-eyed. Ivy had never seen Seb look at a girl that way before.

"My name's Judy, by the way," the girl said. "I work for Mr. Littlefair during Trade time."

"Right, of course. I'm Seb. I'm kinda *new*."

Judy studied Ivy's and Seb's faces. "Wait . . ." She put down her laundry basket. "Are you two the Wrench kids? Ivy and Sebastian?"

Ivy tensed. *Not this again* . . . "Actually our surname is Sparrow, but yeah, we're them."

Judy's ears wiggled as she laughed. It was high-pitched and reminded Ivy of Scratch. "It's so great to finally meet you!" She skated into the room and offered Ivy her hand.

"Er . . . nice to meet you too," Ivy said, a smile on her face. Judy's perfume smelled sweet and fresh like watermelon.

"I have something to thank both of you for," Judy told them. "My mum's been made the new featherlight mailmaster. She's been working in the service for years but never thought she'd reach master. She has you two to thank for unmasking the old one as a member of the Fallen Guild last winter." She put her hands on her hips. "You've earned a friend in me; I owe you one."

Suddenly a shout rose up from the street outside, making the bedroom walls shake. Ivy hurried over to the window. A shiny black 4x4 with huge silver tires was parked in the middle of the road, its engine rumbling. Stern-faced underguards stood at each wheel, scanning the traders with their beady eyes. Everyone had fallen silent.

Ivy wondered if the 4x4 was one of the improvements Selena Grimes had announced; the last time Ivy was in Lundinor the underguards had been using horse-drawn funeral carriages.

"What's happening?" Judy asked, joining Ivy at the window. Seb held the curtain back as Valian craned his neck over Ivy's shoulder.

"I think they're arresting someone," Ivy said. Three underguard constables were escorting a man across the street toward the vehicle. He was floating with his head down, his hands tied behind his back. *Dead—a ghoul, possibly.* Ivy couldn't be sure.

Farther down the road a woman called after him, her voice raw with emotion. "He's innocent!" she cried. "He don't know nothing about what happened to the memorial. None of us do!"

Ivy realized that the woman was dead too: parts of her body were so transparent you could see straight through her to the street behind. A crowd of traders had gathered to view the spectacle, muttering among themselves.

"This shouldn't be happening," Judy said with a stamp of her foot. "It's like the stories my nan told me about when she was growing up and the Fallen Guild were active. *You didn't trust no one,* she said. *Your best friend was a suspect, especially if 'e was dead*." She shook her head. "I hope they don't take him to the Skaptikon."

"This . . . Skaptikon place," Ivy said—the spikiness of the word had made it stick in her head. "What *is* it?"

Valian shivered. "The worst place on earth, apparently. After the Dirge disappeared, the IUC—the International Uncommon Council—were terrified that they might return. They built the Skaptikon to imprison everyone who had served the Dirge."

"Skaptikon means 'a thousand stairs,'" Judy added. "Some say it's a maze that makes you mad, or a hole that goes down into the center of Earth. Others talk about a place so treacherous, it doesn't need walls to keep prisoners in. No one—dead or living—has ever escaped from it."

"Right." Seb nodded. "'Worst place on Earth' sounds about right, then."

And Selena Grimes is using it somehow, Ivy thought with a sinking feeling.

They stepped away from the window, the atmosphere in the room decidedly downcast now. Judy slowly pushed the door open a crack and peeped through the gap. "I'd better get on with the ne—" She stopped before she could finish. "Bother," she snapped. "It's Smokehart. He's searching the rooms for suspects, no doubt."

Ivy closed her satchel. If Smokehart found that book with the smoking hourglass on it, it would be all the evidence he needed to arrest her for being the graffiti murderer.

Valian dropped to his knees and snatched the Great Uncommon Bag from under the bed. "He mustn't find this either," he told Ivy. "And your family history doesn't exactly put you in a positive light. We all have to leave here. *Now.*"

CHAPTER TEN

"This way," Judy whispered. She slipped onto the landing and stuck her head back around the door. "All clear. Follow me."

Ivy's pulse was racing as she secured her satchel across her body. Out in the hallway, the walls trembled with the slamming of doors and the stomp of heavy boots. The sound of Smokehart's voice reverberated down the corridor.

Judy escorted them to a narrow room just off the landing. Inside, several sets of flying salad tongs were beating the dirt from wet bedsheets, dunking the fabric in troughs of green liquid. The air was thick with the smell of laundry detergent, but the green solution was emitting sounds of howling wind and heavy rain, as if there was a storm inside.

"If Smokehart's got the stairs covered, this is the only exit," Judy told them, opening a window in the far wall. She climbed on top of the sill, throwing her legs over the side. "You'll need this to cushion your fall; it's a long way down." She fished a bar of soap out of her apron pocket and rubbed it onto the wheels of her roller skates and placed it on the window ledge. It made a squealing noise as she did so. "See you on the ground!"

"Wait!" Ivy reached forward as Judy cheerily pushed herself off the ledge.

"She'll be fine," Valian said into her ear. "Clean as a whistle, softer than velvet—that's uncommon soap for you."

Sure enough, there was an explosion of little popping noises as Judy landed in the yard.

With Valian's encouragement, Ivy took the soap and began brushing it onto the soles of her shoes. Bubbles appeared around the toes and up behind her heels. Touching one experimentally, her finger rebounded, as if the bubble was made of rubber.

"Hurry up," Seb said, checking over his shoulder.

Ivy threw him the soap before climbing onto the windowsill. It was a good twelve feet to the ground, but she was focused on escaping from Smokehart. She pushed herself off and bent her legs when she hit the ground. The bubbles on her shoes popped, absorbing all the impact. It felt like she'd landed on a giant bouncy castle.

"Over here!" Judy called. She pulled Ivy behind a wooden rack filled with barrels of Hundred Punch. Seb and Valian were soon squashed up beside them.

"It's locked," Valian groaned, trying the handle of the gate behind.

Ivy looked up. The fence surrounding the yard was topped with barbed wire; there was no way they'd be able to climb over. They heard the moan of furniture being dragged across a landing. Ivy spotted a black cloak flashing past the third-floor window.

With a dull thud, the back door that led through to the dining room flew open and a pale-faced figure dressed in black stepped out. Ivy tensed.

Inspector Smokehart scanned the yard slowly with his dark glasses.

"Sir?" came a voice over his shoulder.

He twisted around. Half a dozen underguard constables stood fixed to the spot behind him, awaiting instructions.

"Search every room," he growled. "There is evidence some-where. That symbol didn't just appear on the memorial by itself." The men dispersed, their cloaks thrashing around like a cloud of bats. Smokehart came farther into the yard, sniffed, then rubbed the toe of his boot into the soap residue on the ground. The laundry room window was hanging open above him. . . .

Shouts sounded from upstairs. The inspector scowled and swiftly returned inside. Ivy puffed out a sigh of relief.

"Mr. Littlefair has the keys," Judy whispered, pointing at the gate.

Ivy peered through into the dining room of the inn. It looked nothing like it had the last time she'd seen it. The holly wreaths had been replaced by daisy chains, and now the long wooden tables were covered in white lace cloths and vases of daffodils.

She spotted Mr. Littlefair behind the bar, pouring Hun-dred Punch. A man and a woman wearing yellow hard hats and flowery hakamas perused the menu in front of them. Ivy tuned in to their conversation.

". . . Dragon's Breath Ale," she caught the man saying. "It's meant to be amazing!"

"I'm afraid we don't serve that here." Mr. Littlefair sounded exasperated. "How about Hundred Punch? A hundred flavors, a hundred ways to make you smile!"

The lady raised her eyebrows. "They serve Dragon's Breath at Brewster's across the road. Can't you make it for us too?"

Mr. Littlefair ran a hand through his thinning gray hair. Ivy didn't think she'd ever seen him looking so tired. "No," he said in a tight voice. "It's their own secret recipe—just like Hundred Punch is mine."

With a sigh, he tucked a trash bag under his arm and headed toward the back door. He stared at the barrel of Hundred Punch that was right by Ivy's head. His brow crinkled. "If you're trying to steal from the kitchen," he said in a taut voice, "then you picked a bad day. There are Ugs *everywhere*."

Slowly they all crept out from behind the storage rack.

Mr. Littlefair raised his eyebrows. "*Ivy?* Seb! What are you doing here?"

"We had to hide," Ivy explained. She couldn't tell him the truth about the Great Uncommon Bag, so she told him the next best reason. "Smokehart hates us. He would have found a way to have us arrested."

Mr. Littlefair checked over his shoulder. The doorway was still empty. "I'll let you out the back. Judy, you'd better get inside and try to calm the drinkers down. We could do without this, today of all days."

"Is everything OK?" Ivy asked as Mr. Littlefair pulled a bunch of keys out of his apron.

He sighed. "It's just this new place over the road—*Brewster's*.

It's stealing all my business. Everyone wants this *Dragon's Breath* stuff." He shook his head before pushing the gate open.

Judy turned toward the inn. "You know, you lot might want to lie low at Brewster's for a while. It's the last place Smokehart's gonna search."

"How do you know?" Seb asked.

Judy shrugged. "Because it's the last place he actually *did* search. I heard some guests complaining about it ten minutes ago. Doubt he'll go back anytime soon."

Mr. Littlefair brightened, shooing them out of the gate. "There we go, then, you can hide in there. You'd be doing me a favor; I need someone to suss out the joint."

Out on the dusty Gauntlet, whatever voices Ivy might have sensed with her whispering were drowned by a flood of gossip. Squawks of ". . . Murder!" and ". . . Skaptikon . . ." echoed across the street, while murmurs of ". . . Jack-in-the-Green . . . graffiti . . ." drifted beneath the trees at the roadside. As the three of them headed across the road, an unfamiliar building came into view: a large cottage surrounded by picnic benches and lush grass. Flame-colored bunting hung between the gables, and a satin flag waved proudly from a pole on the lawn.

"Brewster's Alehouse," Seb read. "Come on—let's get inside."

They entered among a whirlwind of other customers. In contrast to the bright fields of Lundinor, the interior—with its dark leather furniture and maroon walls—was gloomy and stifling. The air smelled of charcoal, as if there was an open fire somewhere, or even a barbecue.

Ivy looked around for staff but could only see one man behind the bar in the center of the room: a burly, broad-chested giant with a red beard that trailed down over his sizable belly. It was the same man she'd seen entering the Timbermeal that very morning. His Hobsmatch consisted of a leather jerkin and soot-stained apron—a bit like an old-fashioned butcher's.

Valian spotted a space on the end of a large table, and the three of them headed over. Sitting at the other end was a group of men and women holding tankards filled with a gloopy black liquid. One of the men threw back his head and slugged down the drink. As he put his tankard down, he leaned forward, burped . . .

And a fireball the size of his head erupted from his mouth before disappearing into thin air.

Ivy leaned away as the heat reached her face. She studied the drinkers at the next table. Everyone was sampling the same thick dark liquid and then belching out fireballs. "Dragon's Breath Ale . . . it must be."

Valian grabbed an empty tankard off the table and gave it a sniff. "Hmm. It's weird: I've never heard of it before."

"Why's that weird?" Seb asked. "Are you some secret drinks expert?"

"No, but anything made with mixology gets a lot of news coverage in Lundinor," he replied. "I would have heard of it."

Ivy wrinkled her nose. *"Mixology?"*

Valian slid the tankard over so that she could take a sniff. It smelled like tar and chocolate. "Mixology's the art of combining liquids using uncommon objects. People use it to develop uncommon inks, perfumes, paints, soups—the laundry detergent in the Cabbage Moon, the liquid shadow we used on that ship—anything you can pour, really. It takes a lifetime of experimenting to achieve the right formulas. Concoctions

like Dragon's Breath Ale don't just pop out of nowhere. *That's* why it's weird."

"Looks like it *has* made the news," Seb said. "In the American undermarts, at least." He pointed to a wooden cabinet that was stuffed with framed newspaper clippings and photos of the burly, bearded man behind the bar, grinning. In the center, in pride of place, hung a large poster-sized frame.

It contained the front page of a newspaper, the *Nubrook Observer,* with the headline "Have a Flagon of Dragon!" To the left of the article was a smiling photo of the barman with his hand resting on a bubbling black cauldron.

DRUMMOND BREWSTER INVENTS DRAGON'S BREATH ALE

Prepared from a secret recipe, this uncommon ale allows the drinker to temporarily breathe fire. The discovery was made while Brewster—an ex-chef—experimented in his kitchen at home. The drink has been an immediate success in the United States, and Brewster now has plans to take his alehouse on the road, visiting undermarts across Europe and Asia.

As Ivy finished reading, a boy with scruffy red hair and scorched eyebrows approached their table. A dirty apron—the strings wrapped twice around his skinny body—covered his simple Hobsmatch, and he was balancing several empty tankards in his arms.

Alexander, Ivy remembered. *Drummond Brewster's son.*

"Hello," he said as he reached them. "What can I get you?" There were dark circles under his eyes as if he'd been working around the clock. Ivy thought that was strange—he could only have been around her age.

Seb leaned over and caught a tankard as it toppled out of the boy's arms.

"Thanks," he said, rearranging his burden.

Ivy stood up to help him. "Is there no one working with you?"

Alexander shrugged. "My pa won't allow it. He thinks if we get anyone to help, they'll steal the secret Dragon's Breath recipe."

Drummond's gaze landed on the four of them and he shouted, "Boy, stop chatting!" Ivy's ribs shook, his voice was so powerful. "There's a spillage," he boomed. "Get over here!"

Alexander went pale. "S-sorry," he stuttered. "Gotta go."

Ivy watched him stumble away, clutching his tankards. When she turned back, Seb was flapping a hand in front of his eyes.

"Why do featherlights always fly so close to my face?" A pale blue feather zipped around his head like a paper plane. It swung from left to right, and then, tip down, it began to scribble a message in midair.

Ivy and Sebastian,
  I hope you're both safe and well and have had a good day. Can you please meet me at the House of Bells in an hour?
      With all my love,
      Granma Sylvie x

"Well, we're not far from the House of Bells," Seb said. "We don't have to rush."

Ivy shot a look at the door, wondering if Smokehart and his band of underguards had moved on.

Valian was drumming his fingers on the table, apparently oblivious. "I've been thinking. . . . What if the reason no one recognizes the smoking-hourglass symbol is that it's really, really old?"

"Could be," Seb said. "But if so, how do we find out about it?"

Ivy thought carefully. It was frustrating that uncommoners didn't use the Internet. She glanced back at the framed newspaper cutting. "What about one of the newspapers? They must have offices in Lundinor. Maybe we could search through their archives to see if there's any reference to the symbol in past issues."

Valian brightened. "That might work. There are two papers in Lundinor: the *Lundinor Chronicle* and the *Barrow Post,* but the *Post* is older. We should try there."

"Ivy"—Seb rubbed his face—"that's gonna take ages."

"Have you got any better ideas?"

"No," he admitted, "but the last time I went along with something I thought was a bad idea, I ended up having to eat toenails. Just saying."

Ivy sighed and was about to offer a reluctant apology, when she felt Valian's hand on the back of her head. "Duck!"

She shielded her face as a man belched out another fireball.

CHAPTER ELEVEN

According to a local street bell, the *Barrow Post* head-quarters was on the edge of Stationer's Green in the Great Cavern.

Ivy reached into her satchel for *Farrow's Guide*—there was a map inside that she hoped would help them navigate.

"We can't waste time walking," Valian said, marching beside her. "We're racing against Selena Grimes and Jack-in-the-Green; they don't even sleep."

"And we've got to meet our granma in an hour," Seb reminded. "Can't we just use the Great Uncommon Bag to get around?"

Valian shook his head. "If anyone saw us using it, it'd look suspicious—other uncommon bags don't work within the Great Gates. Somehow, the Great Uncommon Bag can break the rules without being detected. We need a sky stop.

There . . ." He pointed to the roadside, where traders were lining up beside a row of tall metal lockers. Peeking through the doors, Ivy spied various brooms, vacuum cleaners and rugs. A man lifted his leg over a vacuum cleaner, straddling it like a bicycle. The machine made a *vroom* noise as its engines started and it rose into the air.

Seb groaned as the rider zoomed over his head. "Is there any way to get around that's not going to make me feel sick?"

They crossed the road, keeping a safe distance from the underguards' black 4x4, still stationed outside the Cabbage Moon. Valian traded a feather with a young man wearing a khaki bomber jacket who was standing at the sky stop. Ivy imagined how momentous it would be to make her first Trade—like taking a step toward being a real uncommoner.

The man in the bomber jacket turned, took two plastic dustpans out of a locker and passed them to Valian. He approached Ivy and Seb carrying a long-handled mop. "Your friend tells me that neither of you have a license to ride on your own, so you'll have to travel on the back with me." He threw a leg over the mop and indicated the space behind him.

Valian slipped his shoes through a strap on each dustpan, so he was wearing them like slippers. "You'll be able to use these eventually." As he extended his arms on either side, he lifted soundlessly into the air.

Seb mumbled a complaint before swinging a leg over the mop, looking like the kid who had just been humiliated in gym class. Ivy took a seat in front of him.

The mop made a smooth, vertical takeoff. Seb squeezed Ivy's shoulders, his fingernails digging in. "When will this be over?"

"Try not to think about it," she told him. "Valian's right—we're up against people who can walk through walls; we have to take the fastest route."

She peered down as the thatched roofs of Lundinor shrank below her; a patchwork quilt of fields rolled off into the distance. She could see uncommoners below: families going in and out of shops, children tumbling down hills and picnicking on the grass. Three times a year, when the undermart opened, this was their life.

And now it's mine.

As they passed over the Great Cavern Memorial, Ivy noticed that the smoking hourglass still hadn't been removed. She considered what each element of the design might signify—an hourglass represented the passing of time, but smoke was a warning of fire.

"Here's your destination, folks," the sky driver said with a smile as they came to an abrupt halt. He lowered the mop so that Ivy and Seb could clamber off.

They had landed on a patch of grass opposite a huge white windmill painted with the words BARROW POST, EST. 1598. Its crisscross sails creaked as they turned, sending shadows sweeping over the gravel drive in front. Behind the windmill, a vast meadow filled with poppies and checkered black-and-white tents stretched into the distance.

The sky driver collected his dustpan hover-shoes from Valian and shot back off under the cave roof on his mop.

"What shall we say when we get inside?" Seb asked. "They might think it's suspicious if we tell them we want to search the archives for a smoking hourglass."

"Let's pretend we're looking for photos of Granma Sylvie

when she was younger," Ivy suggested. "I don't think anyone will question that."

"Nice idea, but I don't think that's our main problem." Valian pointed to a set of automatic doors at the base of the windmill. Standing in front were two hard-faced under-guards. "Must be an extra security measure because of Jack-in-the-Green or the murders at the memorial. Probably best to avoid them."

Ivy studied the windmill for another way in. A group of scruffy-looking boys and girls stood on the grass beside it, holding dark bundles under their arms. As the sails turned, a child at the front of the line hopped onto one of the lower blades and used it to hitch a lift up to the roof. "Who are they?" she asked.

"Newspaper delivery kids," Valian replied. "Copies of today's edition are expelled from the building through chutes on the roof and the kids distribute them around Lundinor riding on those doormats."

Ivy narrowed her eyes at the slate tiles. "These chutes . . . they go right into the building?"

"I guess so," Valian replied.

She grinned. "I've got an idea."

Hoping their rolled-up coats would pass for doormats, the three of them joined the line beside the windmill. Ivy calculated the time between each rotation. There was only a short window when the sails were close enough to the ground for each child to jump on safely.

"I'll go first," she offered. She waited till the sail was only three feet from the ground, then sprang aboard, hanging on until it reached the windmill roof. She unhooked her legs and dropped down with a scratchy thud. Seb and Valian followed at intervals.

"So which one do we take?" Seb asked.

There were two openings in the gray slate tiles. The *Barrow Post* logo—an old-fashioned cart with a megaphone in the center—was stenciled in white between them.

Bunched around the farther hole, the delivery kids all stepped back as a newspaper came flying out. One of them jumped to catch it.

"That must be the evening *Post,*" Valian said. "Which means, if we want to avoid being hit in the face by the headlines, we should use the empty chute."

Ivy peered in. The shaft was about the width of a wheelie bin, ending in a white fabric surface.

Valian sat on the roof and swung his legs over the edge. "I'll see you two down there."

"Come on," Ivy told Seb. "It looks safe."

At the bottom of the chute she found herself caught by a soft linen hammock. With help from Valian, she climbed down onto a thin wooden balcony constructed under the gables.

She blinked, unable to believe what she was seeing.

Strung between the beams of the windmill were hundreds

of hammocks. Some were perfectly still, but most bounced up and down with great force, making a sound like a twanging rubber band. Newspapers were being tossed between them in a steady stream. Ivy followed the path of one as it sprang from hammock to hammock, making its way toward the base of the opposite chute.

"They must be carried like this up from the printer," Valian said. "I didn't even know uncommon hammocks did that."

Seb dropped down behind them. "Please tell me that's *not* how we're continuing this journey."

Ivy ventured to the edge. A long way below, she could see a white marble floor scattered with desks.

"I can't see any other way down," Valian said, pushing his arms into his leather jacket. "I'll go first if you want."

Seb gave a deep sigh and pulled on his hoodie. "You know your life's really messed up when sliding down a giant hose becomes the most appealing way to get around."

CHAPTER TWELVE

Hammock travel, Ivy discovered, was easier if you were a newspaper rather than an eighty-five-pound girl. The first few bounces were OK, but eventually the hammocks seemed to give up trying to toss the three of them around and just rocked them limply. They ended up having to climb down the ropes, landing in an empty corridor.

"Look for a floor plan or something to tell us where the archives are," Valian said.

Ivy's nostrils twitched from the acrid smell of chemicals in the air. She wasn't sure where it was coming from. A cupboard against one wall housed a set of old-fashioned chemist's jars. Each one was filled with a different colored liquid and labeled in large letters. HEADLINE INK looked thick, dark and murky, while TAGLINE INK was striped and swirling. NOTE-TAKING INK, SPEED-WRITING INK and 24-HOUR TIME-DELAY INK all kept changing color. Ivy wondered what they *didn't* have an ink for. They must all be products of mixology.

Seb disappeared around a corner and called back to them. "Over here."

Fixed to the wall was a list of departments with arrows. Valian tapped the word ARCHIVES and pointed. "That way."

They hurried past an open door. Ivy caught sight of a massive printing machine constructed from a jumble of different objects—a silver dustbin lid, a car windshield, two wooden spoons, a squeaking balloon pump and a toaster among them.

In another room, Hobsmatched uncommoners sat at messy desks with their heads down, jotting featherlights or studying photographs captured in uncommon snow globes. A blackboard on the far wall was being scribbled on by a scraggy gray feather. It read:

Today's top story—GRAFFITI MURDER:
Mysterious vandal kills two underguards.

They came at last to a glass door etched with the word ARCHIVES. Attached to the doorframe were several fridge magnets.

"Careful," Valian warned, eyeing them. "Uncommon magnets attract stolen property. They'll scan us as we go in, and then again when we leave, to prevent us from taking anything."

Beyond the door was a flight of wooden stairs that led down to a small, dimly lit room filled with metal cupboards—the kind used to store flammable materials at school. From the dank smell in the air Ivy suspected that they were in some sort of basement.

"So now we're *underground* underground," Seb mused.

Behind a cupboard door Ivy spotted the back of a man's head: thin gray hair and a roll-neck sweater. A swarm of tiny floating balls orbited his ears. *Marbles.* She shook her head. "Excuse me, sir?"

The man flinched. "Wha—!" *"Oomph!"* He whacked his forehead on the cupboard door, winced and staggered back. Ivy was pretty sure that one of the marbles had zoomed straight into his mouth.

"Oh—sorry!" she said.

He swayed as he turned to face them. He had speckled brown skin and a cheerful face with sharp green eyes. A name badge clipped to his sweater said STANLEY, ARCHIVIST.

"Unidentified Fried Object," he said, smiling.

Ivy raised her eyebrows. Whatever she had been expecting him to say, it wasn't that. "Er, we're here to find some information about our granma. Can you point us in the right direction?" Perhaps the steel cabinets contained the beginning of the archives.

Stanley looked dazed. "Because the lettuce was a *head* and the tomato was trying to *catch up!*"

Ivy turned to Seb and Valian for reassurance. "Any help?"

"To get to the other side!" Stanley continued. "Max no difference, just open up and let me in! When it's ajar!"

Valian tilted his head like he'd been asked to solve a complicated algebra problem. Seb, on the other hand, was grinning. "Don't you guys get what he's saying? They're the punch lines to jokes. Observe." He waved a hand in front of Stanley's bewildered face. "Why did the banana go to the doctor?"

"Because it wasn't peeling well!" Stanley replied.

Seb's grin widened. Ivy considered the marbles still orbiting Stanley's head. "I think he might have swallowed one by accident. What do uncommon marbles do?"

"They're like extra storage space for your brain," Valian said. "You can offload ideas into them."

Like an external hard drive . . . Ivy wondered if Stanley had banked the punch lines to his favorite jokes in the little red marble that had sailed into his mouth. She stepped closer and gave the archivist her most disarming smile before reaching up on tiptoe and slapping him on the back.

Stanley coughed, and something red shot out of his mouth. "Yuck!" he spluttered. "Tastes awful." He batted the other marbles away from his ears, sending them whizzing into the cupboard. Then he shut the door, exasperated. "So sorry about that. Those little things have a mind of their own." He fingered his chin. "Come to think of it, I guess they have *my* mind . . . Ha, oh well!" He looked down at the three of them, smiling warmly. "Information, is it, you're after? Of course— follow me. It's nice to see people your age down here."

He led them past the wooden stairs and through a heavy metal door into an empty room with gray stone walls and a single uncommon lemon squeezer mounted on the ceiling. It bloomed into brightness as they went in.

Seb paused. "Er, are the archives really in *here*?" he asked, his voice echoing. Ivy wasn't convinced either. Stanley didn't seem like the most reliable curator.

Even though the room appeared to be empty, Ivy could sense several uncommon objects close by. The constant din of broken souls was beginning to give her a headache.

"Certainly are," Stanley said. "The *Barrow Post* has been

in print for over four hundred years. A century ago we had to move the archives down here, where there's more space."

Seb frowned at the empty room and lowered his mouth to Ivy's ear. "It'll take forever to find what we're looking for."

Stanley handed a small matchbox to Ivy. She could tell it was ancient, because the packaging was crinkled and brown and she didn't recognize the brand name.

"Sorry," she said. "What's this?"

"The archives, of course," Stanley told her. "Just ask the box what you're looking for and it'll find a match."

Valian gave a smug smile. "Uncommon storage has its uses."

"There's a leaflet somewhere on how to use it," Stanley added. "Stay there—I'll go and get it."

Ivy waited till the archivist had disappeared back into the first room. "Quick—let's ask it about the smoking hourglass before Stanley comes back." Holding the matchbox close to her lips, she said, "We're searching for a symbol: a smoking hourglass."

The matchbox wobbled in her hand and, after only a few seconds, burst open so that Ivy could peer inside.

"A burnt match?" she exclaimed. "That's *it*?"

Footsteps sounded behind her; she slid the matchbox closed.

"Here we are, then," Stanley said cheerfully. He was holding a thick yellowed pamphlet. "Instructions for using a matchbox archive." He handed it over to Seb with a smile. "You're more than welcome to give it a read, but it's fairly simple: the matchbox will find articles relating to your search in ascending chronological order. If there are no matches in the archive, it returns a burnt match."

A burnt match. So there was nothing at all about the smoking hourglass in the archives. . . .

"What are you researching again?" Stanley asked.

"Anything on our granma," Seb replied hastily.

Ivy shook her head clear. "Oh, yes, right. Sylvie Sparrow. Although back when she was a trader, her surname was Wrench."

The archivist threw them a sidelong glance. Ivy tried not to cringe. Would there ever be a time when the name Wrench got a normal reaction?

He shrugged. "Oddly enough, that's what the last gentleman was looking for too."

Ivy jolted. Someone *else* had been searching for information on Granma Sylvie? "The last gentleman . . . ," she said carefully. "Who was he?"

"Never seen him before," Stanley replied. "I can't say I'd want to again either. I caught him smoking down here and had to ask him to leave. I popped his face into a marble so the guards upstairs could stop him from coming back." He signaled to the matchbox. "But don't listen to me go on; ask the box for what you need."

Ivy's mind was still whirring about this mysterious researcher, but she slowly raised the matchbox to her lips. "Sylvie Wrench."

The matchbox made a sound like a cat yowling and then bounced out of Ivy's arms and hit the empty stone floor with a surprising metal clang.

"Give it some space," the archivist advised, stepping back.

They edged away, staring as the matchbox unfolded itself again and again, growing bigger all the time. A neat stack of

papers appeared in the middle, followed by a brown cardboard box.

"Articles your grandmother is
mentioned in will be in that pile,"
Stanley explained. "Journalistic evidence that was kept will be in the box.
Take as long as you need examining
it all; it's forbidden to remove anything." He scratched his head. "I'll
go find that marble; might be able to
tell you more about the gentleman
who was here."

As Stanley left the room, Ivy
knelt on the floor. She could understand now why the place was
empty—you needed as much space as
possible to give the matchbox room to expand. As she picked
up the box of photos, she speculated about who might have
been snooping on Granma Sylvie. All at once this "pretend"
look at her files didn't seem so pointless.

Valian flicked through a batch of papers while Seb examined several documents on the floor beside him. "Lot of stuff
about the Twelfth Night Mystery," he muttered.

Ivy opened the cardboard box. There were two photos
inside. The first showed a rosy-cheeked Granma Sylvie in a
neat school uniform standing outside the Wrench Mansion,
holding hands with her mother. "Seb, look." Ivy passed the
photo across before picking up the next one. When she saw it,
she tensed.

In her hand was a black-and-white picture of a grinning

teenage Granma Sylvie wearing a white petticoat and silver go-go boots. Linking arms with her was another young girl, with slanted cheekbones and long dark hair.

"*Selena Grimes,*" Ivy blurted. "I don't believe it—they're in this picture together."

"*What?*" Valian shuffled closer.

Selena Grimes looked fresh-faced and glowing, smiling with straight teeth instead of the needlelike ones she had now. "You don't think Granma was *friends* with her, do you?" Seb asked.

Ivy didn't know what to think. The thought that her granma had even had a photo taken with Selena left her feeling nauseous. "I guess it explains why Selena appears in Granma Sylvie's new memory of the black door and the smoking hourglass—they must have known each other." Her heart sank. She didn't want to believe that they were friends. They couldn't have been. . . .

"Wait," Valian said. "I think there's someone missing from the photo—there."

Ivy studied the edge of the picture. Beside Granma Sylvie's go-go boots was the toe of another shoe: a black leather brogue. The paper was crisp, brown and flaky. Ivy held it under her nose. "It smells like it's been burned." She examined the inside of the box; there were traces of ash in the corners. "Stanley said that he caught the last man in here smoking. He might have set fire to this."

"There's writing on the back," Seb said, indicating underneath. "I think it might be a postcard."

Ivy turned the picture over. Seb was right. There was an address in London that she didn't recognize, and a short message inscribed in impossibly neat handwriting:

Sylvie,

The nature of my work has finally forced me into hiding.

I am so sorry not to have said goodbye, but the memories of our time together will always make me smile.

Be safe, and know that I miss you.

The tone of the message was so sad, it made Ivy's throat tighten. It was signed at the bottom with a strange squiggle, but as half of it had been burned away, she couldn't make out what it said. "Who do you think sent it? Surely not Selena."

Valian scratched his head. "It's got to be the person who's missing from the photo. Whoever they are, they must be in danger and worried about your gran."

Ivy considered what might have happened to them. There was a stamp affixed to the postcard. Last winter she had discovered that featherlight messages could be intercepted by the mailmaster; perhaps the sender wanted to keep his message away from uncommon eyes.

"Maybe this would trigger Granma Sylvie's memory." She thought about stowing it in her pocket, but then remembered the fridge magnet security door. "If only we could smuggle it out."

"I can take a picture of it," Seb suggested, fishing his phone out of his rucksack.

Valian shook his head. "Common cameras won't work in Lundinor. The pictures always come out blurry so that you can't leave with evidence of what's here. Special Branch have something to do with it." He reached under his leather jacket and pulled out the scruffy Great Uncommon Bag. Then, checking that Stanley wasn't around, he stuffed the photo inside and said, "Sylvie Sparrow's pocket."

Ivy recalled what Valian had said earlier—that the bag could break the rules of Lundinor without being detected. She hoped it would work now.

Just as the photo disappeared, Stanley came back into the room, throwing a small blue marble up and down in one hand. "Got it!" he said, sounding pleased with himself. "The gentleman in here before was a distinctive fellow—smart uniform, curly golden beard and a white line through his eyebrow."

Seb frowned. "I want to say that sounds familiar, but I'm not sure why."

"It's the eyebrow streak," Valian said. "The chief officer of the MV *Outlander* had one, and a blond beard too."

"Yes, but it couldn't have been him," Ivy reasoned. "He's—" She stopped short of saying "dead" in front of Stanley.

"Shall I show you out?" the archivist asked.

Ivy got to her feet slowly, the others rising beside her. Something very confusing was going on.

Back upstairs, Valian pushed his head between Ivy's and Seb's shoulders as Stanley escorted them along the corridor. "The chief officer was definitely dead; I checked his pulse myself. That leaves us with one possibility: someone in Lundinor is masquerading as him."

"Yes, but who?" Ivy asked. "And why?"

Seb grimaced. "Who do we know who is a master of disguise and was on that ship? Jack-in-the-Green—it's got to be."

"Maybe Selena sent him to destroy the postcard, only he got disturbed by Stanley before he could finish the job?" Ivy suggested. "We need to work out who's missing from that photo. There must be a reason Selena wanted it gone."

As they entered the central room of the windmill, Ivy's senses were on full alert. Something was wrong. The journalists were in a frenzy, shouting to one another and milling around. The receptionist kept wiping her brow as she scribbled furiously with a feather.

For a horrible moment Ivy thought the newspaper workers had found out about the missing postcard, but then one of them barged past her, running toward the doors. Ivy clearly wasn't the target of their concern.

A reporter with cropped black hair and square glasses heaved himself on top of his desk and spread his arms wide, addressing the entire room.

"OK, everyone, calm down," he insisted. "We've got no official details as yet, but reports are coming in thick and fast that posters have been put up along the Gauntlet. Rupert?" He pointed to a bespectacled man holding a snow globe. "I want photos of people's reactions to that poster. Get down to the underguard station ASAP; see if it looks like they're setting up for a public announcement. Julia?" He addressed a woman with wavy blond hair in the middle of the group of journalists. "We need vox pops from the traders—I want reactions! Forget the double murder at the memorial—*this* is the biggest story of the week. Why, this is the biggest story of the *year*! Selena Grimes has just announced the first legal Grivens contest in over a century! We need exclusives!"

CHAPTER THIRTEEN

Wiping dust from her eyes, Ivy hopped off the sponge mop onto the gravel. Seb took a few deep breaths, trying to calm his insides.

"Thank you for traveling with Squeegee and Son's uncommon mops," the sky driver said cheerfully. "Don't forget to rate us via featherlight."

"Thanks." Valian slipped his dustpan hover-shoes off his feet and handed them over.

Ivy waited until the driver was out of earshot before speaking. "I don't understand. How can Grivens be legal again?"

Valian shook his head as they headed toward the House of Bells. The Gauntlet was remarkably empty now. Traders had left the street in order to gather under the trees, where linen sheets, fluffy bedspreads and crocheted blankets were floating beneath the leafy canopies like giant butterflies. Projected onto the center of each was a live video feed from the Great Cavern underguard station—Ivy recognized its smooth granite walls and smoked-glass windows.

Seb's forehead creased as they passed a levitating fleece throw. "What *are* those things, exactly?"

"Materializers. They display images," Valian said. "We should see what happens; it might be the public announcement they mentioned at the *Barrow Post*." They made their way under an oak tree, where a pale yellow duvet cover was hanging.

The image on the duvet cover flickered. Ivy flinched as the front door of the station shot open and a dozen underguards came marching through, their tricorne hats fixed to their heads. They formed a line and then parted down the center. Inspector Smokehart and Selena Grimes appeared between them.

Selena raised a conch shell to her lips and cleared her throat. "Some of you will know that Lundinor was established on the site of an ancient Roman undermart; and though its laws and customs have been forgotten, many of them are still honored today. One such rule permits the practice of outlawed celebrations on the occasion of a grand anniversary." She put the shell down and clapped her hands together. "Therefore, in honor of the five hundredth anniversary of the birth of our founder, Sir Clement, I am delighted to announce that a one-off international Grivens contest will be staged in the world-famous West End Stadium the day after tomorrow!"

There was a burst of applause along the Gauntlet. Some people jumped into the air, raising their arms and cheering.

"In keeping with the traditions of the original game,"

Selena continued, "both living and dead players will be welcomed, although we will be using some new rules to safeguard living contestants. The prize—donated anonymously—will be a trove of uncommon objects to the value of ten thousand grade."

Valian's jaw dropped. A few traders standing under the oak tree gasped.

The materializer showed Selena passing the conch shell to Inspector Smokehart. His voice was flat. "Entrants must drink from the contest master's cup. One glove from each participant will be kept until the day of play. Withdrawals are forbidden. Security in the stadium will be tight. For full details, see the posters."

The image vanished with a squeaky *pop,* leaving the duvet cover bare as it folded itself into a neat square and dropped to the ground. The traders left the trees and returned to their businesses in a flurry of whispers.

Valian closed his mouth and stared at the pavement. "She's found a loophole in the law against playing Grivens! I can't believe it."

"Yeah, by going back to Roman times," Seb added incredulously.

Ivy had no idea about Lundinor's ancient history, but she did know that the Dirge had an insatiable thirst for knowledge—if anyone had discovered the forgotten secrets of GUT law, it would be them. "Surely no one is actually going to go along with this?" she asked hopefully. "It's completely irrational. You can't just make something against the law, and then reinstate it for one day."

Seb stared at her. "You seem to be forgetting where we

are, sis: weirdo capital of the world. These are the people who invented the Timbermeal."

Valian smiled sarcastically but gave a grim nod. "He's right. Uncommoners love traditional celebrations; the more eccentric, the better. In any case, people will welcome a distraction from all this news of Jack-in-the Green and the murders at the memorial. This contest has come at the perfect time."

The more Ivy thought about it, the more certain she felt that Selena had planned it that way. She reran the announcement in her head. "The contest will take place two days from now. That's May Day—the same deadline Jack-in-the-Green has for finding the Jar of Shadows." A cold sense of foreboding came over her. "Do you think Selena's planning to use the jar at the contest somehow?"

The three of them looked at one another warily. The people in the street around them had no idea how much danger they were in.

"We've still got time to find that jar before they do," Seb said, gritting his teeth. "Perhaps now that we know more about the Dirge's plan, we should ask Granma for help."

Ivy considered the suggestion carefully. "But Granma Sylvie is already uneasy about being here—if she knows the Dirge are planning something, she'll probably whisk us away before we've had a chance to stop it."

"We need to be careful who we talk to," Valian added. "We've no idea how many disguises Jack-in-the-Green has."

"I guess you're right," Seb said, glancing nervously up at a folded materializer hanging in a tree. "He could even have been one of the officers standing in the background at the announcement."

"Even scarier than that," Valian said, "he could be that tree."

Ethel and Granma Sylvie were sitting on the large front porch of the House of Bells when Ivy, Seb and Valian arrived. Ivy almost didn't recognize the building in its spring incarnation—a timber-framed three-story house painted cornflower blue and covered in climbing roses.

"Ivy! Sebastian!" Granma Sylvie leaped up from her seat. Strands of long white hair had come free of her neat bun and her cheeks were flushed, as if she'd just run the length of the Gauntlet. "I'm so happy to see you." She squeezed Ivy tightly and then pushed her back for inspection. "Are you OK? Where have you been since the Timbermeal?"

Ivy brushed the dried mud from the last mop landing off her knees. "Just exploring the Great Cavern. We didn't go far." She greeted Ethel with a hug and sat down on the bench beside Granma Sylvie. Ethel patted Seb fondly on the shoulder as he took a chair. Her hand froze when Valian appeared behind him. They gave each other a wary scowl, and he joined the others around the table.

"What happened to you?" Seb asked Granma Sylvie, glancing at her disheveled hair and clothes. "You look a bit—"

"I've had a difficult morning," Granma Sylvie said, cutting him off. "This business sorting out the Wrench estate has been exhausting. Only an hour ago, the underguard escorted me into the family mansion."

Ivy had often thought about that strange old house on the hill; Granma Sylvie would have only been a teenager when she lived there.

"More like *you* escorted *them*," Ethel corrected. "They couldn't have got in if you hadn't given them access—that place only opens to a member of the family." Her flinty eyes narrowed. "If you ask me, all this cataloging-the-estate business is a cover for what Smokehart and the underguard really want—access to that building and all the secrets inside."

Granma Sylvie pursed her lips. "Even if you're right, I can't get out of it now; they made me shake on it. At least I managed to convince them that the four of us were at the Timbermeal when that graffiti appeared this morning, so they can't hassle us for statements." Her lip quivered. Ivy guessed the murders at the memorial and their connection with the smoking hourglass had been troubling her.

Ethel huffed and began pouring tea. "You can't have them bullying you like this." She passed Granma Sylvie a cup of pale green steaming liquid. Seb eyed it suspiciously. "It's only peppermint," Ethel told him. "Even uncommoners don't mess around with tea."

Granma Sylvie's face darkened as she took the cup. "We've been logging the contents room by room, starting on the ground floor, but neither I nor any of the underguards have found anything of great value so far. I overheard a few of them talking—they suspect that my family stored any high-grade objects in secret locations around the world." The teacup was shaking in her hands, so she put it down. "I hope they're not expecting me to know where they are."

"That does it," Ethel said. "I'm coming with you tomorrow, whether they like it or not." She leaned back in her chair, a satisfied expression on her face.

Granma Sylvie pulled several objects out of her handbag:

a small drawstring purse made of blue velvet, a waxy old tape measure and a stainless-steel saltshaker—the kind you'd find in a fast-food restaurant. "I'm only allowed to take a few things out of the house each day. Here—these are for you." She handed the saltshaker and tape measure to Seb and the purse to Ivy.

Ivy peered inside. The purse was filled with a handful of small feathers, some buttons, a teaspoon, a china napkin holder and a broken pencil. She sensed they were all uncommon.

"I thought it could be your allowance," Granma Sylvie said. "Ethel told me that most children who take the glove are given one the season after."

"My *allowance*?" Ivy queried.

"I added it up earlier," Ethel explained. "You've got five grade in there."

Ivy's face flushed. *I can trade.* She flexed her gloves; now that she had something to barter with, they would record what deals she made.

Seb scrutinized the saltshaker. "*OK, so what does this baby do?*"

"Uncommon saltshakers are viewing devices," Valian said.

"And yer gran 'as the matching pepper pot," Ethel added. "Tip some out and you'll see."

Seb turned the object upside down and gave it a shake. The salt looked like snow as it fell. An image appeared in the crystals: it showed the porch of the House of Bells, with the five of them beneath it, as they were right then. "OK, that is totally cool."

"I'm not sure if I'll get a chance to send many featherlights over the next few days," Granma Sylvie said. "The shakers should allow us to check up on each other."

Ivy shared a nervous smile with Seb and Valian. They'd have to be careful.

"What does the tape measure do?" Seb asked, stuffing the saltshaker into his rucksack.

"Resizes stuff," Ethel said. "You wrap it around something to make it bigger or smaller. I've never used one myself, but 'eard others talk about them. You'll 'ave to get that one graded; see 'ow much it's worth."

Valian caught Ivy's attention and then pointed to Granma Sylvie's pocket.

"Er, we found something today, Granma," Ivy said softly, "while we were exploring. This is going to sound strange, but it's in your pocket."

"What?" Granma Sylvie pushed her hand inside her jacket and drew out the half-burned postcard. She blinked twice before examining it.

"We're not sure who the sender is," Ivy prompted, "but the photo shows you and Selena Grimes."

"Yes, but I don't recall Selena Grimes at that age," Granma Sylvie remarked. "I have no memory of her at all, apart from the one you already know about."

Ethel leaned over. "The picture must've been taken before you and I became friends, Sylv. You didn't 'ang around with Selena Grimes when I knew you."

"What about the shoe?" Valian asked, pointing to the toe of the mysterious black brogue. "Do you know who it belongs to?"

Granma Sylvie looked blank.

So much for that idea. Ivy was about to slip the postcard into her satchel, when she noticed another piece of paper on the table and dragged it toward her. It was the smoking hourglass that Granma Sylvie had scribbled that morning. The other hourglass symbols—on the leather notebook and on the memorial—had been drawn with straight edges and clean lines, but Granma Sylvie's freehand sketch was wonky.

"Maybe it's just me, but do these two look similar?" Ivy positioned Granma Sylvie's sketch next to the postcard and pointed to the burn marks at the bottom of the message. "I thought that was the sender's initials, but perhaps I was wrong."

Seb squinted. "Ivy, that's the same symbol! Whoever wrote the postcard signed it with a smoking hourglass."

Ethel fumbled with her teacup. "Sorry—*what* did you say?"

"A smoking hourglass . . . ?" he repeated.

"I knew it!" Ethel sprang to her feet and scuttled into the House of Bells without another word. There was a muffled chorus of oohs and aahs from the bells inside the shop, and then she returned carrying a newspaper and a small bell that looked like it had been carved from some sort of crystal. It was translucent yellow in color, with creamy white veins marbled through it.

"I knew there was something familiar about that symbol on the memorial," Ethel said, opening the newspaper. "It's on the front page of this afternoon's *Chronicle*. *Murder at the memorial*," she read. *"Deplorable vandal draws burning sand timer across the stone. Underguards suspect victims were poisoned."*

Ivy read the headline, feeling a surge of excitement. "Are you saying you've seen the smoking hourglass before?"

Ethel shook her head. "No, but I 'ave 'eard of it—I didn't make the connection at first because the *Chronicle* called it a burning sand timer. Here, listen . . ."

She held the crystal bell over the center of the table and gave it a shake. A child's voice rang out, singing a nursery rhyme:

> *"The 'vatum men come a-hunting to town*
> *And we will go to see*
> *In tent or thatch or burrow or cart*
> *Who knows where they will be, will be,*
> *Who knows where they will be?*

> *"With flourish and fizz the 'vatum men mix*
> *For five wonders of light,*
> *So stirs a dream, so flares a hope,*
> *What will they show tonight, tonight,*
> *What will they show tonight?*

"But 'vatum men no more we see
Now grips a crooked fear
More powerful than e'er before,
How long will the dark live here, live here,
How long will the dark live here?

"Farewell to those great 'vatum men,
We shall see their kind ne'er more . . .
So hide your smoking hourglass,
And lock the secret door, the door,
And lock the secret door."

As the bell fell silent, Ivy's mind was reeling, wondering what it all meant. Ethel rang the bell again, as if double-checking what she'd heard.

"Weird . . . but catchy," Seb decided. "Anyone know who the 'vatum men are?"

"The *Rasa*vatum," Ethel corrected, "to give 'em their proper name. When I was a girl, they were a guild of mixologists famous for staging secret demonstrations. They'd drift into an undermart without announcing their arrival, put on a spectacular show—brewing everything from dream elixirs to waters of eternal youth, then give 'em away free to the audience. The following day they'd be headline news."

"Like rock stars," Seb said. "I'm guessing you had to do some seriously impressive mixology to be a member of their guild."

"I'd say so," Ethel agreed. "They were rumored to store all their recipes in a vast library, which only members 'ad access to."

Valian shook his head. "But I've never heard of them before. Not even from my parents. What happened to them?"

"Once the Dirge rose to prominence, the Rasavatum stopped appearing." Ethel sighed. "Evidence of mixology was found at the scene of the Dirge's crimes—it was said that the Rasavatum 'ad joined them. Mixology fell out of favor in a big way. The Rasavatum were never spoken of again."

Ivy reran the last verse of the nursery rhyme in her head, trying to understand the connection between the smoking hourglass and the Rasavatum. *"So hide your smoking hourglass . . . ,"* she murmured. "When the Rasavatum disappeared, so did the symbol. Could the smoking hourglass be the Rasavatum's coat of arms?"

Ethel shrugged. "The only people who'd know that would be Rasavatum members themselves. They didn't use their coat of arms in the same way as other guilds. They existed by word of mouth." She tapped the newspaper again. "That's why no one's recognized it."

Granma Sylvie's gaze was far away. Ivy wondered if she was thinking about her memory of the smoking hourglass on the black door. If the Rasavatum had worked for the Dirge, it meant another troubling connection between them and her past.

Seb leaned closer to Ivy and Valian, keeping his voice down. "We know the Dirge once had an army of the dead. What if they're using the smoking hourglass to call back their old followers in the Rasavatum and rebuild their forces?"

Valian tapped Ivy's satchel. "The owner of that notebook and the sender of the postcard must both have been members of the guild. We need to know more about the Rasavatum in order to understand how the notebook works."

"Ho hum." Granma Sylvie inserted her head between the three of them. "Whatever you're plotting, you can just unplot it. It's dinner and bed for the two of you."

Seb groaned. "But—"

"No buts." Granma Sylvie patted him on the shoulder. "Whatever it is, I'm sure it can wait till tomorrow."

Valian smiled thinly. "Meet me at my place in the morning?"

Ivy nodded. They had work to do.

CHAPTER FOURTEEN

Seb held the door of the Cabbage Moon open as Ivy followed him outside. "Worst night's sleep ever."

"Tell me about it." Ivy rubbed her temples. The garbled voices of trapped souls had rattled around in her head all night, waking her several times in the early hours.

As they moved onto the Gauntlet and turned in the direction of the Market Cross, Seb studied his feet. "I kept dreaming about the chief officer lying there, dead."

"We've still got another day and a bit to stop the Dirge from killing anyone else," Ivy reminded him. "The Jar of Shadows is out there; we've got to learn how to find it."

Lundinor was just waking up. Groggy shouts and clinking tent poles pierced the morning quiet, along with the sizzle of open-air cooking. Ivy stared across the patchwork fields and saw a thread of smoke rising from almost every camp. She thought of all the people who called Lundinor home at certain times of the year, and just how many lives were at risk from the Dirge and their vile plans.

On the opposite side of the road she spotted Alexander Brewster collecting glasses from the tables outside the alehouse. His apron was stained and his fiery hair looked as if he'd just battled through a storm. He caught Ivy's gaze as she looked over.

Hey! she mouthed, waving. Alexander returned her smile before sighing and continuing with his duties. It seemed like he never got a break. Maybe, when this was all over, Ivy could invite him for a Hundred Punch at the Cabbage Moon; he was new to Lundinor—he probably hadn't made any friends yet.

Seb slipped his rucksack off his shoulder. "I'll say this for our innkeeper," he decided, unwrapping the foil from a fried-egg sandwich, "there's nothing *little* about Mr. Littlefair's food." He took a massive mouthful, sending ketchup squirting down the front of his black T-shirt.

Reaching inside her satchel, Ivy tickled Scratch hello, then felt past him for Granma Sylvie's postcard. She studied the photo and reread the message, which had been playing in her mind. If it had been sent by a member of the Rasavatum, then the "dangerous work" the author spoke of could have been something carried out on behalf of the Dirge.

But . . . Ivy still didn't want to believe that Granma Sylvie had known anything about it. "Why would Selena want this destroyed?" she wondered. "Perhaps the person missing from the photo is someone who knows something about her involvement with the Dirge?" She massaged her forehead, trying to lessen her headache.

Seb stopped. "You all right?"

"It's just my whispering; it makes my head hurt."

He scanned the road purposefully. "Violet Eyelet's Button Apothecary is over there—she might have a button to help."

Ivy headed over to a rickety wooden cart standing beside the road. It was painted pale green and lilac, and resting on top was a chest of what looked like a hundred tiny drawers, each with a little label hanging from the handle.

Violet was standing behind the stall, her fluffy white hair piled on top of her head like a huge dollop of meringue. Three pairs of different-colored spectacles jangled around her neck. "Hello, petal! Give me one moment and I'll be right with you."

Ivy waited while Violet served another customer. The apothecary was busy. Among the shoppers was a hunched old man with crooked teeth and deep wrinkles in his tanned skin.

Something about him was familiar. . . .

Mr. Punch?!

No one else would have recognized the quartermaster of the Great Cavern, but Ivy's whispering allowed her to see Mr. Punch's true nature—he was a Hob, a race of the dead formed from several souls who all looked and spoke differently. On other occasions she'd encountered Mr. Punch as a wise old shop assistant; a pale red-haired young man in a ringmaster's tailcoat, which was how he appeared as quartermaster; and a skinny guy with dark skin and a fuzzy beard. His eyes were always the same swirly blue-green color, like a tropical lagoon.

"Sir?" Ivy asked, going up to him.

The old man winked. "Nice to see yer back in Lundinor, Ivy Sparrow." His voice was coarse, like a trader who'd been shouting to his customers all day.

Ivy broke into a smile. *I'm right. It* is *him.*

"Lundinor looks a bit different this season, eh?" Mr. Punch said.

Ivy wasn't sure what he meant, but she didn't have time for any more riddles. "My *abilities* have started to change," she whispered. "I can hear voices all the time now—not just when I'm touching an uncommon object. And I can sense the dead too. Do you know why?"

Mr. Punch rubbed a hand across his chin. "Not exactly, but if I had to guess, I'd say that the longer you are exposed to fragmented souls—both those trapped inside uncommon objects and those transformed as races of the dead—the more acute your whispering becomes. It is a sense, after all—just like your sight or smell; it is a way to read the world around you. The more you use it, the stronger it will get." His eyes flashed. "It's a pity you don't have a tutor—someone with the same gift as you."

Ivy sighed, doubting she'd ever find another whisperer. It wasn't as if she could place an advertisement in the *Barrow Post.* Fear of the Dirge kidnapping people like her had kept them silent for years.

"Ivy!" Violet panted, shuffling over. "Sorry—I was in the middle of an exchange. What can I do for you?"

Ivy hesitated. There was so much more she needed to ask Mr. Punch. "Um, I need something for a headache," she said hurriedly.

"But of course!" Violet pushed two pairs of spectacles higher on her nose, squinting at the chest. Eventually she selected a drawer and picked out a handful of square gray buttons. "Is it for you, dear?"

Ivy nodded.

"Oh." Violet smiled kindly. "I'm sorry to hear that. Here you go." She assessed Ivy's outfit and tucked one of the gray buttons into the top pocket of Ivy's sweater.

The throbbing in Ivy's temples lessened almost immediately. She started to get her allowance out of her satchel, but Violet shook her head. "There's no charge for friends, Ivy. Now, what can I do for you, si—?"

Violet looked up to where Mr. Punch had been standing, only to find that he had vanished. She looked along the road in both directions, but he was nowhere to be seen.

She placed her hands on her hips. "Must have been dead," she told Ivy. "Those ones disappear all the time."

As Ivy and Seb continued along the Gauntlet toward Valian's, Ivy couldn't help but notice the number of GRIVENS CONTEST posters fixed to tree trunks and tent poles. Bunting decorated with Grivens pieces was strung between some of the shops, and there were at least two stalls offering reductions on newly minted Grivens sets, displaying hastily written signs saying: GET PRACTICING!

She caught snatches of excited conversation, the traders speculating on who might enter the contest or taking bets on the final winner. Ivy tensed, knowing what might really happen that night if she, Seb and Valian failed in their search. *All the fears in the world . . .* Opening the Jar of Shadows would be like releasing a nightmare into Lundinor.

They slowed as they approached Hoff & Winkle's Hobsmatch Emporium, heading for the staircase at the back that led to Valian's room. Ivy had passed the store during the winter, when it had taken the form of a crumbling house with dusty leaded windows. Now it was a huge wooden barn with a steeply sloping roof. Chickens pecked at the hay bales outside. Ivy brightened; she was beginning to enjoy discovering how everything had changed.

A very short woman with shiny brown hair was sweeping up by the wide barn doors as they passed. She wore a sleeveless beaded dress, golden sandals and a pale pink cloche hat. When she spotted them, she waved. "Yoo-hoo!"

"Is she talking to us?" Ivy asked.

They stopped as the lady came trundling up to meet them.

"It *is* you!" she declared in an Irish lilt. "Oh, how exciting! Known Valian since he was a tadpole and he's never had friends before. Miss Hoff will be so thrilled!" She rested her broom beside her; it was at least two feet taller than her.

Ivy looked at the barn. "You're . . . Miss Winkle?"

The lady held out her hand. She was wearing small pale pink suede gloves embroidered with daisies. "Delighted to meet you both."

"We're here to see Valian," Seb said, smiling thinly as he shook her hand.

"Yes, he was called out on urgent business this morning," Miss Winkle explained. "Told us to let you know that you should wait for him here." She scrutinized Seb's plain black T-shirt, muddy jeans and scruffy sneakers and smiled weakly before turning with similar disappointment to Ivy's outfit. "You'd better come inside."

As Ivy stepped over the threshold, a bell called out, "Miss Hattie Hoff and Miss Gabriella Winkle wish you the best of the Trade!"

"Miss Hoff!" Miss Winkle shouted, leading them into the middle of the barn. "Look who I found—it's Valian's friends!"

The floor was filled with clothes rails. Ivy spotted a

tall, slim lady with vibrant red hair raise her hand. "Right with you, Gabi!" She finished helping a man in purple yoga pants adjust the fit on his astronaut helmet before dashing over. Her Hobsmatch consisted of a white Formula 1 racing driver's suit emblazoned with brightly colored logos, crimson cowboy boots and leather biker gloves. She gasped when she saw Ivy and Seb. "But my dears—you're not in Hobsmatch!"

Before Ivy could offer an explanation, Miss Winkle tutted, "My thoughts exactly. But we can sort that out in no time. We'll add it to Valian's account." She pulled a plastic twelve-inch ruler out of the pocket of her dress and held it to Seb's head.

He shied away, looking at her out of the corner of his eye. "What exactly are you doing?"

"I'm taking the measure of you," Miss Winkle explained. "Finding out what you're made of. Haven't you ever noticed that uncommoners wear Hobsmatch that expresses who they are? The ruler helps us find what's inside so we can match what's on the outside. Why do you think it's called Hobs*match*?" She held the ruler lower for Miss Hoff to examine.

"Oh yes, yes," Miss Hoff said. "What about the black and red"—she swept her hands down her sides—"with the stripes and the large . . ." She gestured in circles on her shoulders.

Seb's eyebrows slowly climbed higher up his forehead. Ivy couldn't help giggling.

"Just you wait here. I'll bring our suggestions forthwith," Miss Hoff told him.

While she was gone, Miss Winkle took Ivy's measurements with the same ruler. Even without it touching her skin,

Ivy could sense that it was uncommon. Mr. Punch had said that her whispering was a way to read the world around her, and it got her thinking.

She concentrated on the nearest couple of uncommoners browsing through the clothes racks, trying to reach out with her senses and detect any fragments of broken soul. It was tricky. She couldn't control her whispering in the same way as her other senses—it wasn't like focusing her eyes or tuning her ears. Instead, it came from somewhere deep inside her. After a moment's struggle she gave up.

"Interesting," Miss Winkle said. She peered into Ivy's green eyes and smiled, dimples appearing in her cheeks. *"You're courage and tall and love above all."*

Ivy frowned. "I'm *what*?" She craned her neck to examine the ruler. The black inch lines had re-formed into words, spelling out the phrase Miss Winkle had quoted. "What does that mean? I'm not tall."

"I don't think it means physically, dear," Miss Winkle said.

Seb folded his arms defensively. "So what did the ruler say when you measured me?"

"Oh yes," Miss Winkle twittered. *"Rhythm and grit and filled with wit."*

"Has a good ring to it, if you ask me," said a familiar voice from behind them. Ivy turned to find Judy balancing a small barrel of Hundred Punch in her arms. She smiled at them and set the barrel down. "I got my first Hobsmatch outfit here too."

"You did?" Ivy said. "What did the ruler say about you?"

Judy tucked a strand of poker-straight hair behind her ear, darting a look at Seb. *"Daring and grace and glowing of face,"* she said in a small voice. "I'm delivering Hundred Punch in exchange for replacement trousers for Mr. Littlefair. Anyway, what are you two doing here?"

Before Ivy could give an answer, Miss Hoff returned with an armful of possible Hobsmatch garments for her and Seb. Ivy spied a frilly white cuff and the corners of some pointy shoulder pads among them. Seb's legs twitched like he was about to turn and run, but Judy put a hand on his shoulder and escorted him and Ivy to the changing rooms.

Half an hour later, Ivy found herself standing in front of a long antique mirror while she waited for Seb to emerge from his cubicle. She smoothed down the arms of her cropped black jacket with its smart Eton collar, which complemented the casual pair of stonewashed jeans underneath. Ribbon-laced brown leather boots and a red satin neck scarf completed the outfit. The color made her smile; it reminded her of the poppies in their garden at home. Altogether she thought Miss Hoff and Miss Winkle had done a good job. She'd never thought she'd feel comfortable in Hobsmatch, but now she could see why the traders liked it; it was as if she was wearing an extension of who she was.

"OK, this is the last one," Seb called from the changing room. "If this looks stupid, erase it from your mind." He poked his head around the curtain and looked at Judy. "Especially you."

Judy laughed as he shuffled out wearing black three-quarter-length shorts, a baggy L.A. Lakers basketball jersey, scuffed vintage sneakers and a straight-cut, loose-fitting long black mandarin coat. It was embroidered with gold thread and he'd turned the sleeves up, like he did when he was drumming. "Well . . . ?"

Ivy cocked her head, taking it all in. She liked the combination of modern sportswear and traditional Chinese dress. "Actually . . . this one kind of suits you."

"Yeah," Judy agreed. "It's a good mix."

"Really?" Seb opened the coat, showing them the gold satin lining. "The cool thing is, there're these long pockets inside that I can put my drumsticks in."

Ivy was just hanging a swimming cap back on a hook when something in the corner of the barn caught her eye. Inside a large glass case, an ivory leather jacket with long red sleeves was draped over a mannequin. There were gold buttons around the collar and leaves embroidered in jade thread on the cuffs.

She walked over to take a closer look. A brass plaque attached to the case read: JACKET WORN BY SIR CLEMENT, CIRCA 1560. "Is this *real*?" she asked Miss Hoff. "It's amazing."

"Absolutely," she replied with a smile. "We inherited it from our fathers, Mr. Hoff and Mr. Winkle."

"And they from *their* fathers," Miss Winkle added, appearing at Miss Hoff's side. "Our ancestors were the foremost Hobsmatch traders of their time. Apparently Sir

Clement bequeathed the jacket to our family before he Departed."

"Here, you can take a closer look if you'd like." Miss Hoff unlocked the cabinet using a small silver key from her pocket. Very carefully she slid the jacket off the mannequin and hung it over her arm. "The leather jerkin is over four hundred years old," she said, pointing to the chest piece. "Sir Clement added the sleeves later; they're made of Chinese silk. Have a feel—it's just like new."

Ivy ran her fingers down the front. The leather was soft but didn't feel as if it was about to crumble. She guessed uncommon methods had been used to preserve it. Her fingertips grazed something rough under the lapel, so she lifted it up.

Hidden underneath was a symbol embroidered in gold thread:

A smoking hourglass . . . !

Ivy drew her hand back, her mind whirring.

"Lovely, isn't it?" Miss Hoff cooed, brushing the jacket down before returning it to the glass case. "We really don't take it out enough."

Had Sir Clement been a member of the Rasavatum? He was one of the most famous uncommoners in history; there was bound to be tons of information available on him in Lundinor. Ivy needed to find out more.

The floor shook with the thud of running footsteps. A familiar voice called into the barn, "Ivy? Seb?" Valian came tearing in, zigzagging between the clothes racks in order to reach them. "Sorry I'm late."

"You all right?" Seb asked.

"Yeah, fine." Valian started as he caught sight of Seb's Hobsmatch. "Nice. Suits you."

Ivy doubted Valian would have the same opinion when he realized the outfit was being charged to his account. "Listen—I think Sir Clement could have been one of the Rasavatum," she said in a hushed voice. "Is there somewhere we can go to learn more about him?"

Valian shrugged. "I suppose we could ask at the tourist information van in the Market Cross. They offer historical tours for visitors. How did you find out?"

"I'll explain on the way," Ivy said. "We've got no time to lose."

CHAPTER FIFTEEN

As they hurried along the road, Valian zipped up his jacket. "Someone from the Scouts' Union contacted me earlier—that's why I had to leave. A rare uncommon sundial was being sold in the East End; scouts use them to pinpoint the location of objects."

"Did you manage to get hold of it?" Ivy asked. "Did it find the Jar of Shadows?"

Valian scowled. "Sundials are normally highly accurate, but when I got it to search for a jar within the walls of Lundinor, it couldn't fix on a single location. If the Jar of Shadows is here, it's being hidden by powerful uncommon forces." He hesitated. "It's a bit like what happened with Rosie."

"Your sister?" Seb asked. "What do you mean?"

"Before I went to the Scouts' Union I wrote Rosie's name on the label of the Great Uncommon Bag to see if it would find her," Valian explained. "The bag took me to Montro-quer undermart in Paris, but Rosie wasn't anywhere to be seen, so I tried the bag again and found myself in Mai Masima undermart in Thailand. After that it took me to undermarts in Germany, Lithuania and Portugal. It was like it couldn't settle on one location."

From the set of Valian's jaw, Ivy could tell how frustrated he was. "Maybe we can mark on a map all the places the bag has taken you to so far, and see if they're connected?" she suggested. "If we can find a pattern, we might be able to predict where Rosie will be next."

Seb gave her a wary glance. She knew what he was thinking: there was a strong chance that Rosie might not even be alive; she'd gone missing so long ago, and in the Dead End too. After their own experiences in that place, Ivy knew how dangerous it was.

The three of them slowed as they came to the Market Cross. There was little evidence of yesterday's Timbermeal other than a few patches of flattened grass. Valian pointed to a dented old ice cream van standing on the edge of the green and they headed over.

The vehicle was decorated with advertisements for things to do in Lundinor. There were guided tours for the living—WALK THE WALLS OF THE GREAT UNDERMART OF LUNDINOR—and the dead—WALK THROUGH THE WALLS OF THE GREAT UNDERMART OF LUNDINOR—as well as suggestions for places to stay and awards for Lundinor's top restaurants.

At the rear of the van was a notice board covered with announcements from different guilds. Ivy paused to take a closer look. The top of every notice showed the guild's coat of arms, and below, the times and dates of the next guild meeting. The Ancient Order of Chestnut Roasters were due to vote for a new guild leader.

"Does every guild have a leader?" Ivy asked Valian, thinking uneasily of the Dirge.

"Yeah, that's the rule. They have the final word on any guild decisions. There's a fixed number of members too; a space only becomes available when someone has Departed."

That was why there were only six members of the Dirge, Ivy thought. The code name Wolfsbane could have been taken by several people before Selena Grimes started using it.

Seb read one of the notices. "So . . . are you in a scouts' guild?"

Valian scoffed. "No. You have to be invited by the other members."

Ivy searched for disappointment on his face. He caught her looking at him and shrugged. "I'm used to working on my own. Anyway, it's hard to feel lonely when you live in busy undermarts all year round."

"All year round?" Seb repeated. "But Lundinor's only open three times a year."

"There are hundreds of other undermarts around the world. When one closes, another one opens; there's a kind of circuit."

The lady behind the counter of the tourist information van had flowers in her fluffy brown hair. "There's a Sir Clement museum," she told them. "I haven't sold any tickets for a long while, but I'm sure they're still valid." She rooted around in the van and reappeared with a small book of perforated paper tickets. "They're half a grade each."

Ivy couldn't understand why the place didn't have more visitors. The tourist information lady held out a patchy velvet glove expectantly. Ivy felt herself going red, realizing she meant to trade.

"Don't look at me," Valian said with a shrug. "That sundial cost me an arm and a leg—I'm broke."

Ivy remembered the allowance Granma Sylvie had given her and got the purse out of her satchel. Ethel had said there was five grades' worth of objects inside it, but Ivy wasn't sure which item to pick. She hastily selected a china napkin holder and handed it over.

The lady examined it carefully. "Hmm. Let's check the current market grade." She took a stainless-steel fork off the counter and, very gently, tapped the prongs against the side of the napkin holder. A clear, high-pitched chime rang out and, as the sound died away, Ivy caught a number being sung: *"One point eight."*

"Excellent. That'll do nicely." The lady smiled and shook Ivy's hand.

Ivy's wrist went weak. This was it: her first Trade. She was now as much an uncommoner as anyone in Lundinor. She didn't have long to dwell on the moment.

"The museum is in Sir Clement's old house, high up in the West End," the lady told her. She scribbled the directions down on a piece of paper and handed it over. "Have fun!"

To reach the West End the three friends had to walk through a huge archway of flowers that spelled out the words THE BEST END. Once inside, Ivy didn't know where to look first. White pavilions bordered gleaming marble courtyards and lawns so neat and green, the grass could have been made of plastic. People in huge Hobsmatch hats strolled around carrying parasols and walking tiny dogs, while others sat at tables, sipping tea and nibbling fancy cakes. Ivy noticed several underguards erecting temporary street bells directing people to the Grivens stadium. Preparations for the big contest were already under way.

"Well, it's exactly where that lady said it would be," Valian said, craning his neck. "High up."

In front of them stood the biggest tree Ivy had ever seen—the trunk was as wide as a car, and the branches reached so high, the top wasn't visible.

Seb screwed up his nose, peering into the dark canopy. "There's a museum in there?"

Ivy looked closer. Nestled between the branches were some wooden platforms, with rickety rope ladders and bridges made of chain and driftwood. A long sign had been nailed to the rough brown bark.

THE GREAT OAK TREE

LEVEL 1: *Cog & Caster, wheelmongers*
LEVEL 2: *François Filigree's Furniture Jamboree*
(also former residence of Sir Clement)
LEVEL 3: *Muddled Melodies—uncommon objects*
with musical means

The list continued to Level 21, but Ivy's attention had already focused upon something. *"François Filigree,"* she read. "I've seen that name before—yesterday, at the Timbermeal. It was written on that patio chair you were sitting on."

A varnished wooden staircase spiraled up around the trunk. After fifty steps or so they reached a large, wide platform set among the branches. On it stood a forest of black iron spindles—some as tall as a door, others the size of cotton reels. Each spindle was stacked with a different type of wheel; there were brightly colored skateboard wheels, wooden cartwheels, bicycle wheels and supermarket shopping cart wheels, among others.

"Turn your life around with a new uncommon wheel!" called a voice from somewhere behind them. "Best quality in Lundinor!"

Valian growled and sped up. "Quick—we haven't time to talk."

As they climbed the next set of stairs, the foliage of the Great Oak Tree grew denser and more tangled. Eventually the noises from the street below were muffled and it became so dark that uncommon lemon squeezers had been fixed to the branches to light the way.

"Whoa!" Ivy exclaimed, coming to a halt. In front of her, the stairs turned into a rickety rope bridge, crossing over to the other side of the tree. On each side hung nets topped with an assortment of chairs and tables piled up on top of one another as if they were about to be used in a bonfire. At the sound of Ivy's voice, they started shuffling around, kicking their legs and jostling for attention.

"The way's blocked," Valian said, pointing to a tangle of thorny branches in the middle of the bridge.

Seb pulled out his drumsticks. "Not for long."

"Careful," Ivy said, laying a hand on his arm. "It's still part of the tree."

Seb thrashed his drumsticks through the air, aiming at the thicket. There was a loud crunch as, with an explosion of leaves and splinters, a hole appeared in the center.

They continued over the bridge in single file. Halfway across, Ivy heard a voice:

"Helloooo there! Are you on your way to François Filigree's Furniture Jamboree?"

She stopped, gripping the rope rail tightly and looking around. She couldn't see anyone. "Um, actually we want to visit the museum at Sir Clement's old house."

"Oh," the voice said. "You're not lost, then?"

Ivy nudged Valian. "I don't know. . . . *Are* we?"

There was a shuffling noise behind them, and a short, dumpy man dropped out of the branches, bounced onto the net and somersaulted over them onto the end of the bridge.

"Most people who wind up in my shop are lost," François Filigree said in a sad voice, brushing down his long purple overcoat with a pair of thick, fire-retardant gloves. He had a small pear-shaped body with virtually no neck, and tiny arms and legs. Covering his face was a smooth white porcelain mask with small eye holes, painted lips and a black mustache.

He must have caught Ivy staring at it because he said, "It's from Japanese Noh theater. Excellent Hobsmatch, of course. There aren't many people who dare to wear them, so I really do stand out."

"Yeah . . . see what you mean," Seb said slowly. He edged up behind Valian, his knuckles white on the rope. "Er—the museum?"

"Right . . ." François Filigree's shoulders sagged. "Have you got tickets?"

Ivy felt around in the pocket of her new jacket. "Yes."

"Then I'll show you the way," he said, sounding dejected. "Come in, come in."

He led them on a twisting route, past a graveyard of broken table legs and more cluttered bridges, to a ramshackle multistory tree house. The walls were covered with holey strips of moldy bark, and thick spiderwebs filled the empty window frames. Crumbling chimneys, crooked roofs and half-demolished balconies poked out of the dark green leaves.

"Leave your tickets on the table inside," François Filigree told them.

"*This* is the museum?" Ivy exclaimed.

He tilted his strange white mask. "I understand that it might look a little unloved, but there are plenty of Sir Clement's original possessions to check out inside, along with a few of my own knickknacks. Everything's for sale; let me know if you want to strike a deal!"

Ivy climbed the dusty steps toward the front door.

"Careful," Filigree warned, batting a branch away from her hand.

She felt her left glove catch on something as she withdrew it. A small hole had appeared in the thumb.

Filigree winced. "Ah, sorry; the tree grows at such a rate."

As he bounded off, Ivy poked her thumb, assessing the hole. Seb yanked on the handle of the tree house door and a cloud of dust puffed out. "This place can't have had any visitors for years."

"I'm guessing access was difficult," Valian said drily. "I don't know why Filigree doesn't cut things back. It's almost like he doesn't want customers."

The entrance hall was covered in vines and weeds. A solitary stool tottered in one corner and a cracked ladder hung down in the center, leading to the upper floors.

"We'd better split up to save time." Valian jumped for a rung on the ladder and pulled himself up. "I'll search upstairs. Let me know if you find anything down here."

Seb walked over to a rectangular hole in the wall, which had clearly once been a doorway. "Here goes," he said, ducking under what was left of the rotting frame.

Ivy followed him through. The room beyond was decorated with sun-bleached maps and vintage posters, and the air smelled musty and dank. A balding velvet couch rested against one wall and a moth-eaten Chinese rug covered the floor. Ivy examined one of the sideboards, which displayed a selection of objects labeled with price tags. "François's collection," she said, wiping the dust off a box containing a spun-glass paperweight.

"Any sign of the smoking hourglass?" Seb stood on tiptoe, looking into the rafters. "Or anything to do with mixology or the Rasavatum?"

Ivy spotted a checkered wooden board set with marble chess pieces. Or at least, she *thought* they were chess pieces. She read the label: ORIGINAL 1604 GRIVENS SET—7.4 GRADE.

"Know what that reminds me of?" Seb said, appearing

at her shoulder. "Toenails." He reached for a tarnished silver photo frame by her elbow. *"Rare Victorian photo frame, circa 1879,"* he read out loud from the tag. *"Frames an image by a minute either side—5.6 grade."*

Ivy frowned. "What do you think that means?"

"Dunno. Maybe it changes the way a photo appears somehow."

Ivy thought of the postcard of Granma Sylvie and Selena. She'd hidden it under her mattress before leaving the Cabbage Moon that morning. "Do you think the frame could tell us who Jack-in-the-Green burned off that postcard?"

"It's worth a try," Seb said with a shrug. "Do you have enough grade to trade for it?"

Ivy shook her head. She'd spent 1.8 getting them tickets for the museum.

Seb turned out the pockets of his jeans, but all he found were a few feathers and his phone, which he swiftly clutched to his chest. "Er . . . no."

"The only other uncommon thing I have to trade is Scratch," Ivy said. "And there's no way that's happening."

"We'll have to ask Valian," Seb decided, his mouth curling in disappointment. He tucked the frame under his arm. "Keep looking for Rasavatum clues."

Ivy studied the faded posters on the walls. One promoted the opening of the West End of Lundinor: MARVEL AT THE WEST END, LUNDINOR'S GRAND NEW SPACE FOR TRADERS! The watercolor painting in the center depicted children playing with hoops and sticks, running on a green lawn beside a row of striped pavilions. "Seb, how much do you remember of that nursery rhyme?"

"A little bit," he said. "It starts: *The 'vatum men come a-hunting to town.*"

"Yeah . . ." Ivy's mum had once told her that nursery rhymes sometimes had hidden meanings. "It doesn't say what they were hunting for, though, does it?"

Scratch vibrated within her satchel. "Repeating rhyme to Ivys can nursery!" he announced proudly as she scooped him out. "Memory excellent Scratch."

Ivy hugged him. *Of course.* He'd been in her bag when they'd first heard the rhyme. She hurriedly got out a pen and paper. "OK, Scratch, go slowly."

Once he had finished, Ivy read the rhyme back carefully, trying to identify something they might have missed, but the poem only echoed the story Ethel had already told them.

There was a creak above her head, and more dust fell down onto the sideboard. Ivy was about to brush it off her piece of paper when she noticed that only some of the words were now visible. "Wait . . . What if we're reading it wrong? What if only certain lines are important?"

Seb scanned the page a few times, reading the poem through in his head. "The only pattern that makes sense is if you take the first line from the first verse and the second line from the second verse and so on. . . ."

Ivy tried it, reading aloud: *"The 'vatum men come a–hunting to town . . . for five wonders of light . . . more powerful than e'er before . . . and lock the secret door, the door, and lock the secret door."* Her skin prickled. "Seb, it works!"

"Yeah, but what does it mean?"

Ivy's voice went hollow. "Oh no. The Rasavatum were searching for *five wonders more powerful than ever before.* . . . That can only be one thing—the Great Uncommon Good!"

Seb's eyes widened. "If the Rasavatum were hunting for the Great Uncommon Good even before the Dirge, that might be why the Dirge recruited them."

"And it would explain why a formula from the smoking-hourglass notebook would help Jack-in-the-Green find the Jar of Shadows," Ivy added. "It must have belonged to a member of the Rasavatum who was searching for it."

A tremor ran along the floorboards and Valian appeared in the doorway. "There's nothing useful up there," he said, running a hand through his hair. "Have you had any luck?"

"Ivy found a secret message in that nursery rhyme," Seb explained. "Also, we're buying this." He held up the silver photo frame. "Except that neither of us has enough grade to trade Filigree for it, so"—he grinned—"we'll owe you. . . ."

CHAPTER SIXTEEN

The second she poked her head out of the Great Uncommon Bag, Ivy spied Judy's roller skates. "Judy!" Her mind raced to find an explanation as she crawled out onto the floor of their room in the Cabbage Moon. "Er . . . this isn't what it looks like. . . ."

Judy stared at the sack by Ivy's feet. She was wearing an apron over her waistcoat-tutu combo, and in one hand held a rustling brown feather duster. As Ivy clambered to her feet, the duster gave a noisy *squawk,* which seemed to bring Judy out of her stupor.

"Ivy? What's going on? How are you bag-traveling in here?" She opened her mouth to say more, but was cut off by a loud scratch and thump over Ivy's shoulder. Valian and Seb appeared through the opening of the Great Uncommon Bag in quick succession.

"I knew no one would see us leaving that overgrown tree," Valian said, dusting off his knees as he got up. Seb threw a hand over his mouth and staggered to the open window, mumbling something about fresh air.

The feather duster squawked again, attracting both boys' attention.

"What's going on?" Judy demanded, putting her hands on her hips. "You're breaking GUT law by using that thing. You'll get Mr. Littlefair into trouble."

The duster screeched loudly. "Breaking the law, breaking the law."

Judy frowned. "I don't understand—uncommon bags don't work inside undermarts. Is there something special about this one?"

"Special about this one," the duster wailed. "Special about this one."

Seb hastily slid the window closed. "Can you ask that thing to be quiet?"

Judy stuffed it in among the mesh of her tutu without taking her eyes off them. "Look, if you're in some kind of trouble, just tell me. I might be able to help."

Ivy knew they weren't meant to be trusting anyone, but she couldn't think of an explanation that Judy would believe— apart from the truth. Plus, it would be good to have someone else to talk to about what was really going on. "Maybe we *should* tell her," she suggested nervously.

Seb smiled at Judy. "OK by me."

Valian narrowed his eyes, his expression switching from anger to mild annoyance. Eventually his shoulders slumped. "Fine," he told Judy. "But you're not going to like it."

Judy hid the feather duster in the wardrobe to keep it quiet, and as the bearskin rug lay snoring in the corner of the room, Ivy, Seb and Valian recounted everything that had happened last winter.

She rolled anxiously back and forth on her roller skates. "Ivy's a whisperer. . . . You own one of the Great Uncommon Good. . . . Valian fought wraithmoths in the Wrench basement. . . . You played Grivens with Jack-in-the-Green!" She shook her head. "What's next?"

"Well, we're hoping to use this," Ivy said, slipping the silver photo frame from her satchel.

Seb lifted her mattress and pulled out the postcard. "We think that whoever's missing from the photo can tell us more about Selena's past and her connection with our granma."

"Let's have a look at them both," Judy said.

Seb passed her the postcard, Ivy the photo frame. Judy teased the back of the frame away and tucked the postcard facedown inside so that the photo would appear on the front.

Ivy watched her curiously. "Have you used one before?"

"No," Judy admitted, "but whenever I have to use something uncommon that I'm not sure about, I just act as if it was a common version and hope for the best."

At first nothing happened. Ivy drew closer to Judy and studied the image. Granma Sylvie and Selena Grimes were standing on a cobbled road with a redbrick wall behind them.

"Uh, guys?" Seb asked. "Are you seeing that?"

Ivy looked up and realized that something had happened to their room. She could still see the walls and floor, but the duck-egg-blue wardrobe and bedside chair were slightly faded. If she turned her head, the wooden floor appeared to be made of cobblestones, and the walls flickered between sunflower wallpaper and red bricks. Ivy squinted. It was a bit like looking at a hologram. From one angle she saw their room, but from another she saw the eerie setting of the photo. "Are we inside the photo somehow?"

Valian tilted his head. "I don't think so. It's more like the photo's being projected around us."

Ivy heard muffled footsteps, and a girl with golden hair came running through the bedroom wall and across the cobbles. The four of them shuffled back to the edges of the room, but Ivy was too slow and the girl ran straight through her—as if she was made of nothing but air.

"Is that *Granma*?" Seb asked.

The young girl *was* Granma Sylvie. Ivy could tell by the shape of her face and her amber eyes. She was wearing the same Hobsmatch as in the photo—a frilly white petticoat, a denim shirt and silver go-go boots. Ivy waved a hand in front of her, but the young Sylvie remained oblivious.

"It's like some sort of recording," she decided. "Remember: it frames the picture by one minute either side. I think right now we're seeing the minute before the photo was taken."

Young Sylvie cupped her hands around her mouth. "Come on, Lena!" she called in the direction she'd just come from. "We've got to be quick—the door only appears for a few minutes; that's why it's a *secret* sweetshop!"

A second girl came racing into the room. The young Selena Grimes had freckles over her pale nose, and her dark braid swung behind her shoulders as she ran. Ivy shivered; it was disconcerting to see her with so much life in her cheeks. "Sylvie, hang on!" Selena panted. "I promised we'd wait for Amos."

"Amos *Stirling*?" Young Sylvie put her hands on her hips. "He *likes* you."

"What do you mean?" Selena asked, smoothing down her dress. She was wearing a gray pinafore over a silver blouse, with long Victorian leather riding boots laced up to the knee.

Sylvie giggled. "You *know* what I mean. He's always asking questions about you, following you around. He *likes* you."

Selena blushed. "Well, he's never said anything to me." She flashed her bare fingers while adjusting her black satin gloves. Her hands were not yet riddled with maggots. Ivy couldn't believe this was the person who would grow up to join the Dirge and become Wolfsbane.

"Selena's still touching the ground; she hasn't become a ghoul yet," Seb commented.

"What do you think came first," Valian said, "Selena dying or her joining the Dirge?"

Ivy did the math. "They must have both happened sometime between when this photo was taken and when the Dirge were last seen on Twelfth Night 1969."

A tall boy with a mop of jet-black hair came hurrying into the room. He was wearing a white shirt, navy breeches and polished black brogues. "Lena—sorry I got held up." He was well-spoken and looked a few years older than Sylvie and Selena.

Seb pointed at the boy's shoes. "They're identical to the shoe in the photo!"

Amos was clutching a leather-bound book to his chest.

"What's that?" Sylvie asked, tilting her head. "Don't tell me you brought *homework*?"

Amos reddened. "No, it's just my journal. I take it

160

everywhere. You never know when you'll need to write down a new mixology formula."

"You're a mixologist?" Sylvie's face brightened. "That's so interesting! I know what you mean about the journal—it's the same with this. . . ." She pulled a snow globe out of her pocket. "I want to be a photographer, so it's important to carry it on me at all times." She grinned. "Hey, let's get a picture now! I can take before and after shots." She set the snow globe on top of a fence post by the brick wall, then huddled between Amos and Selena.

"Say 'Uncommon Cheese,' " she called.

"UNCOMMON CHEESE!"

The snow globe vibrated, and a puff of tiny snowflakes shot out of it. Sylvie stepped forward, removed the globe from the post and peered inside. "Looks great," she declared, showing the other two.

As Amos put his journal in his other hand, Ivy gasped. Embossed onto the dark leather cover were the familiar lines of the smoking hourglass.

The notebook! It was the same one.

Judy flinched, allowing the frame to slip from her fingers. As she fumbled to catch it, Amos, Sylvie and Selena swiftly disappeared and the room returned to normal.

Ivy retrieved the notebook from her satchel urgently. *"That's* why the initials *AS* are written on every page," she said, running her fingers across the cover. "They stand for Amos Stirling. This isn't just a notebook; it's his *journal*."

"He said he was into mixology," Seb commented. "Do you think he was a member of the Rasavatum? That might explain why the smoking hourglass is on the front."

"But it still doesn't tell us why Selena would want to remove him from the postcard," Valian pointed out. "Or help us understand how we might use the journal to find the Jar of Shadows."

Ivy opened the journal and flicked through the blank pages. She could sense a soul trapped within it somewhere, but the pages didn't feel warm and tingly. "We need to find out what happened to Amos. On the postcard he mentioned that he'd been forced into hiding. Did he ever come out? Did he see Granma Sylvie again?"

Judy opened the wardrobe door and retrieved the feather duster, which began squawking. "I've got an idea that might help," she said. "We just can't do it while my mum's around. She takes a lunch break at two p.m. Meet me at the featherlight mailhouse then."

CHAPTER SEVENTEEN

Granma Sylvie slid onto the bench opposite Ivy, Seb and Valian, placing a bowl of soup on the table. All around, the dining room throbbed with activity—families chatting at tables, people serving drinks and collecting plates. The air smelled like a better version of Ivy's school canteen—gravy and roast meat without the stark after-smell of disinfectant.

"I hoped I'd catch you three in here," she said, smiling. "I checked your room before I left this morning, but you were both still asleep. And I used that pepper pot yesterday afternoon. You were buying ice cream, I think."

The tourist information bureau. That had been lucky; if Granma Sylvie had looked in on them at any other time of the day, the scene would have been far more incriminating.

"What are you doing here?" Seb asked, looking up from his chicken sandwich. "I thought you'd still be at the mansion."

"I've only come back briefly," Granma Sylvie explained. "Ethel made the underguard agree to give us a lunch break. We began cataloging the first floor this morning; then it's the study and the library, and finally the third-floor bedrooms." She examined Ivy's jacket and red neck scarf. "Hobsmatch?"

Ivy brushed down her dungarees, smiling. "You like it?"

"It suits you."

Granma Sylvie's outfit was similar to the one she'd been wearing yesterday—a stiff pencil skirt and crisp blouse.

Ivy hesitated before saying, "I have to ask you something; it's about the postcard again."

Granma Sylvie straightened. "Fire away."

"Is the name Amos Stirling familiar?"

"Amos Stirling . . ." She shook her head. "No, I'm sorry. I've never heard it before."

Ivy looked at the others, her shoulders slumping. If only Granma Sylvie could remember.

Outside, Ivy peeled off her jacket and stuffed it into her satchel.

"It's heating up," Valian said, pulling a newspaper out from under his arm.

"Tell me about it." Seb's mandarin coat was tied around his waist.

"Not the temperature," Valian groaned. "The Grivens contest." He showed them the newspaper: the contest was the top story, splashed across the front page. "Famous players have been arriving from all over the world where the game is still played legally. Late last night four people drank from the contest master's cup and two again this morning. Add those to the other four who've already entered, and we have ten contestants so far."

The photo accompanying the main article showed a man with a chiseled jaw and slick black hair taking a sip from a huge brass cup. He was surrounded by snow globe photographers and screaming fans. Ivy swallowed, trying to dispel the bitter taste at the back of her throat. If they wanted to stop the Dirge from opening the Jar of Shadows at the contest, they were running out of time.

Hearing a clatter across the street, she glanced around. Brewster's Alehouse was packed, as always—revelers released flaming burps as they lounged at picnic tables outside. Ivy spied a scrawny figure hunched over a row of metal bins in the alley beside the building.

Alexander Brewster. He swayed on the spot, a mountain of bulging bin bags in his arms. His thin legs wobbled as he took a step. . . .

"Hold on!" she called, hurrying over.

Alexander's pale face poked out from behind the black bags. "I think I've picked up too many," he fretted.

Ivy grabbed the top bag, and together they unloaded the rest into the dustbins.

"There's no time to take the rubbish out," Alexander said, sighing once they'd finished. "We're so busy that Pa is having to whip up batches of Dragon's Brew overnight. Every day we're selling out."

Ivy brushed her hands clean on her dungarees. "That's good, isn't it?" she said. "It's a great achievement. Everyone wants your dad's ale."

Alexander's mouth twitched. "I guess." He set the last lid back on a dustbin. "Thanks for helping, er . . ."

Ivy held out her hand. "It's Ivy—Ivy Sparrow."

He shook it with old leather gloves the color of oxblood.

Ivy helped him collect the glasses from the outside tables before wishing him luck with the rest of his shift and going back to join Seb and Valian. The featherlight mailhouse was only a short walk away.

"Isn't this better than skyriding?" Seb asked as they came to a fork road off the Gauntlet. "We have our feet on the ground, our lunch still in our stomachs. . . ."

Standing on the corner in front of them was a dilapidated wooden hut. A mosaic sign propped up behind the dusty window said POTTER'S POINT. The weedy garden was packed with eager customers and stallholders selling empty plant pots of all different shapes and materials—terra-cotta, plastic, glazed pottery and glass.

As Ivy searched for some indication of what they did, her eyes picked out a face among the shoppers and she froze. "No way . . ." She pointed with a shaky hand. "Is that . . . ?" She was too shocked to finish the question.

Seb followed the line of her finger and his brow crinkled. "The chief officer of the *Outlander* ship?"

Ivy examined the man's features carefully, making doubly sure that it was the same person. *White line through his eyebrow, curly blond beard* . . . "It's definitely him," she decided. "I don't understand—he's *dead*."

Valian narrowed his eyes. "We have to follow him. Judy can wait."

Head down, the chief officer shuffled away from the plant-pot sellers, his hands in the pockets of his smart black uniform. As he turned toward the East End, Ivy, Seb and Valian kept their distance, using trees and clusters of crowd as cover. The shabby quarter had undergone a spring transformation into a patchy forest of silver birch trees, complete with ramshackle cottage shops and ragged tents. Scarlet toadstools poked out of the ferns in the undergrowth, and wind rustled through the spindly branches.

The traders here all wore a similar style—their Hobsmatch was Victorian and tatty: mud-stained tailcoats, threadbare trousers and moth-eaten petticoats were the favored choices.

The chief officer emerged from the forest at the edge of a vast swamp. Ivy squinted into the thick white mist. Small groups of men and women sat fishing in the tall reeds. In the distance, on the far bank, lay the misshapen silhouettes of shepherds' huts. The chief officer trudged around the swamp and entered a green hut, third along from the left. There were dim lights on inside.

Ivy approached one of the fishermen. "Excuse me," she asked politely, "do you know whose hut that is?"

The fisherman lifted his cap to see. "The green one? Not sure, love, sorry." Ivy was about to step away when he added, "Only two fellas have gone inside since I got 'ere, and that was hours ago. Both of 'em were dead: one sticky and yellow; the other 'ad an extra arm."

Ivy had a horrible feeling she had met those two characters before. "Why is the chief officer meeting *them*?" she asked Seb and Valian.

Valian glanced at the fisherman's rod. "Can I borrow that for a minute? I'll owe you one grade."

The man shrugged and shook his hand. "I haven't caught a bite for a while anyway."

Valian took the rod and started around the edge of the

swamp. "Come on—we can use this rod to find out what's being said inside."

They snuck up to the green hut, ready to spring into action. The frilly curtains at the windows were all drawn, but smoke rose steadily from the chimney.

"Uncommon fishing rods catch bites," Valian explained, keeping his voice low. "It can be a bite of anything: cake, data . . . even a bite of conversation." He raised the rod toward the chimney and lowered the hook into the smoke. In seconds, something was tugging on the line. Carefully Valian reeled it in toward where they were crouching. A set of voices emerged from the hook as if it was a speaker:

"Glad you got my message," one said. It sounded like Mick the Stretch. "I received your payment. Here's what you asked for: coordinates for where my sources think this jar of yours is being hidden."

There was a pause, then another familiar voice. "*There? How did you find it?*"

Jack-in-the-Green. Ivy shivered.

"Squasher's friendly with one of the guards," Mick answered. "The jar was smuggled in there last night."

Suddenly the front door of the shepherd's hut swung open and Jack-in-the-Green stepped out. Valian lowered the fishing rod onto the ground, and they all ducked.

Huge yellow eyes scanned the mist over the swamp. Jack-in-the-Green adjusted his emerald suit before taking a feather out of its pocket. Ivy squinted, desperately trying to make out what he was writing, but only one word at the top was clear: *Selena*.

"He's sending her the coordinates," Valian hissed.

To Ivy's annoyance, the broken soul of one of the dead flitted into her ear, making her skin prickle. She tried to ignore it, but it was close by. . . .

Jack-in-the-Green suddenly shook himself like a dog with wet fur. In an instant, the seven-foot green-skinned creature was transformed into a man with a curly blond beard. The chief officer of the MV *Outlander*.

Ivy, Seb and Valian remained quite still until he had tramped most of the way back around the swamp. Then, very quietly, they left their hiding place and began to trek after him. Ivy sensed the dead creature start to move too, following.

"We've got to get those coordinates," Valian said. "If the Jar of Shadows—"

"Shh," Ivy hushed, raising a finger to her lips. "There's someone else here." She tried reaching out with her whispering, this time focusing on her immediate surroundings.

Perhaps all the adrenaline running through her system had sharpened her senses—because it worked: she could pinpoint the presence of one of the dead approaching through the long grass. She spun on her heels and stamped into the bog.

"Ouch!" cried a shrill voice. A wobbly red and blue jester's hat loomed out of the shadows. "What do you think I am? An ant?" Johnny Hands had a scowl on his face and a hand to his chest.

Ivy squared her shoulders. "You were following us! And you were hiding outside the shepherd's hut."

Johnny Hands folded his arms. "What if I was? A ghoul has to work. There are several parties interested in Jack-in-the-Green's whereabouts, I'll have you know. I don't suppose you saw what he wrote in that featherlight . . . ? My patron would be very interested to find out."

Ivy narrowed her eyes, wondering who Johnny Hands's patron was. Still, if Johnny was spying on Jack-in-the-Green, at least he wasn't working for the Dirge.

"I can pay you for the information," he added. He reached into his pocket and pulled out a candy-pink plastic yo-yo.

Ivy gasped. "But that's *mine!*" The yo-yo had saved her life on several occasions. She hadn't forgotten the confident feeling it gave her.

"I'm afraid, my dear, that it *was* yours," Johnny Hands said. "You lost it and I claimed it. Uncommoners pretty much invented 'finders keepers.'"

"What will you trade for it?" she asked through gritted teeth.

"I'm only exchanging it for one thing," Johnny Hands told her. "The contents of that featherlight."

Ivy kept her face blank. There *was* a way to intercept featherlight messages, she knew. "The yo-yo first, then I'll tell you what was in that message."

Johnny Hands smirked. "The message first, then I'll hand over the yo-yo." He held out a gloved hand.

"I don't technically have the message yet," Ivy admitted. "We're on our way to get it. Do we have a deal or not?"

Johnny Hands's dark-ringed eyes narrowed. "Well played, Ivy Sparrow." He shook her hand and slammed the yo-yo into her palm. "But I'm coming with you."

CHAPTER EIGHTEEN

The tall, wobbly brick tower of the featherlight mailhouse was now covered in dark vines, and there was moss on the tiled roof. Multicolored feathers of different sizes flew in and out of the building through teacup-sized holes.

Judy was waiting outside when they arrived, one roller skate resting up against the mailhouse wall. "You're late—what happened?" She spied Johnny Hands. "Oh."

"Glorious to meet you too, my dear," he said, tipping his jester's hat in her direction.

"He's going to wait outside," Seb explained in a strained voice.

Johnny Hands muttered something that sounded like "Rude" before gliding off.

Judy led Ivy, Seb and Valian into a small circular room at the bottom of the mailhouse. The last time Ivy had seen it, her great-uncle Cartimore Wrench—aka Ragwort—was living there, and it had reeked of unwashed clothes, rotting apple cores and filth. Now the space was clean and bright, and the air smelled of ladies' perfume and coffee. Jars filled with different feathers were arranged on shelves, each labeled with neat handwriting. Ivy read, among others, *Long-Haul Albatross, Quick-Noting Pigeon* and *Send-a-Song Nightingale.*

"There's no time to explain, but we need you to intercept a featherlight for us," Ivy told Judy hurriedly. "Can you do that?"

"Er—technically yes, but my mum will kill me."

"It was sent a few minutes ago to Selena Grimes," Seb added. "We think it gave the location of the Jar of Shadows."

Judy frowned. "I see. I'll try my best. Do you know what feather he used?"

"Greeny yellow with a fluffy gray tip," Valian said. "I memorized it."

She nodded. "Sounds like parakeet. We'll need to go upstairs; you can help."

A set of winding timber stairs led them to the top of the tower.

"I'm afraid it's bad news about Amos Stirling," Judy said as they climbed. "I sent him a featherlight with a special long-distance feather—it would have found him anywhere. But . . . it didn't even leave the mailhouse."

"So he's Departed," Valian said. "They're the only people you can't send messages to. When they're gone, they're gone. I've tried it with Rosie. The feathers always leave. That's how I know she's still alive."

Ivy turned around. "You *know* Rosie's alive? Why didn't you say so?"

Valian blinked. "Of *course* she's alive. Did you think it was just wishful thinking? Why would I have been looking for her all this time if she was . . ." He shook his head without finishing.

"Valian, we're sorry," Seb said behind them. "We should have had more faith. We'll help you find her when this is over, we promise."

Judy called down from the top of the stairs. "Come on, we haven't got long!"

An even smaller room sat beneath the circular roof. The floor was carpeted in fluffy down, which whirled into the air every time the tower shifted.

"The only way to intercept the message—if it hasn't already been received—is to call all traveling feathers back here," Judy explained. "Between us, we'll have to grab any parakeet ones that come in, and then resend the others. It will only amount to a short delay for most messages; I doubt anyone will notice." She cringed. "Except my mum, but I'll deal with her later."

Judy unhooked a horn hanging in the middle of the room and put it to her lips. Ivy expected to hear an ear-piercing sound, but when Judy puffed out her cheeks and blew, she heard nothing at all.

"Quickly," Judy instructed, hanging the horn back up. "Stand by the holes. Get ready to catch anything green. It's easier than it sounds; you just need to be focused."

Ivy stood by six holes, arms outstretched. For thirty seconds or so nothing happened, and then a storm of dull *thuds* encircled the roof and feathers began swooping in through every hole.

"Grab them!" Valian yelled.

Ivy caught the first two by mistake—they weren't even green—and dropped them onto the floor. She shook her head, trying to concentrate.

"Got one!" Seb shouted over her shoulder.

"It'll only last a few . . . more . . . seconds," Judy called, her voice strained.

The thudding stopped abruptly and the air cleared. Ivy turned around empty-handed, looking disappointed. "I didn't get any—sorry."

Judy and Seb were holding one green feather each; Valian had a peacock plume. When he saw everyone staring at it with quizzical expressions, he gave a thin smile and dropped it onto the pillow of feathers at his feet. "Similar color. My mistake."

"You open the message like this," Judy told Seb, stroking her green feather backward—from tip to quill. With a quick swish, it wrote a short message in the air.

> Dear Cecil,
>   You won't believe this, but they've got one
> of those sports commentary bells in . . .

Ivy shook her head. "It's not that one."

Judy snatched back the feather and ran her fingers along it in the opposite direction. It immediately disappeared with a tiny puff. "Seb, try yours."

Seb was holding his feather as if it was a priceless sword, balancing it between both palms. Taking a breath, he stroked it as Judy had instructed and it began to write:

> Selena Grimes,
>   Griddlex-gump, gallen-glow, murdle-pop,
> saddle-blow . . .

✕ ✕ ✕

Ivy's senses prickled. "That's it! But . . . what does that mean? It's nonsense."

Valian stepped closer, watching the feather write two more lines. After it had finished, it bounced gently on the spot, the text glowing with a faint golden light. "Looks like Dead Man's Code," he said. "It's an ancient language the dead developed in order to keep secrets from the living."

Judy examined the message. "My mum had to study Dead Man's Code to be mailmaster. She taught me how to read it." Her eyes widened as they followed the writing. "The Jar of Shadows is being hidden. . . ." She put a hand to her mouth before continuing to read faster. "Jack-in-the-Green asks Selena to join him there this afternoon to search for it together!"

"So," Valian said, "where is it?"

Judy grabbed the green feather, stroking it quill to tip so it vanished. "Sorry—if Selena doesn't receive the feather soon, Jack-in-the-Green will know it was intercepted," she explained. "He might come here for my mum."

"Good thinking," Seb told her. "Er . . . where is the Jar of Shadows?"

Judy knelt down and began stroking each of the feathers, sending them back on their way with a little puff every time. "You can't go there. It's too dangerous."

Ivy crouched to help her. "Judy, we have to," she said firmly. "Someone's got to stop the Dirge from getting their hands on the jar. The lives of all the uncommoners in Lundinor are at stake. You've got to tell us."

Judy sighed. "It's hidden in the Skaptikon."

CHAPTER NINETEEN

"Wait ... that 'living nightmares' place?" Seb asked. "How are we going to search fo—?"

He was cut off by a loud crackle as Johnny Hands floated *through* the roof and hovered in the middle of the room. "Visiting the Skaptikon is not like going on some jolly holiday," he declared in a deep voice. "Don't be fools."

Ivy fell onto her bottom. "You were listening!"

"Of course I was listening." He stared at them. "You *can't* go to the Skaptikon. The less said about that place, the better. It still gives me nightmares, and I don't even *sleep*."

Valian cocked his head. "Hold on ... you've *been* to the Skaptikon?"

Johnny Hands rubbed his gloves together nervously. "Not as a prisoner, but I was there when they built it. The IUC recruited me to test it out."

The International Uncommon Council . . . Ivy didn't know

what to say. Testing the Skaptikon couldn't have been a pleasant experience.

"One of the designers once told me that the way to fight the Skaptikon was to beat it at its own game. To fool it, like it fools you." He shook his head. "Of course, he also said that old socks made great tea bags, so who knows?"

Valian said, "So you're saying there *could* be a way to get into the Skaptikon safely?"

Johnny Hands raised a scruffy eyebrow. "My dear boy, like I said, the Skaptikon is no place for a jolly holiday. It has its own atmosphere inside—not even gravity behaves in the same way. It's all back to front and upside down."

Back to front . . . Ivy knew someone who saw the whole world that way.

"Anyway, this is a pointless conversation," Johnny Hands said, fixing his jester's hat tightly over his straggly hair. "Even if you find the place, it's deep, deep below Lundinor. You'd never get in or out undetected." He began dissolving back through the rafters. "I've got to alert my patron with this information. Till our paths cross again, Ivy Sparrow!"

Once he'd gone, Ivy, Seb and Valian were quiet for a moment, then Valian pulled the Great Uncommon Bag out from under his jacket.

Judy looked up. "You can't be serious."

"If we leave now," Valian said, "we might have a head start. Selena can have only just received Jack-in-the-Green's featherlight."

"I think Scratch might be able to help us when we're inside," Ivy suggested, stuffing him into the left pocket of her dungarees, and her yo-yo into the right.

Seb pulled on his mandarin coat, stowing his drumsticks within.

Judy's mouth fell open. "You're all stupid," she said. Her eyes lingered on Seb. "Braver than anyone I've ever met . . . but still totally stupid."

Ivy wasn't sure where her earlier surge of confidence had come from, but once she'd crawled out of the Great Uncommon Bag and into the Skaptikon it swiftly left her.

At once her ears were assaulted by noises: a roaring wind, the distant clang of metal bars and incoherent shouting. The sounds seemed to permeate right through her skull, stifling her thoughts and blurring her vision. "Argh—" She rubbed her temples as a hand pulled her up off the cold stone floor.

"Just stay still," Valian said, his voice trembling. "It gets a bit better after a minute or so."

They were in a windowless room about the size of a changing cubicle. The air was warm, as if they were standing close to an open fire.

"The Skaptikon is messing with our senses." Valian was shivering. Ivy reached out to him; his skin was like ice.

Seb arched his back and rubbed his shoulder. "I feel bruised. Like I've just fallen down some stairs."

"It must be affecting us all differently." Ivy was starting to sweat beneath her jacket but decided against taking it off. Johnny Hands had said that the Skaptikon fooled you; perhaps it was tricking their senses, telling them one thing when the reality was quite different.

Valian picked up the Great Uncommon Bag and stuffed it inside his jacket. "There's no alarm going off; the bag must have worked."

The three of them examined their surroundings. A ragged

hole in one wall appeared to lead out onto a dusty stone staircase covered in thorny weeds. Wind whistled through the opening.

"What do you think this room is?" Seb asked, wincing as he bent to pick up his rucksack. "A cell?"

"The Skaptikon famously doesn't have cells," Valian said. "It must be an old warden's room. They stopped using them after a while; not even the wardens lasted long in this place." He pulled a small garden trowel out of his inside pocket. Ivy recognized it—Johnny Hands had given it to him last winter; it glowed pale blue when it sensed the presence of the dead. "Hopefully we can use Ivy's whispering to find the jar and get out of here ASAP."

Ivy's face flushed. She didn't like the thought of them relying on an ability she didn't fully understand; she'd only really been able to harness her talents once. "I'll try," she said with a forced smile. "If the broken soul inside the Jar of Shadows is powerful enough, I could use it as a homing beacon and pinpoint where it's coming from." The soul inside the Great Uncommon Bag was stronger than most; she didn't see why it shouldn't be the same with the Jar of Shadows.

"Let's stay close," Valian suggested, zipping up his leather jacket and rubbing his gloves together to keep warm. "It'll be better if we face this place together."

Ivy was still sweltering. Seb drummed his fingers against his thighs, trying to relax. "Think of Johnny Hands's advice," she told him. "Try and fool the Skaptikon like it fools you. Beat it at its own game."

Seb looked at her blankly. "Yeah. Because we all totally understand what that means."

Ivy led the way out into a series of interweaving staircases,

doors, platforms and porticos—all constructed of the same gray stone. Light and shadow fell strangely, so it wasn't clear where one structure ended and another began. Wind screeched in her ears; she couldn't tell where it was coming from.

"It's like this artist I studied at school," Seb said. "Escher. He painted all these illusions and impossible constructions—stuff where it looked like a staircase was going down, when it was actually going up."

No wonder it sends you mad, Ivy thought.

She tried to concentrate on her feet, treading carefully over the weed-covered stone. Taking a few steps forward, she reached out with her senses. Echoing voices murmured all around her—the fragmented souls of the dead.

Valian's trowel glowed brighter. "Could be inmates," he said. "Or could be Selena and Jack-in-the-Green. Be on your guard."

Ivy listened carefully to each voice, checking for the jar, but couldn't find it. After a while searching, she sensed a strange whisper carried on the wind. She closed her eyes and concentrated, trying to distinguish it from the others. It didn't seem like the mutterings of one of the dead because it wasn't moving. Instead, it felt trapped. Older. Darker, like someone chanting deep under the earth.

Ivy's eyes snapped open. "I think I've got it," she announced, surprising herself. It *had* to be the Jar of Shadows; it sounded similar to the Great Uncommon Bag. "But sensing it isn't the problem; it's locating it that's going to be difficult. We need to go farther in."

They moved onto a platform with a sheer drop on both sides. Beneath them, a tangle of staircases twisted down into the shadows. Ivy's sense of perspective warped every time she looked up from her shoes—the gray paths and steps seemed to fracture into jagged pieces and overlap. She didn't suffer from vertigo, but the feeling was very similar, like seeing your surroundings through a kaleidoscope.

Seb rubbed the space between his eyebrows. "Is it me or does it feel like we're walking upside down?"

Valian swayed. "Or like the ground is moving."

"Time to call on a friend, I think." Ivy reached into her satchel and pulled out Scratch, who was trembling.

"Ivy don't likings in the Skaptikon," the bell said, whirring nervously. "Gettings of out?"

"No, Scratch," Ivy said. "We have to stay in here till we find the Jar of Shadows. Can you help us? What does this place feel like to you?"

"Normals not," he said in an unsteady voice. "Scratch sensings storm can."

At that moment a deafening clap split the air. Ivy threw her arms out for balance, the sound reverberating through her bones. "Was that *thunder*?!" she exclaimed.

"No way." Seb tipped his head back. "This is impossible."

It was raining.

Droplets fell from nowhere, spitting off the gray stone. Ivy felt her cheeks; her skin was bone-dry. *It must be some kind of illusion.* She searched for clouds and instead spotted two figures standing on a platform high above her. One was incredibly tall and green; the other hovered over the floor, robes flapping in the wind. Even through the rain Ivy could see them glaring down at her.

No! Her legs jerked. "Seb! Valian!" she shrieked. "We need to run. *Now!*"

CHAPTER TWENTY

Ivy lurched into a sprint, her heart pounding, Scratch clutched tightly in her hand.

"They're coming!" Seb shouted, chasing her down. "Faster!"

She glanced over her shoulder. Jack-in-the-Green was airborne, shooting toward them with his spiky limbs tucked under his torso like a giant green dart. Alongside him, Selena sped through the rain, her dark braid lashing whiplike over her shoulders. She bared her needlelike teeth as she locked eyes with Ivy. "Your bodies will rot in here!" she shrieked. "No one will ever find you!"

Ivy thumped into Valian's side.

"Ivy—look out!"

But she had already overbalanced.

"Whoa!" She felt her feet slip from beneath her. . . .

And then she was falling.

"Seb!" The gray stone blurred past her on either side. Her limbs flailed. "Valian!"

She hit an invisible surface and stalled in midair, as if she was floating. She couldn't see anything supporting her. After a few seconds she began sinking again, but this time there was something cold pressing against her body.

She wriggled frantically. "Scratch!" she screamed, bringing him to her ear. "What's happening?"

"State changings Skaptikon," he cried. "Ivy needs be swimmings!"

Swimming! Ivy kicked her legs. She stretched her hands above her head and hauled them down to her sides in powerful strokes. Her body surged upward.

At first she couldn't see the surface of the water—she could only feel the change between air and liquid—but then she angled her head and spotted the ripples made by the rain. The water came up to her shoulders.

She took a deep breath and started treading water to stay afloat. She wasn't sure how, but as she was falling, the air must have changed from gas to liquid.

The nearest solid surface was a tall stone staircase thirty feet away. At its summit she saw the underside of a circular platform, spilling over with weeds. Ivy paddled desperately toward it. With Scratch still locked in her grasp, it took all her energy.

She yanked herself onto the bottom step and lay back, panting. Her clothes and skin were dry; around her was only air. "Can you see Seb and Valian anywhere?" she asked Scratch. "Do you know where I am?"

"Goings where Scratch try to see," he said somberly, "but fallings too fast went."

"It's all right," she said, giving him a squeeze. She was grateful just to have him there; she couldn't imagine a worse place to be alone.

As she recovered her senses, she considered how she might reach Seb and Valian. She had no clue how far away they were, and she had no feathers left with which to contact them. She regarded the endless maze of stairways and viaducts surrounding her and tried to dispel the feeling of panic.

"Ivy?" Scratch trilled in her hand. "Beings don't sad. All is not losings."

Ivy sniffed, fighting the urge to cry. She clutched the little bell to her chest, using her whispering to sense the fragment of broken soul inside him. It was so warm and chirpy that it gave her hope.

She thought about her whispering. Perhaps she could use the Jar of Shadows to help navigate; it was a fixed point in the Skaptikon. She wiped her nose with the back of her hand and tried to refocus. *Keep it together,* she told herself.

Thunder rumbled overhead as she got to her feet and plodded up the stairs to the circular platform. She concentrated on trying to control her senses—though in the thunderstorm it was difficult. Eventually she fixed on the heartbeat of the Jar of Shadows. . . .

And it was closer than before—*much* closer.

As Ivy reached the top step, she hesitated. The platform was covered with weeds and pockmarked with crevices, as if an ancient battle had once taken place there. In the center, standing by itself in its frame, was a wooden door painted powder blue and decorated with pale dancing figures. It was the only structure not made of stone that Ivy had seen in the Skaptikon.

She lifted Scratch to her chest. "The jar is here," she decided. The heartbeat was stronger than ever before, and a mournful voice began to crystallize in her mind. She caught words, but they weren't English. "It feels like it's right in front of me."

Suddenly the floor tipped and Ivy dropped to her knees, clinging to the weeds for support. Her vision wavered.

Scratch jangled. "All in Ivy's head it's beings!" he told her.

His voice sounded warped. The Skaptikon must be playing tricks on her hearing as well as her balance, Ivy realized. She knew she had to fight against it. She curled her hands into fists and summoned all her strength, focusing hard on the Jar of Shadows. Its voice tapered into one clear pulse. It was coming from behind the door.

She approached it slowly. The broken soul within the jar sounded louder and clearer with every step. *This is it.* Her stomach fluttered as she reached for the brass handle and pressed down.

"Ivy, no!" Scratch screamed.

She drew her hand back, feeling his anguish. "Scratch, what's wrong?"

"Scratch not understandings," he said, his voice brittle. "Ivy not wantings to open jar. What Ivy thinks doing?"

"Open the jar?" Ivy repeated. "I don't want to—" She froze and stared at the door handle, suddenly remembering one of the punch lines from Stanley's jokes. *When is a door not a door? . . . When it's ajar.*

Her chest tightened as she took a step back, realization

sweeping through her. The Skaptikon was tricking her. . . .
The door *was* the jar. She'd been about to open Pandora's box!

She steadied herself. *Fool the Skaptikon like it fools you*—that
had been Johnny Hands's advice. Perhaps she had to make the
Skaptikon believe that she could see the truth—a jar, not a
door?

Imagining hard, she reached down to the base of the door
and spread her arms wide as if she was about to lift the entire
doorframe into the air. As her hands touched the wooden surface, it transformed into porcelain, and a large jar—covered
in the same white and blue patterns as the door had been—
appeared before her. Ivy strained to lift it but managed only to
slide it to the very edge of the platform.

Behind her she heard a rustle, and she swiveled on her
heels, reaching for her yo-yo.

"Ivy, you found it!" said a familiar voice.

"Seb?" Her eyes glowed with relief as he came into focus.
"Thank goodness! Are you OK? What happened?"

"We tried looking for you," he told her, stepping closer.

Ivy felt so thankful, her legs went weak. "It's all right. I
had Scratch with me."

"You should get away from the jar," he urged, staring at it
over her shoulder. "It's dangerous."

Ivy frowned. She wanted to run over to him, but there was
something about his voice that made her hesitate. She couldn't
quite put her finger on it. "Are you . . . OK?"

Behind Seb, Ivy spied Valian heaving himself up onto the
platform. He caught her eye immediately and put a finger to
his lips. Ivy wasn't sure what was going on. His uncommon
trowel was glowing brightly, but it didn't make sense; there
were no dead people nearby.

"Just step away from the jar," Seb repeated.

As Valian stalked up behind him, a cold chill ran down Ivy's spine. She raised her yo-yo in her right hand, Scratch clutched tightly in her left. "Why do you want me to get away from the jar, Seb?" she asked.

He scowled and came nearer.

It's not him, she thought with a start. *It's definitely not him.*

Against all her better judgment, she flicked her wrist in the direction of her brother, sending a torrent of wind spinning toward him. Seb made a horrible hissing sound and dived aside, dodging its path. Then, with a swift shake, he shifted into Jack-in-the-Green.

Valian charged him from behind while Ivy did a loop-the-loop with her yo-yo, blasting off another cyclone.

"STOP!" screeched a voice from above. Selena Grimes hovered down to meet them, the real Seb struggling in her arms. Jack-in-the-Green snatched Valian in a razor-sharp grip.

Valian screamed as if he'd been stabbed.

"You ignorant little children," Selena spat. "You really thought you could stop me from getting hold of the Jar of Shadows?" She laughed and gripped Seb even tighter, making him yelp in pain.

Ivy gritted her teeth, knowing she had to keep Selena talking to give herself time to think. "What are you going to do with it?" she asked.

"Break it open," Selena replied, her eyes glinting. "In the Grivens stadium. All around the world millions of uncommoners will be watching the contest. It will be the ultimate demonstration of the Dirge's power."

Ivy thought of all the traders who would be at the stadium, her friends among them. "But everyone will be killed!"

Selena grinned. "Of course. The Jar of Shadows contains the greatest fears of everyone on the planet. With its power, we will overwhelm anyone who dares oppose us, and the Dirge will finally rule Lundinor."

No matter what, Ivy knew she couldn't let Selena take that jar—there were too many lives at stake. She wouldn't be able to overcome Selena and Jack-in-the-Green by force; she needed some other leverage. . . .

"This can all be over in matter of seconds," Selena said with a nasty smile. "Step away from the jar and tell me where you've hidden that journal."

Amos's journal? Ivy didn't know why Selena was asking about that now. She looked at the Jar of Shadows, standing close to the edge of the platform. Perhaps that was her leverage. . . .

"You can't use the jar if I destroy it first!" Ivy shouted, stuffing her yo-yo and Scratch into her pocket and putting both hands on the jar. If she gave it a hard enough shove, she could push it over the side.

Selena's eyes flashed with panic. "No!"

"She's bluffing," said Jack-in-the-Green. "If she destroys the jar, she will kill herself and her two friends."

Ivy turned and put her back to the jar so that they knew she meant business. "But at least then you won't be able to use it. The Skaptikon might even contain its power, and no one else would be hurt." She looked down. If she pushed the jar in the right direction, it would land in that patch of water she'd been floundering in a few minutes earlier and wouldn't break.

Selena scowled and put her sharp teeth to Seb's neck, hissing.

Hoping her plan would work, Ivy pushed with all her

might. With a loud scraping sound, the jar toppled over and disappeared into the abyss.

"Idiot!" Selena shouted. She threw Seb aside and leaped over the edge of the platform. Jack-in-the-Green unfolded his wings and took to the air, Valian clutched tightly in his second set of arms.

Ivy fumbled for her yo-yo, but Seb was quicker. He rolled to his feet and in one fluid motion, like a trained swordsman, drew his drumsticks. Aiming at Jack-in-the-Green, he struck the first blow decisively, beating both drumsticks double-time. The mantis's wings twisted and he tumbled off course. Valian wriggled free and dropped down onto the stone with a thud.

"Over here," Ivy cried, beckoning them to her side. She got to her knees and looked over the precipice. Half-submerged in invisible liquid, Selena Grimes was locked in a strange dance with the Jar of Shadows. "We can still stop her." She turned, expecting to find Seb at her side, but he was kneeling sixty feet away, Valian slumped limply in his arms.

"IVY!" he yelled.

Ivy got to her feet and rushed over. Valian's jacket was hanging open and there was a large dark patch on his gray T-shirt. *No, Valian. Not that . . .*

"He needs help," Seb said, tugging the Great Uncommon Bag out from inside Valian's jacket. "There's so much blood. We need to get him to a hospital."

Valian's eyes flickered open. He batted an arm at the bag and, understanding his meaning, Seb held it under his lips. Valian coughed and croaked, "Lundinor Infirmary."

"I'll go through first," Seb suggested. "That way I can pull him through from the other side."

Once her brother had disappeared, Ivy used the last of her strength to push Valian into the bag. Tears ran down her cheeks as she guided his basketball shoes into the darkness.

Malicious laughter erupted over her shoulder and she turned to see Selena Grimes rising through the air, Jack-in-the-Green flying beside her with the Jar of Shadows in his arms.

There was an empty feeling in the pit of Ivy's stomach as she crawled into the bag.

They had failed. The Dirge now possessed one of the Great Uncommon Good.

CHAPTER TWENTY-ONE

Ivy wiggled her toes, feeling crisp sheets. Her head was resting on something soft. She opened her eyes and saw that she was lying on a narrow camp bed in a large canvas tent. The walls were covered with hundreds of pockets, each containing a flask, vial or bottle filled with a different-colored liquid, some bubbling or steaming. The air reeked of antiseptic, and there was a chatter of voices outside.

With difficulty, she turned her head and spotted Seb and Valian asleep on camp beds beside her, their faces shining with sweat. "Seb?" she hissed.

She remembered Valian's wound but guessed, from the peaceful expression on his face, that he had received treatment. *The Lundinor Infirmary.* That's where Valian had sent them.

All at once she recalled what had happened to the Jar of Shadows. She had to warn people! She tried to sit up, but immediately her vision swirled. Instead she reached for her satchel, which was sitting at the end of her bed. Scratch trilled as she tugged him out.

"Safe Ivy's," he said in a relieved voice. She hugged him tightly, grateful for his help in the Skaptikon. "Nurses tent bringing to you," he explained. "Knowings of your face, so sendings featherlight to Sylvie Granma."

"Granma Sylvie—is she here?"

Scratch vibrated. "Visitings once she but sleepings were you."

Slowly Ivy grasped what he was saying. The infirmary staff had recognized Ivy and Seb—doubtless from pictures in the newspapers last winter—and contacted Granma Sylvie. Ivy wondered if anyone had figured out that they'd come from the Skaptikon. She didn't know how long they'd been there.

She rummaged through her satchel, searching for something she could use to attract attention. Amos's journal and the photo frame would be of no help; she had no feathers left, and her allowance bag was full of tiny low-grade objects she had no idea how to use.

Then she spotted a piece of black card with gold writing on it in one of the inside pockets and pulled it out.

Johnny Hands's business card. Ivy recalled his words: *"I desire to inquire."*

The tent walls suddenly flapped and Johnny Hands appeared out of thin air, sitting on a chair at the foot of Ivy's bed. "Good evening, Ivy Sparrow," he said, crossing one leg over the other and removing his jester's hat.

Ivy wasn't sure how he'd got there so quickly—some trick of the dead, no doubt.

"I'm guessing you want to inquire about my tutoring services."

Ivy frowned. "*What?* No, I need your help. . . ." She wasn't sure what to tell him—that they'd been to the Skaptikon and failed to stop Selena Grimes from finding the Jar of Shadows?

"Ah, my mistake." Johnny Hands traced the brim of his jester's hat with his bony fingers. "I heard you were in the market for a tutor and presumed that, since I'm probably the only other whisperer you know, you'd need my services."

Ivy choked. "*You're* a whisperer?" She hadn't even considered that the dead *could* be, let alone . . . Johnny Hands.

"But of course," he said, twirling a hand through the air. "If you don't believe me, ask yourself how it is that I know you're looking for a teacher."

The only person other than Seb with whom Ivy had discussed her whispering was Mr. Punch. The quartermaster had suggested finding a tutor, but surely he wouldn't have revealed Ivy's secret to Johnny Hands unless . . .

She remembered Johnny Hands spying on Jack-in-the-Green outside the shepherd's hut. "Your patron . . . is it Mr. Punch?"

He flashed his crooked teeth.

There was obviously more to him than Ivy—or Valian—knew. If he had the trust of Mr. Punch, perhaps it was safe to accept his offer of help. "I have so many questions," she admitted. It was amazing to meet someone with the same gift as her. "How do I turn it off? Do you suffer from the headaches too?"

"I'm afraid you can never turn it off," Johnny Hands said, "but you can increase or decrease your field of sense. For example"—he floated off the chair and rose toward the tent roof, turning slowly in midair—"I can control my whispering so that I only sense what's inside this tent. It's always easier to use the natural barriers around you—walls, lines in the pavement, furniture; that kind of thing." He floated back to his seat. "Your turn."

Ivy looked at Seb and Valian, who were still asleep. She had time for one attempt.

All around her she could sense the voices of broken souls in the infirmary. She tried to ignore anything beyond the tent walls, imagining the whole world only existed within that small space. Slowly the muttering began to fade.

"I think it's working!" she exclaimed.

"Good," Johnny Hands said. "Now try to direct your senses toward me. Tell me—how many uncommon objects do I have upon my person right now?"

A few voices began murmuring as Ivy concentrated on Johnny Hands. They sounded shrill and metallic; the trapped souls of uncommon objects.

She counted. "Three?"

Johnny Hands clapped. "Well done!"

There was a rustle outside the tent. Ivy tensed as she saw the silhouettes of two people talking in hushed voices.

One was tall and slim. "I understand what you're saying, but I can't take you with me." *Granma Sylvie*—Ivy would recognize her voice anywhere. "The deeper we go into that place, the more I worry about what we might find—what I might have hidden from you."

"Hidden from me? Pish," the other figure remarked with a familiar Cockney drawl. *Ethel*. "Believe me, I knew you, Sylv.

There's no way you were involved with the Dirge, no matter what this memory of yours means."

Granma Sylvie sighed. "I keep thinking of Selena Grimes's deception. What if I was lying to you all those years, like she was?"

"Ridiculous," Ethel snorted. "You've got to trust in who you are. You're scared, is all."

There was a long *vrrrp* as someone unzipped the tent opening. Ivy's eyes shot to the chair. Johnny Hands had vanished . . . and there was so much more she wanted to ask. "Ivy?" Granma Sylvie smiled. "You're awake!" She came hurrying over and hugged Ivy tightly, then ran a hand across her forehead. "How are you feeling?"

Ivy shrugged, sending pain shooting between her shoulder blades. Her body ached, but she had no idea how bad anything was. She hadn't felt this awful inside the Skaptikon—but that place had completely messed with her senses.

"Here—this should help." Ethel handed Ivy a pewter flask filled with warm liquid.

Ivy held it under her nose. It smelled like ladies' perfume.

"It's called Raider's Tonic," Ethel said. "Mr. Littlefair mixed it. Takes its name from the scouts 'oo drank it after storming ancient sites looking for uncommon objects 'undreds of years ago." The corners of her eyes crinkled. "It'll have you feeling better in no time." She covered her mouth with her hand. "Much better than the stuff they give you in 'ere."

Ivy took a sip. The tonic was honey-sweet with a spicy kick. As it warmed her insides, she felt her senses sharpening.

"Granma?" rasped a voice. Seb sat up, blinking. "That

you?" He gave Ivy a quizzical expression, then turned to Valian. "Valian!" He shook him gently by the shoulder.

"Careful," Granma Sylvie warned.

Ethel handed Seb a flask of Raider's Tonic as Valian eased himself up, rubbing his head.

"Argh—I feel like I've been punched in the gut," he groaned.

"What happened to you three?" Granma Sylvie asked. "The infirmary staff couldn't tell me where you'd been or how you got here. They said they just found you in a tent, passed out."

Thank goodness, Ivy thought. The Raider's Tonic gave her an idea. "Hundred Punch," she said. "We accidentally drank a bit too much of it, and then we rode an uncommon rug and started feeling sick, and then . . . I think Valian fell off into some bushes."

Ethel raised her thin eyebrows. "Must've been very thorny bushes."

Valian winced. "They were."

Granma Sylvie put her arm around Ivy and kissed her forehead. "I'm just glad that's all it was." She looked at Ethel. "Let's take them back to the inn—get them into a proper bed."

Ethel nodded. "Right you are."

Ivy figured the Raider's Tonic had done its job because, by the time they reached the street outside the Cabbage Moon, her head was clear, the ground had stopped moving and she felt in control of her senses again. The evening light was dim and the Gauntlet had quieted. There were a few last-minute shoppers picking up bargains, but most of the stalls were vacant.

"Ivy!" Alexander Brewster raised his hand in greeting. Ivy glanced at Seb and Valian, who were wearily trudging through the front door of the Cabbage Moon. She desperately needed to talk to them about what had happened in the Skaptikon, but she didn't have the heart to ignore Alexander. "I'll be two minutes," she told Granma Sylvie. "I'm just going to say hi."

"*One* minute," Granma Sylvie said. "I want you in bed ASAP."

"Hey," Ivy called to Alexander, hurrying over. "How're you doing?" The walls of the alehouse shook with noise.

Alexander shrugged. "All right. Have you had a good day?"

Ivy wasn't sure what to say. "Er . . . I was at the infirmary. I haven't been feeling well." She rubbed her belly.

Alexander winced. "Won't offer you any Dragon's Breath, then—not a good idea if you've got an upset stomach." He cocked his head toward the alehouse. "Great for singing, though."

Ivy smiled, hearing the laughter and out-of-tune voices coming from the revelers within. She caught the distinctive bass of Drummond Brewster, and the patrons quieted as he started singing on his own. Ivy couldn't catch all the words, but the tune and the rhythm were familiar.

The *'vatum men nursery rhyme* . . . Ivy was sure of it. "That song your father's singing . . ."

Before she could finish there was a loud *smash,* the singing ended and the back door of the alehouse burst open. Out stormed Drummond.

"Boy, get back in here!" he raged, arms in the air. "I can't do everything!"

Ivy edged away as he came toward them.

"Who's this?" he demanded, pointing at Ivy.

"She . . ." Alexander didn't finish.

Drummond studied Ivy more closely. "I've seen you at the Cabbage Moon. Asking questions, are you?" He poked a huge sausagelike finger into Ivy's chest, knocking her satchel off her arm. "Well, you can keep them to yourself!"

He stared down his nose at his son. "Inside. Now." As he returned to the alehouse, Alexander rushed to help Ivy gather up her belongings, which had spilled out onto the road.

"I'm . . . sorry," he managed.

Ivy reached for Amos's journal, but Alexander grabbed it first.

His eyebrows twitched as he saw the smoking hourglass on the front. "Sorry—you'd better put this away."

As he handed the journal back to Ivy, a huge whooshing sound filled the air like wind filling a sail. Someone screamed in alarm behind them.

"Fire! FIRE! BLACKFIRE!"

CHAPTER TWENTY-TWO

A smoking hourglass was lit up in fire across the front of the alehouse. The building was engulfed in seconds. People started running away, shouting.

"Ivy, help me with these!"

She turned to find Mr. Littlefair staggering out of the Cabbage Moon carrying four buckets of water. Ivy hurried over and grabbed two. Alexander followed, with more buckets.

"Hurry!" Mr. Littlefair shouted. "We need to douse the flames!"

"What kind of fire is that?" Ivy asked. The flames weren't orange; they were plum and crimson colored, with licks of black. They seemed to be consuming the place more quickly than regular fire could.

"Blackfire," Mr. Littlefair said. "Deadly. It can only be made using mixology."

Ivy placed one bucket at her feet and swung the other toward the fire. Customers were still running out of the building as the water hit.

"It's no use," Alexander shouted. "Look!" He pointed to the roof, where the fire was rapidly eating through the thatch.

Ivy grabbed the second bucket and swung it toward the alehouse just as a red-faced Drummond Brewster came barreling through the front door. He was clutching to his chest the charred framed photo of him inventing Dragon's Breath Ale.

"SOMEBODY DO SOMETHING!" he boomed, charging out among the fleeing crowd. He grabbed a man by his lapels and began shaking him. "My alehouse is burning down! The Dragon's Breath is fueling the flames; it'll be ashes in a matter of minutes!"

Alexander hurried to his side, tugging on his apron. "I'm here, Pa. I'm OK."

"Do something useful!" his father snapped, eyes still fixed on the alehouse. Ivy couldn't help but notice the look of disappointment on Alexander's face.

Suddenly she heard a siren. *The underguard. About time.*

Two black 4x4s came rumbling into the street and the remaining traders formed large circles around them. The passenger door of one opened and Inspector Smokehart stormed out and began shouting.

"Castleguards—get control of this blaze!" he commanded, pointing to the team who had just emerged from the other vehicle. Ivy noticed they had slightly different uniforms to normal underguards—a castle design was embroidered on the backs of their cloaks. "You three," he called to the trio of constables from his own car. "Cordon off the area, get everyone inside. We need to have this blaze under control before any pyroaches arrive."

"Pyroaches?" Ivy said.

"A race of the dead," Mr. Littlefair mumbled, fetching more water from the tap outside the Cabbage Moon. "They can only exist in extremely high temperatures, so they live in volcanoes, incinerators, power plants—those kinds of places. You only find them in undermarts when something's burning."

"Are they dangerous?" she asked, filling one of her buckets.

"They eat living flesh." Mr. Littlefair strained under the weight of two sloshing pails. "You don't want to meet one."

Johnny Hands had once told Ivy that smoke in an undermart was a bad omen. It made sense now.

The castleguards opened the trunk of their vehicle and each picked up something brightly colored, and carried it toward the alehouse.

"Are those *buckets and spades*?" Ivy exclaimed. The plastic shovels were luminous shades of pink, blue and yellow and the buckets were just like those used by children to build sandcastles at the seaside. When the castleguards were in position, some aimed their spades at the alehouse, holding them to their shoulders like rifles, while others turned their buckets upside down on the dusty road: an unending stream of sand and water spouted from the spades toward the flames.

A hand gripped Ivy's shoulder.

"What's going on?" Seb asked. The others came rushing through the doors of the Cabbage Moon behind him.

Granma Sylvie put a hand to her chest. "Ivy—you're OK." She clasped her in a hug.

"I'm fine," Ivy said, pulling back. "I was just talking to Alexander when the alehouse burst into flames. The smoking hourglass materialized out of thin air like it had been lit on a timer."

The underguards started shuffling back, and Inspector Smokehart appeared in the space. "We will be taking witness statements from anyone who may have seen something," he announced. "Whether you think you did or not, it could all be important. A murderer is on the loose, and I suspect we will be adding arson to the list of charges against them."

He caught sight of Ivy and Seb and curled his lip. "You two. Again. I saw you at the memorial; you're making quite a habit of appearing at crime scenes. Do you expect me to believe that it is just a coincidence?"

Seb shifted his weight, eyes down. Ivy didn't bother offering a defense; Smokehart wasn't going to believe her.

Remembering something, she felt for her satchel and clicked the clasp shut. . . . Amos's journal was inside.

One of the castleguards approached the inspector, clearing his throat. "We think it's some kind of time-delay blackfire concoction, sir. Never seen the formula before; must be the work of a highly skilled mixologist. It'll take a good ten minutes to get those flames under control with our buckets and spades."

The alehouse thatch was still smoking and the walls were charred, but the majority of the strange purple flames had disappeared.

Drummond and Alexander appeared in front of Brewster's. "Well?" Drummond cried, charging up to Smokehart. "Have you found out who did this?"

The inspector stiffened. "We are just beginning our investigation, sir," he said tightly. "You need to step aside and let us continue."

"Step aside?!" Drummond thrust his charred photo in front of Smokehart. "Have you seen what has happened here? My reputation, my livelihood! I will not step aside! What are you doing just standing there?"

Ivy noticed that Smokehart's neck was now speckled with blood-red dots, which only happened when he was seriously angry. She shuffled back.

The sound alerted Smokehart. "You!" His head shot around. "Don't think you're getting away. I want you searched." He pointed to one of his constables, who promptly strode up to Ivy and patted her down before lifting her satchel over her head.

"Wait!" she said, pulling it back. "That's mine! You have no right to do this!"

Seb tugged on the strap. "Oi! Give it back!"

"Excuse me," Granma Sylvie said in a firm voice, stepping forward.

The constable scowled and swept aside his black cloak, giving a glimpse of his uncommon toilet brush. Ivy hadn't forgotten the horrific pain she'd felt when she was attacked with one before. She hesitated before laying a hand on Seb's elbow.

"Let him have it," she said softly. "It's not worth it."

Smokehart snatched Ivy's satchel, ripped it open and yanked the uncommon photo frame out first.

"Hold this, boy," he barked, shoving the satchel into the arms of the closest bystander, Alexander Brewster. Ivy tried to attract the boy's attention, but he was looking at his father. She tensed as Smokehart inspected the photo frame.

"Really, Inspector! Is this all you can think of?" Drummond protested. "Examining the contents of a little girl's bag? You should be hunting for the real culprit. This is the work of a master criminal, not a child."

The insult bounced off Ivy; she was much more concerned about Smokehart finding Amos's journal. He took the satchel back from Alexander and rooted through it, dropping Ivy's belongings one by one. She flinched when Scratch hit the dusty ground; she could see him trembling. Finally, Smokehart turned the bag upside down and shook it. Ivy studied the pile at his feet. The journal wasn't there.

Had she lost it? If Smokehart had found it, the smoking hourglass would be all the evidence he needed to connect her with the memorial murders. More worryingly, in the wrong hands the journal could be dangerous. Amos might have recorded any number of powerful secrets inside.

Ivy tried to think back. The last time she'd seen it was when Alexander had handed it back after it had fallen out of her satchel, but in all the commotion she could have dropped it again. She scrutinized the closest bystanders; perhaps one of them had picked it up.

Seb nudged her in the ribs and nodded at Alexander. Ivy spotted the corner of Amos's journal protruding from the pocket of his dirty apron. She relaxed and tried in vain to catch his eye. She couldn't understand why he'd helped her, but she was thankful that he had.

Smokehart clenched his teeth, his dark glasses fixed on Ivy.

Drummond Brewster gave an exasperated sigh. "Well, I could have told you you'd find no evidence in there. Who-ever's behind this has obviously been plotting my downfall for some time." He waved the framed clipping in Smokehart's face. "They're jealous of my success! See!"

The inspector looked at the uncommon photo frame in his hands. "I have a suggestion," he said, snatching the burned newspaper cutting out of Drummond's grasp. "Why don't we put your special picture in this, if your frame is too damaged?"

Ivy could only watch in stunned silence as he inserted the clipping into the uncommon frame.

Instantly the dusty street was covered with an image of a stainless-steel kitchen. The crowd hushed, and Smokehart's eyebrows disappeared below the top of his dark glasses.

The ghostly image of a fresher, thinner Drummond Brew-ster popped up from behind a countertop. He was carrying three bottles of different-colored liquid.

"What else do you need, son?" he called. "How about some of this silver stuff?"

Alexander walked into the room, carefully balancing a cauldron in his arms. He put it down on the stove. "No thanks, Pa," he said. "That will dull the effect of the fire. You need just

the right balance of ingredients for it to work. I've been experimenting with this formula. We need it to be fiery but not to
burn the drinker's throat." He added two drops of a fizzy black
liquid. The cauldron started to emit steam. "Almost there."

Drummond peered in and rubbed his hands together. "If
this works, I'll be famous. We could take the alehouse around
the world. Quick—let's get a picture of the moment I in-
vent it."

Alexander kept his eyes on the contents of the cauldron,
but Ivy noticed a line appear on his brow. She couldn't believe
what she was seeing. Drummond hadn't invented the ale at all.
Alexander had!

Drummond left the scene and came back carrying an
uncommon snow globe while Alexander stirred the mixture
with a spatula. Ivy gathered it was uncommon because the
cauldron started floating.

"OK, it's done," Alexander said with a sigh.

Drummond grinned. "Move out of the way, then—let's
get this picture."

Alexander stepped back, head down, and aimed the snow
globe at his dad.

At that moment the scene evaporated and there was only
the road before them. "That is PRIVATE!" Drummond
raged, snatching the frame from Smokehart and pulling out
the newspaper clipping. "How *dare* you!"

There was a smirk on Smokehart's face. "My apologies,"
he said. "Though I must say, that was illuminating."

CHAPTER TWENTY-THREE

Granma Sylvie stood in the doorway, the amber light from the landing spilling over her shoulders. She tapped her slipper against the floor. "I understand that you want to stay up, but you're both getting an early night. No arguments." A loud scratch reverberated around the room. Granma Sylvie's gaze flicked to the chimney breast. The uncommon wallpaper was busy rearranging itself into an elaborate re-creation of Van Gogh's *Sunflowers*. "The rest will do you good," she continued in a taut voice. "You've had a long couple of days. I'll see you in the morning. Good night." She blew them each a kiss before shutting the door.

Ivy heard Seb shuffling in the bunk above. "Hang on. Give it a few seconds."

She waited for Granma Sylvie's footsteps to fade away before pulling back her covers and tiptoeing across to the window. She drew back the curtain and looked out. It was dark outside; Brewster's Alehouse had stopped smoking. A quiet stream of people flowed down the Gauntlet.

There was a dull thud and the Great Uncommon Bag appeared in the middle of the bedroom floor. It rustled as a shape appeared within it.

"All clear?" Valian asked, poking his head out.

Ivy raised a finger to her lips. "Keep your voice down." His straggly dark locks hung in front of his face as he padded out softly on hands and knees. Behind him, a head of shiny dark hair popped out, followed by a pair of almond-shaped eyes.

"That bag is unbelievable!" Judy whispered, smiling broadly. Her tutu sprang out as she got to her feet. She was wearing bright purple leggings and a gray T-shirt with the sleeves rolled up. The wheels of her roller skates thrummed as she glided into the center of the room and plonked herself down on the rug. "Thanks for the invite. I love a good emergency meeting."

Seb leaped quietly down from his bunk. "Glad you came," he said, flashing her a smile. He sat cross-legged on the floorboards next to her.

"First things first," Ivy began, shuffling up between Valian and Judy. "How are you feeling? That injury in the Skaptikon looked really serious."

Valian tapped his jacket. Ivy heard the clink of metal. "The Raider's Tonic has been helping," he said. Ivy realized he had a flask tucked inside. "When I got back to my room, Miss H and Miss W had left me several bottles of the stuff. They must have heard about me being admitted to the infirmary."

Ivy could have sworn she'd seen Ethel sending them a featherlight earlier, but she decided not to bother mentioning it.

"What about you two?" he asked.

Seb rubbed the back of his neck. "Feels like I just played a really hard game of football . . . and I was the only player on the team."

It was Ivy's head that hurt more than anything. Sensing the broken soul inside the Jar of Shadows had been like standing next to the speakers at a gig by Seb's band. Her head was still buzzing. "Something like that."

"What about that Alexander Brewster kid?" Seb remarked. "Can you believe it? It was him all along—he's the real genius behind Dragon's Breath Ale."

Ivy looked at her satchel, which was lying on the floor by her bunk. "And he helped me. After the underguards had gone he gave me back Amos's journal. He didn't ask any questions either."

"Maybe he didn't care," Seb said. "His dad's just been exposed as a massive liar. That's probably his biggest concern right now."

"I suppose so." Ivy was shocked to find that Alexander's own father had exploited him so callously.

Judy's hazel eyes sparkled. "I'm still getting over the fact that you three have been into the Skaptikon and survived!"

"We failed, though," Ivy said glumly. "Selena and Jack-in-the-Green got away with the Jar of Shadows, and they're planning to open it at the Grivens contest tomorrow night. How are we going to stop them now?"

"If we even survive till then." Seb propped an elbow on his

knee, and rested his chin on it. "Selena's gonna try to get rid of us before then, I just know it."

"There's still hope," Judy told them. "There's always hope." She pushed a small brown paper bag into the middle of the floor. "I made these. Try one—they're meant to be good for thinking."

Ivy peered closer. The bag was stuffed with dusty white cubes. "Are they . . . marshmallows?"

"Made with mixology," Judy explained, grabbing one and holding it in front of her nose. "Mr. Littlefair gave me the recipe when I was practicing for my exams."

Ivy reached into the packet and took one. It felt just like a regular marshmallow. She gave it a sniff. *Vanilla.* "What do they do?"

"I don't know," Judy said. "I was too busy studying to make them before, but like I said—they're meant to help you think; to give you ideas. That's why I've made them now."

Valian and Seb grabbed one each. "It can't make our situation any worse," Seb decided. "After three? One, two . . ."

On *three,* Ivy took a bite of her marshmallow. At first it was just gooey and sweet, but then it started fizzing. With a *whoosh,* her bottom lifted off the floor as a dense pillow of steam appeared beneath her.

"What *is* this stuff?" Seb was wobbling around on the small white cloud that had formed under him.

Judy dipped a gloved forefinger into it and rubbed it against her thumb. "Not sure. Perhaps it's meant to be a cloud of thought. . . ." She took another bite of marshmallow. Ivy, Seb and Valian copied her.

A ball of cloud now appeared under Ivy's satchel, tipping

it up and spilling out the contents for the third time that day. Amos's journal and the postcard were lifted up and carried into the center of the room.

Ivy watched them as she bobbed up and down. The movement was soothing, helping to focus her mind. Floating toward her on a soft white wave, the journal seemed to be calling out to her. "When we were in the Skaptikon, even though she'd already found the Jar of Shadows, Selena still wanted to know where the journal was," Ivy remarked. "It must have another value that we don't know about."

Valian's face brightened. "First Selena tries to destroy the postcard, and now she desperately wants the journal. The only connection is Amos Stirling. He's the key to the whole mystery."

The postcard bobbed over to Judy and she picked it up. "Oh, now that's interesting," she commented, reading the message again. "Before my mum began her training in the Featherlight Guild, she worked at the Lundinor Registry, where the births and deaths of every uncommoner are recorded. You didn't mention the posting date before—the twenty-seventh of December 1967. That's two days before Selena Grimes died."

Ivy's skin prickled; she thought they might be close to a breakthrough. The rocking motion of the cloud allowed her imagination to drift.

"This would be a whole lot easier if Amos Stirling wasn't Departed," Seb said, swaying gently. "He'd have all the answers. There's nothing uncommon that lets you go back in time, is there? Then we could go and ask him what's going on."

Valian snorted. "I wish."

Ivy's thoughts were being guided by a gentle tide, pushing

her in one direction. They gradually gathered themselves around a single extraordinary concept.

She pondered the riddle they'd had to answer to get into the well at the World's End.

> *I have no wings and yet I fly.*
> *If you master me, you will never die.*

"You don't think we could use the Great Uncommon Bag, do you?" she said.

The other three turned to her.

"To do what?" Judy asked.

"To discover why Selena doesn't want anyone to know about Amos," Ivy said. "To travel back in time."

CHAPTER TWENTY-FOUR

The next morning, the inn was quiet.

"She's gone," Ivy said, trudging back into the bedroom. She closed the door behind her, sighing with regret. She'd wanted to see Granma Sylvie before they left. "There was a note on her pillow explaining that the underguard had called her in early again and she didn't want to wake us. They're exploring the bedrooms of the mansion today."

Ivy could tell from Seb's expression that he was just as disappointed. As things in Lundinor grew more dangerous, spending a few moments with Granma Sylvie seemed even more important. Ivy knew that they might not see her again.

"I've still got the saltshaker. We can check on her when we get back from . . ." Seb's face hardened as he looked down at the Great Uncommon Bag.

"I suppose so," Ivy agreed. She thought about her mum

and dad too; they were so far away. "According to the note, Ethel's coming to collect us after breakfast."

Valian was sitting on the bottom bunk. "We'd better be quick, then. It'll be easy to avoid Ethel afterward. There's always a big sale along the Gauntlet today; the House of Bells will be packed."

"Hmm." Judy held a faded denim shirt against Seb's chest. "You can't wear the L.A. Lakers shirt; it's too modern. What about this one? It's from the 1950s."

Smiling, Seb shrugged off his mandarin coat. "Good idea—thanks." Judy's cheeks flushed.

Ivy smoothed down the long sleeves of the black kurta tunic Judy had given her, along with some khaki combat trousers and canvas pumps. *Hobsmatch outfit number two.* She liked this one because the tunic was loose-fitting and easy to move around in.

"This won't be like looking at the photo in the uncommon frame, will it?" Seb said darkly, arranging the Great Uncommon Bag.

"If it even works," Ivy pointed out. They still couldn't be certain of the bag's capabilities.

Valian stood up and wiped his hands on the back of his vintage Levi's. "But if it does, just imagine what we could do. I could go back to the day Rosie disappeared and find out what happened. I could even go back and stop my parents—"

"This is *dangerous*," Ivy cut in, glaring at Valian and her brother. "You're right: this won't be like looking at shadows of the past. This will actually *be* the past. We can't afford to let anyone see us in case it *changes the course of history*. Anything we do could affect what happens now." The back of her neck tingled. They were messing with things more powerful than any they'd encountered before.

"All right," Valian muttered. "If we risk disrupting the past, we'll leave straightaway and come back to the present. Hopefully we can find Amos before that happens." He took a luggage tag and pen out of his jacket pocket. "I'm using a label to be accurate."

"Are you sure I can't come with you?" Judy asked. "I want to stop them as much as you three do."

"We need you to stay here in case something goes wrong," Valian said, gulping. "You're the only other person who'll know what's happened to us." He scribbled on the luggage tag and tied the label to the side of the old burlap sack. "If this works, we'll arrive in Lundinor two days after Amos sent the postcard—the twenty-ninth of December 1967, the night Selena died."

Ivy fiddled with her gloves as Valian and Seb crawled into the bag before her. If the experiment went wrong, she didn't know what might happen to them. . . . She gave Judy a thin smile before putting her head inside.

The bag dragged her forward at high speed and whipped her around in a dizzying pattern of twists and turns—like the teacups at a fairground, except in pitch darkness. Pressure squeezed her face and chest, making her feel queasy. She caught the faint whiff of burning in the air. Just when she thought something might have gone seriously wrong, there was a flash of light and the bag spat her out at the side of a dark cobbled street.

Ivy scrambled to her feet, snatching the Great Uncommon Bag off the ground. From the silver bells glinting on

the buildings she could tell that she was in Lundinor, but the undermart had a wintry feel: cast-iron streetlamps stood guard on the pavements, and the air was full of the scents of cinnamon and roast chestnuts.

She gawped at the frost-topped roofs. The bag might just have worked. . . .

"Over here!" Valian waved to Ivy from behind a stack of empty wooden crates beside the road. Stuffing the Great Uncommon Bag into her satchel, she dashed over and tucked herself down beside him.

Crouching on Valian's other side, Seb looked like he was trying not to throw up. Ivy remembered the teacups sensation and guessed that his journey had been particularly awful. "Do you think this is it?" she asked Valian, adrenaline surging through her. "Are we in 1967?"

Valian seemed lost for words. He shook his head and pointed to the crates, which were each stamped with the logo of the business opposite: MR. SNIPPETS. Hanging in the pristine shop window were photographs of men sporting elaborate mustaches; one gentleman had two hairy galleons sailing on his upper lip; others had the roaring head of a dragon or the body of a vintage racing car. Ivy couldn't decide if they'd been fashioned with an uncommon object, or if the resident barber was just incredibly talented. She searched for her reflection in the glass, but it wasn't visible; no one would be able to see them from the street.

"My dad used to get his hair cut here when I was little," Valian managed, his voice disbelieving. "But it didn't look as new as this. We *must* have gone back in time."

"So it worked!" Ivy couldn't believe it. *Time travel.*

"You know what this means," Valian said. "I can return to my childhood and save them—Rosie and my parents . . ."

Ivy didn't think it was wise to get his hopes up; there was so much they still had to learn. She squeezed his shoulder. "We've only been here a minute—we don't know what's going to happen. Let's get this over with first."

She locked eyes with him, and his expression hardened. "Yeah, OK. You're right."

The clip of heels suddenly disturbed the quiet street.

Ivy tensed. "Someone's coming."

Seb—who had finally regained his composure—craned his neck around the corner of the crates to get a better view. Ivy lowered her head, peeking through a gap.

Someone wearing a long gray cloak and red stilettos swept along the road. As the figure turned, Ivy, Seb and Valian glimpsed a pale face and a long dark braid.

Selena Grimes. She looked *exactly* the same as she did in Ivy's time, almost fifty years later—except that in sixties Lundinor her feet touched the ground. Ivy was looking at a *living* Selena Grimes. "What's she doing here?"

"I don't know, but I can't see Amos yet," Valian whispered. "Let's follow her—she might lead us to him."

Seb got to his feet. "She's heading down the street opposite."

They pursued Selena from a distance, mixing with the traders on the main roads and hiding in the shadows, where it was quieter. Selena's heels were so noisy, they were always able to locate her, even if she occasionally drifted out of sight. The other uncommoners didn't give them a second glance. Ivy hoped none of them had a good memory for faces. Her mind kept returning to the consequences of their time travel, but she tried not to dwell on it.

"Look at what they're using to fly," Seb said. "Vintage." He signaled toward a stream of traders sweeping over the rooftops on vacuum cleaners with flowery fabric bags hanging from the back.

As they continued, Ivy noticed further evidence of the fact that they were walking through a Lundinor of another era—shop signs painted in old-fashioned lettering, and goods displayed in wicker baskets behind dusty wood-framed windows. Traders called, "Cheerio!" as they left buildings; fashion pieces from later decades were missing from their Hobsmatch.

All at once Valian pointed to a recess in the wall. "Quick—in there. I think she's going inside."

They watched from the shadows as Selena stopped outside a door. Instead of producing a key to open it, she stamped one of her stilettos twice on the ground, and they saw a circular metal panel set into the cobbles beneath her feet.

"Drain cover?" Seb mouthed.

With a swish, the disk slid open and Selena Grimes descended into the ground as if there was a platform under her feet, lowering her down. Ivy tensed. The only thing she knew about the drains of Lundinor was that they were inhabited by foul races of the dead.

"We'd better find out what's down there," Valian decided.

They waited thirty seconds before sneaking after Selena. The drain cover was only big enough for one person to stand on at a time. Ivy went first. She held her yo-yo in front of her, ready for anything that might jump out when she reached the bottom.

An empty stainless-steel tunnel welcomed her. She pressed herself against the cold wall as she waited for Seb and Valian to descend behind her. The air smelled musty and the floor was wet.

"Ivy—anything down here?" Seb asked, appearing in a crouch on the drain cover. He aimed the light from his cell phone ahead of them.

The end of the passageway was shrouded in shadow; there was no sign of movement. "Nothing yet." Ivy touched her satchel, thinking of the Great Uncommon Bag inside. If anything happened, they would need to escape fast.

Valian joined them as they crept nervously along the tunnel. The farther they went, the closer the walls seemed to draw in. Eventually the ceiling was so low, Seb had to bend his knees. "OK, this place is definitely getting smaller. What's going on?" He directed his phone into the distance. The tunnel appeared to shrink to a point at the very end.

"I don't get it," Ivy said. "There's no way out. Where did Selena go?"

Valian narrowed his eyes. "There must be a clue some-where."

They continued as far as they could, crawling on their hands and knees when there wasn't enough room to stand. At the very end of the tunnel Seb swept the light across the wall. Writing had been scratched into the surface, but there was so much, and in so many different hands, that it looked like one huge scribble.

"The crooked sixpence," Ivy said shakily. "Look." The coin appeared six times in a circle, the face of each featuring the masked head of a different member of the Dirge, with their code name written below.

"Over here—there's something written on the other wall." Seb lifted his phone to illuminate words etched into the steel.

> Sing a song of sixpence
> A pocket full of spies,
> Tell us what you're seeking
> And someone shall reply.

"It's like the creepiest answering machine message ever."

Valian scrutinized the tunnel. "This *has* to be where the Dirge's followers came to contact them. They had a whole army working for them in the sixties—*a pocket full of spies,* like the message says. They must have built secret gateways like this all over Lundinor in order to communicate."

"So that's what Selena was doing down here—trying to contact the Dirge." Ivy picked up a jagged piece of flint and held it to the wall. "You must have to scratch your response; that's what all this writing is. If only Selena's wasn't lost with the others."

Valian patted his jacket pocket. "I might have something

that can help with that." He retrieved a small plastic flashlight and aimed it at the wall. "People claim you can find a needle in a haystack with an uncommon flashlight. I've only ever found stuff that I'd misplaced in my room."

Seb folded his arms, impressed. "I swear you've got more gadgets in that pocket than Q from the James Bond films."

"Who's James Bond?" Valian asked, flicking the flashlight switch back and forth.

Seb stared at him. "You're kidding, right? First Scratch doesn't know about *Star Wars,* and now this?"

"Valian, is it working?" Ivy asked. No light was coming from it.

"Shhh." Valian flicked the switch one last time. "It works with sound, not light. I've told it to find Selena's handwriting."

Ivy listened carefully. The flashlight was clicking. As Valian waved it over the walls, the clicking sped up or slowed down depending on where he positioned it. In no time at all he'd pinpointed Selena's response.

"I still can't see it," Ivy said, shuffling closer. "There's too much other writing here."

Valian flicked the flashlight switch again, and the pattern of clicks changed. "It's in Morse code now; it should spell out the message for us. Seb—write this down."

Seb made notes on his phone as Valian deciphered a string of letters from the pattern of dots and dashes.

"*I ask the masters of death to change my future,*" Seb read when the flashlight had finished. "The 'masters of death' must mean the Dirge—it's as if Selena wanted their help."

The sound of a knife being sharpened filled the tunnel, and the floor trembled. Ivy steadied herself. "What's happening?"

The walls drew back and the tunnel got bigger. There was

a loud *clang* and the end of the passageway expanded like the pupil of an eye into a dark cave with a low ceiling. The three of them got to their feet and edged in slowly.

The air was cold and damp. Pillars of sandy rock stood sandwiched between floor and ceiling, casting strange shadows. Somewhere in the distance, water was dripping. Ivy flinched as the tunnel entrance closed behind them with a loud scrape. "Where are we?"

Valian stuffed his flashlight back into his pocket and retrieved his uncommon trowel. It was glowing. "Dead here. Hide."

They managed to dive behind the nearest pillar just in time.

A man in a long-tailed velvet coat stepped *through* the cave wall close by. He had a handsome face with deep-set dark eyes and thick black hair. His high leather boots didn't touch the ground.

Ivy squinted. There was something familiar about the line of his jaw.

Amos Stirling . . . ?

She studied him carefully. He was much older than the boy from the postcard, but it was the same person—except that now he was dead. The Great Uncommon Bag must have delivered them to Amos; he'd just been following Selena.

Amos crouched, his eyes shifting from side to side. From his pocket he produced a glass conical flask containing a measure of glittering blue liquid and placed it on the cave floor. Out of his other pocket he took a lightbulb, which he balanced in the neck of the flask. Protecting his fist with his sleeve, he smashed the bulb.

Two streams of white light shot out, twirling in midair. They contorted into the shapes of two people—one hooded and wearing a mask, the other a woman with a long dark braid.

"A mixologist's lightprint," Valian whispered excitedly. "I've never actually seen one before. The light re-creates whatever just happened in this room."

The hooded person began talking. "There will be no turning back, Miss Grimes. The process is irreversible." He had a deep, coarse voice that set the liquid in the flask trembling. "The trade is simple: we will turn you into a ghoul and, in payment, you will serve us in any way we require."

Ivy shuddered. Why on earth had Selena Grimes *asked* the Dirge to turn her into a ghoul? She watched curiously as Selena's figure handed over what appeared to be a violin.

"Your soul will fracture in two," the masked man told her, holding the instrument aloft. "The larger part will form a ghoul, but the other piece will remain trapped inside this object, which we shall keep. If you decide to break our agreement at any time, we will reconnect the two parts of your soul and you will become Departed. You will cease to be."

Ivy couldn't believe it. The Dirge could turn the living into the dead *and* they had mastered the secret of turning the dead into the Departed! Perhaps that was what all their forbidden research had amounted to.

Amos shook his head.

With a loud crackle, Selena's form dissolved and another stream of light surged out of the broken bulb, shaping itself into a different person in a hood and mask.

The original masked man lowered his head. "My leader, Blackclaw. The contract with Selena Grimes is done." Ivy realized with a sinking feeling that they had been joined by her great-grandfather Octavius Wrench: he was the Fallen Guild's leader! "I am also pleased to announce the successful capture of two additional members of the Rasavatum. As with the others, if they will not swear loyalty, they will be disposed of."

"Good work, Monkshood," Blackclaw remarked in a clear, rich voice. "Pity about Amos Stirling. So talented a person would have been useful. Still, the library is the only prize of interest. Given access to a thousand years of mixology, we can master the art ourselves."

Ivy swallowed. The Dirge hadn't persuaded the Rasavatum to serve them at all; they'd dismantled their guild, picking off members one by one—and Amos Stirling had been one of their victims.

A high-pitched metallic scrape resonated through the cave. Immediately Amos knocked the smashed bulb onto the floor and stowed the conical flask back in his pocket. The figures of light vaporized.

A circular stainless-steel panel appeared in the cave wall and started opening. Ivy pressed herself back against the pillar. The three of them were within sight of whoever was about to enter, but if they tried to move, Amos would see them. She pulled the Great Uncommon Bag out of her satchel, reminding herself that if they were discovered in 1967, the ramifications would be catastrophic.

"We're going," she decided. "Now."

CHAPTER TWENTY-FIVE

Crawling out into their room at the Cabbage Moon, Ivy found Seb and Valian glowering in the direction of the bunks.

"Johnny Hands?" she exclaimed, getting to her feet. The ghoul was sitting on her bed, his feet hovering a few inches off the floor. He glimpsed the Great Uncommon Bag and a line appeared between his brows.

"Welcome back," he said, adding, "I'm here to escort you to my master. We don't have much time."

Valian folded his arms. "Your *master*? I thought you were an independent scout, like me."

Ivy recalled her conversation with Johnny Hands in the infirmary. With everything that had happened since, she'd forgotten to tell Valian or Seb. "Why does Mr. Punch want to see us?"

Johnny Hands rose to his feet. "He will explain himself, but we have to be quick," he said urgently. "Follow me."

"Whoa—hold everything," Valian said, gesticulating wildly. "*You* work for *Mr. Punch*? Since when?"

Johnny Hands counted on his fingers. "Let me see . . . Probably for coming up on two hundred years." He went to open the door. After seeing him dissolve through the roof of the featherlight mailhouse, Ivy wasn't sure why he was bothering. "Now please, come along."

Seb scanned the room. "Hang on, where's Judy? She was meant to meet us here."

"Mr. Littlefair sent her on an errand," Johnny Hands said dismissively, brushing a hand through the air. "Now, I really must insist: *hurry!*"

Outside Mr. Punch's curiosity shop, a green silk ribbon was writing in the air:

Welcome, welcome, one and all! Curiosity awaits!

The last time Ivy had visited Mr. Punch's shop it was a small brick house—painted fig-purple—with a slate roof and wrought-iron shop sign. Inside, Ivy had discovered a collection of uncommon objects stored in glass cabinets, wooden trunks and jeweled chests.

That was then.

Facing Ivy *now* was a colossal purple big top, the kind you'd see at a circus, the peaks so steep and tall, they looked like a mountain range at dusk. Waving furiously atop each one was a white flag decorated with Mr. Punch's logo—a black top hat.

"I'll wait here," Johnny Hands said, hovering by the entrance.

Ivy smoothed down her kurta before heading in, Seb and Valian trudging along behind.

It was dark and quiet inside the tent. Boxes sat in shadow around the walls while, in the center, a white spotlight lit up the sandy floor. On either side stood two towers accessed by rope ladders, with a trapeze hanging between them. The sounds of Lundinor were muffled by the thick walls, so the crunch of their footsteps echoed loudly.

"Hello?" Ivy called.

There was a clatter, and then the spotlight moved slowly across the tent, coming to rest on a platform at the top of one of the towers. Ivy saw a man in a black top hat sitting there, his legs hanging over the edge.

"That's him," Valian said quietly. *"Mr. Punch."*

"It's safe to climb the ladder," a deep voice called down. "I knotted it myself."

Ivy surveyed the platform from a distance. It was a strange place to have a meeting—but, hey, this was Lundinor. At the foot of the rope ladder she swung her satchel around and began to climb, Seb and Valian following behind. From the top, the tent looked even bigger.

"Here you go," Mr. Punch said, shuffling along to make room. The platform was crammed with cases and boxes stuffed with uncommon objects. "Sorry about my collection—it never seems to fit in here as well as it does in a proper building."

Seb sat down beside a gray stone plinth, his knees drawn up to his chest. Valian shuffled up between a rusty oilcan and a large model sailboat. Ivy took the space beside Mr. Punch.

"I was told that *you* were behind the transformation of Lundinor," she said, letting her legs hang over the edge like his. "Can't you just change the tent whenever you want?"

"Ah, but it doesn't work like that," Mr. Punch told her, tipping his hat to Seb and Valian. "Good to meet you both at last." He pointed to the plinth beside Seb. "That stone does all the work."

Ivy regarded the gray stone plinth. The pedestal was carved with winged horses and five-pointed stars, and an old book with yellowed pages was lying open on top of it. "The plinth?" she asked.

"You could call it a plinth," Mr. Punch said. "Over the centuries it's had many names: lectern, podium, easel . . . I call it a stone."

"Hang on—this plinth transforms the whole of Lundinor?" Seb leaned away from it, staring. "I don't understand."

"The stone is fond of books," Mr. Punch explained with a shrug. "If you lay one open on top of it, the stone manifests certain aspects of that book in real life."

Ivy considered the grassy meadows, trees and flowers growing in Lundinor; one uncommon plinth had done all that. "So you lay a different book on top of the stone every season?" she asked.

Mr. Punch opened a gleaming mother-of-pearl chest beside him. It was full of objects, including several leather-bound books. "A Dickens every winter," he explained. "That's traditional. Something sunny for spring—this year I used *Mary Poppins in the Park*—and in autumn it's whatever takes my fancy. The stone is very rare, as you can imagine. I wouldn't be able to sell it for less than ten grade."

There was a clatter as Valian knocked over the oilcan. "What?!"

Ivy felt like she'd just had the wind knocked out of her. She scanned the big top, checking they were still alone. There were only five objects in existence that had a ten-grade value. "The stone is one of the *Great Uncommon Good*?"

Mr. Punch's eyes twinkled as he took a Russian doll out of the chest—a man in traditional Russian costume. "Let me tell you a little about where that phrase comes from," he said, holding the doll on his flattened palm. "Many hundreds of years ago, when tales of five ten-grade objects first surfaced, one man decided to collect the stories together and give each object a name. The bag that you and your friends possess was called the Sack of Stars, and sitting behind us is the Stone of Dreams. It was this same man who named the objects the Great Uncommon Good, believing that they would do extraordinarily good things."

The Sack of Stars. That's what they should be calling it. Listening to the story, Ivy guessed that the Jar of Shadows still had its original name. She wondered what the other two objects might be.

"But of course the story collector soon realized that, in the wrong hands, the Great Uncommon Good could do extraordinarily *bad* things," Mr. Punch continued, opening the Russian doll to reveal a set of ever-smaller figures. "So he set about forming a guild of uncommoners who would hunt down the five objects and keep them hidden from the rest of the world. The guild was called the Rasavatum."

Ivy shared a look of confusion with Seb and Valian. "I thought the Rasavatum were mixologists."

Mr. Punch blew on the Russian dolls and they began moving of their own accord. A lady in a red dress curtsied to Ivy; a man brushed down his suit, stretching his legs. "The original members *were* talented mixologists," Mr. Punch explained. "They needed to conceal the work they were really doing, so they used their mixologist skills to build a reputation as a troupe of mysterious showmen. It allowed them to travel from undermart to undermart, gathering information on the Great Uncommon Good without anyone knowing what they were really up to. It was a fantastic *disguise*." At that word, the Russian dolls' faces froze and they jumped inside each other in ascending order of size, till only the original man remained. Mr. Punch tapped him on the head, smiling. "Over the centuries, members of the Rasavatum have come and gone, but two things remain: our masquerade as mixologists, and our promise to conceal the Great Uncommon Good."

"*Our?*" Seb cocked his head. "*You're* a member of the Rasavatum?"

Mr. Punch put the Russian doll back into the chest and closed the lid. "The very last one. The Dirge made it their mission to discover our identities and hunt us down, but it was against our oath to fight—we are a peaceful guild committed to nonviolence."

"So *that's* why the Rasavatum went into hiding," Ivy said. An army of questions marched into her head. She guessed there were few people Mr. Punch could trust with the truth, especially with half the Dirge's identities still a mystery. She peered into his swirling eyes, contemplating the multiple souls coexisting inside him. She couldn't imagine the extent of his knowledge or the number of secrets he was guarding.

"Sir Clement was a member of the Rasavatum," Mr. Punch said. "He used the Stone of Dreams to build Lundinor, and the object has been under the protection of our guild ever since. Fifty years ago another of our members tracked down the Jar of Shadows. Since then, I have endeavored to keep it out of the Dirge's reach."

Ivy blushed. "So it was *you* who hid it in the Skaptikon?"

Mr. Punch nodded solemnly. There was no anger on his face, only regret. He pulled his legs up onto the platform, turning around so he was facing Seb and Valian. "Under no circumstances must the Dirge be allowed to wield the power of one of the Great Uncommon Good. As guardians of the Sack of Stars, you three must keep it hidden from Selena at all costs."

Valian's expression hardened as he poked around in his inside pocket, checking that the Great Uncommon Bag—the Sack of Stars—was still there. "Selena Grimes—you know who she really is?"

"I have known since you three unmasked Cartimore Wrench as *Ragwort*," Mr. Punch said with a scowl. "I discovered Selena's true identity by tracing the grim-wolf back to her. The creature has since left her employment."

"If you know who she is, why can't she be arrested?" Seb asked. "The underguard will believe *you*, surely."

"The underguard will *listen* to me," Mr. Punch agreed. "But they will not take action without proof. Selena Grimes won their trust years ago; it will not be brushed aside so easily. In any case, the entire force would be unable to stop her on their own." He fastened his cord jacket. "After I discovered Selena's true allegiance I began hunting for an object that I knew would vanquish her. Only this morning I got word that it has been found."

Ivy wondered what Mr. Punch could be talking about. She had the feeling that he knew everything they'd been getting up to over the last couple of days. Perhaps Johnny Hands had been spying on them.

"The reason I have summoned you here," Mr. Punch went on urgently, "is because I am leaving Lundinor immediately in order to retrieve the object. I hope to be back before the Grivens contest begins so I can stop Selena Grimes from opening the Jar of Shadows. Whatever happens while I'm gone, you must keep the Sack of Stars safe. I fear there are other members of the Dirge in Lundinor right now, and they will be watching you three."

Mr. Punch's story of the Rasavatum and his warning about the Dirge were still running through Ivy's head when she left the big top. Out on the lawn, people stood in small groups discussing the evening edition of the *Lundinor Chronicle*. Ivy couldn't see the headline, but she noticed a few of the traders gawping at her. A cold feeling seeped into her bones. "Er . . . What's going on?"

Valian's eyes narrowed. "I don't know, but I don't like the look of it."

Johnny Hands came shooting across the grass, his jester's hat wobbling. When he reached them, he dithered, apparently trying to tell them something, but in the end he just shook his head and held up a crisp copy of the *Lundinor Chronicle*.

On the front page was a photo of Ivy in the dungarees and cropped black jacket she'd been wearing yesterday. She was grinning from ear to ear, a large bronze trophy cradled in her arms.

Seb read the headline, his voice growing higher with every word. "*'Eleven-Year-Old Girl Becomes Final Competitor in Grivens Contest'*?!"

Ivy was trying to gasp and speak at the same time. "But—that's not me!" She grabbed the newspaper to examine it more closely. OK, it did look *exactly* like her, but unless she had an extreme sleepwalking problem that she didn't know about, she hadn't entered herself into the Grivens contest. There had to be another explanation.

"Shape-shifter," Valian muttered bitterly. "It must be."

Ivy scanned the article. "It says here that to enter the contest, players had to deposit one of their gloves in the contest master's cup and then drink from it."

"Yuck." Seb pulled a face. "Soggy glove juice—what's that all about?"

"The drinking part is customary," Johnny Hands explained. "Grivens contests were always presided over by a contest master—a referee. They were chosen from a handful of retired ex-players, and it was traditional to use one of their old trophies as a cup into which new contestants could deposit their gloves."

"The cup is uncommon," Valian added. "Once a glove is placed inside, its owner is bound to enter the contest. Withdrawals are forbidden. If a player fails to show up . . ." He grimaced. "Well, you've seen what happens to people's hands when they make a bad Trade—imagine that happening, but to *all of you*."

As Ivy remembered Selena Grimes's rotting hands, her throat became dry. "But—look," she said, wiggling her fingers. "I've still got both my gloves."

Johnny Hands studied them carefully. "That damage—has it always been there?"

Ivy appraised the small hole in the left thumb. She'd almost forgotten about it. "No. I snagged it on a branch a few days ago."

"*What* did you say?" Valian asked.

Ivy held out her hand so he could see the hole for himself. "You remember—in the Great Oak Tree, at Sir Clement's old house."

"But . . . part of it's *missing*," he said, throwing Johnny Hands an uneasy look.

"What does that mean?" Ivy asked slowly, already fearing the answer.

"It means that if we check inside the contest master's cup, we're likely to find a scrap of your glove," Johnny Hands said. "And the cup needs only a thread in order to register entry."

Valian stared at Ivy. "It means you're going to have to play, Ivy. Tonight."

As she recalled just how confusing the game in the carousel had been, Ivy's legs went weak. "But—I can't. I don't know how. I'll be—"

"Killed," Johnny Hands finished matter-of-factly. "And though I hate to point out the obvious, that's exactly what whoever is behind this deception wants."

Suddenly they heard a commotion behind them. Ivy spun around as excited shouts filled the air. A large group of people were running backward onto the lawn. As heads turned, Ivy recognized some of the faces—they were journalists from the *Barrow Post*. Some were shaking snow globes while others were holding feathers, scribbling madly in midair. A few of them rushed to join the crowd as it parted.

Selena Grimes appeared in their midst. Her dark hair had been styled into an elaborate braided updo and she was wearing a long silver gown with flared sleeves, like a medieval queen. Ivy recalled Mr. Punch's warning to keep the Sack of Stars away from the Dirge. Immediately she grabbed Seb's sleeve and turned to run.

"Well, this *is* fortuitous!" Selena declared. "We are joined by our final contestant!"

Ivy froze as several photographers broke from the pack to swarm around her, shaking their snow globes in her face. She cowered, shielding her face.

"Stop it! Go away!" Seb tried to elbow them aside—but there were too many.

Selena Grimes glided toward her, the horde following.

"Ivy Sparrow," she said in a honeyed voice, "may I offer my sincerest congratulations." She hovered closer and spread her arms wide as if to give Ivy a hug.

Ivy went rigid with shock. She tried to step back, but there was a journalist right behind her. Selena's cold, hard arms came around her shoulders. Ivy gave a muffled shriek but was too angry and scared to even move.

Selena's cold breath kissed Ivy's cheek as she lowered her lips to Ivy's ear. At an almost imperceptible volume she said, "Enjoy the game, child. It'll be the last you ever play."

CHAPTER TWENTY-SIX

Valian's eyes flicked from left to right as he checked the contest rules. The newspaper supplement was so long, the paper flapped over his shoulder like a scarf in the wind. "Here it is—they're operating a forfeit system. Living players are allowed to have a spotter with them to stop them from being killed." His face brightened as he turned to Ivy. "You're gonna be fine."

She gave him a doubtful smile, keeping her head down as they approached the House of Bells. Everyone was staring at her. She wished she could become invisible like one of the dead.

"What does this spotter thing entail?" Seb asked, peering over Valian's shoulder. "Could *I* do it?"

Valian read back through the rules. "Ivy has to play the game by herself, but the spotter stands behind her, outside the chalk circle, and pulls her out of the Krigvelt if it appears she isn't going to make it."

Seb shrugged. "OK . . . that's doable. Valian's right, Ivy. You're gonna survive this."

Ivy held out her hand. Her fingers and thumb were trembling so much, she could see ten of them. "If Selena Grimes is behind this, I don't think it matters *what* we do," she said quietly. She glanced warily at Johnny Hands, wondering if it was wise to reveal everything they knew about Selena Grimes and the Dirge. . . . If he had earned Mr. Punch's confidence, she reckoned he could be trusted. "She's probably devised a plan to get rid of the three of us once and for all." Now that she thought it through, it all made sense—the shape-shifter who had impersonated her must have been Jack-in-the-Green.

Seb gritted his teeth. "Can't Mr. Punch stop this?" he asked Johnny Hands. "He's meant to be the most powerful man in Lundinor."

"Unsurprisingly I'm a step ahead of you there," Johnny Hands replied, adjusting his gloves. "As soon as I read the head-line, I sent Mr. Punch a featherlight. It must have been only moments after he'd left Lundinor. I've received no response as yet."

Ivy paused on the steps to the House of Bells. She could only hope that, wherever Mr. Punch had gone, he'd find what he needed and get back in time to stop Selena. As she opened the shop door, the bells inside sprang into fevered conversation. They trembled as she passed, chattering about the Grivens contest. Ivy tried to ignore them.

"Ivy?!" a voice cried. "Is that you?" The door at the back swung open with a bang, and Ethel rushed out, her headscarf flapping. Under her arm she was carrying a square piece of wood.

She stopped in front of them, hesitating. She frowned at Valian and Johnny Hands, then turned to Ivy. Her lip wobbled. "I've been to the underguard station. Your gran is still at the mansion; she asked to stay behind after they left. I've sent her three featherlights already, but I think they're having trouble getting through. I'd go and fetch her myself if the place would let me."

Ivy knew that the Wrench Mansion would only reveal itself to a member of the family; it had been built with uncommon bricks that liked to move—that was no doubt part of the problem.

Seb slung down his rucksack. "Maybe I can use the saltshaker. If Granma's still got the pepper pot with her, we might be able to see what's going on."

"Good thinking." Ethel pointed to the desk at the rear of the shop. "Do it over there. We need the space 'ere to practice." She held out the piece of wood—a chopping board.

Ivy edged away.

"Now don't worry—it's a common one," Ethel said. "I just thought we should sit down and review everything. The contest begins at eight; that means we've got a little under two hours." She raised an eyebrow at Johnny Hands. "As you're 'anging around, you can 'elp. I'm a little rusty with Grivens. I s'pose you've played it before?"

He smoothed down his waistcoat. "Madam, I've been playing it for the best part of five centuries."

Ethel pursed her lips. "Well then."

They sat cross-legged in the middle of the shop floor,

with Johnny Hands hovering above it. He spread a handful of wooden figures across the chopping board in the middle. "Every Grivens game begins in the same way."

Ivy tried to ignore her nerves and pay attention. Having seen the game played on the carousel, she found some of what Johnny Hands told her familiar.

"Each player chooses a bell, a suitcase and a glove from a box of Grivens pieces."

"Does it make any difference which pieces you choose?" Ivy asked.

Johnny Hands twisted a bell piece between his fingers. "Yes, but there is no way of telling which piece will be strongest; it's all down to luck."

Ivy's spirits sank. "I see." It was like most card games—there was no way to control the hand you were dealt, only what you did with each card afterward.

Johnny Hands rotated the chopping board. "When all four players have chosen their first piece to put in the red zone, the board is spun to activate the next stage of play."

"In the Krigvelt," Ivy remembered. She would never forget seeing Seb appear on the helipad of that skyscraper.

"The Krigvelt will be in a different place every time," Ethel explained, "with different challenges. I've 'eard of everything from a tropical island and an underground sewer to the top of a mountain. You 'ave to withstand the dangers of the environment, not just the attacks from the other players."

"When you go into the Krigvelt, your first aim is survival," Johnny Hands told Ivy. "You have to work out what your Grivens pieces can do—they might be able to attack one of your enemies or protect you from attack. Each Grivens piece has a different characteristic. Gloves are usually defensive, while suitcases are attacking. But there are exceptions."

Ivy recalled Seb finding an American football helmet in his suitcase.

"Bells are the weird ones," Valian added. "I've been reading about famous Grivens games, and bells can mess with your mind. Some of them have hypnotic voices—they make you so disorientated you can't defend yourself."

Johnny Hands cleared the board. "If you survive your first visit to the Krigvelt, you play again with your remaining two pieces. Occasionally, games aren't over even after three rounds—so you keep picking pieces until one player is victorious."

Ivy tried to store the information into her memory. It was like cramming for the world's worst exam.

"It's a pity there's no way to cheat," Seb remarked. He was holding up the saltshaker. "I can only see shadows with this. I guess the mansion is blocking it somehow."

Ivy's forehead crinkled. She hoped Granma Sylvie was safe.

"Actually there *is* a way to cheat at Grivens," Johnny Hands announced. He pointed at the wooden pieces on the board and Ivy looked at them again. "Grivens pieces are made of common materials—paper, stone, plastic. However, you can use *uncommon* materials—the marble from an uncommon statue, the wood from an uncommon table leg. Playing with an uncommon piece puts you at an advantage because it tends to be more powerful in the Krigvelt."

"If only there was a way for us to smuggle some into the stadium," Ethel muttered. Ivy wasn't sure if she was being serious.

Seb placed a hand on Ivy's shoulder. "Hey, we've faced worse situations than this . . . right?"

She forced a smile, thinking of the one thing everyone seemed to be forgetting: it wasn't her surviving the Grivens contest they had to worry about—it was the Dirge opening the Jar of Shadows in the stadium.

The light from the cave ceiling had faded and the evening air was cool. As the five of them made their way through the West End, Ivy's feet felt like lead. Underguards stood at street corners, directing the last few spectators toward the Grivens stadium. She could hear the noise of the crowd—like a distant storm—growing louder as they approached.

She rubbed her neck. "I guess I should say thank you," she muttered to Johnny Hands, floating beside her. "For the Grivens advice."

He tipped his hat at her. "You're welcome. I forgot to mention—Selena Grimes doesn't know that you're a whisperer. Perhaps you can use that to your advantage."

Ivy didn't know how. She peered into his dark eyes, something puzzling her. "Can I ask you a question? It might sound stupid. . . ." With her attention focused on the contest, Ivy hadn't had time to analyze what she'd seen in 1967. She was still trying to understand why Selena would have gone to the Dirge to be turned into a ghoul. "Do you *like* being dead?"

"Do I *like* it?" Johnny Hands chuckled, wiping a tear from his eye. "You are funny."

"Well . . . ?" Ivy was still waiting for an answer.

"Being dead has allowed me to see much more of this fine world than is possible in one lifetime," Johnny Hands said.

"And I've been fortunate enough to call some extraordinary people friends."

Ivy could feel a "but" coming.

He pointed to his shoes, which were hovering over the dusty road. "And yet despite all that I haven't felt grass under my feet or sand between my toes for five hundred years. I can't sleep, which means I can no longer dream, and everyone I once loved is Departed." His expression hardened. "The answer to your question—whether I do or do not like my situation—is irrelevant. This is my *forever*."

Ivy looked away, worried that her question had been insensitive. She hadn't meant to upset him.

All at once they saw lights flickering at the end of the road and Johnny Hands stopped. "The stadium is only a block away now. It's time for me to go." He raised a hand over Ivy's head, unsure what to do, then ruffled her hair. "Farewell, Ivy Sparrow, and good luck."

Johnny Hands dissolved into thin air, and at the next corner the Grivens stadium came into view. It looked like a huge conservatory with a domed roof, the colored shapes of thousands of people moving behind the misty glass. Spiky-leafed exotic plants were arranged on the lawns outside, depicting the three Grivens pieces—the glove, the bell and the suitcase.

There was a massive throng of people still lining up to go in, and a bank of reporters stood beside a green carpet, shaking snow globes at glitzy stars in outrageous Hobsmatch who glided past, waving to the masses. Stationed around the stadium, platoons of underguards observed everything stoically, toilet brushes strapped to their chests rather than tucked into their belts.

Ivy took off her satchel and gave it to Valian for safekeeping. "I'll be watching," he said, putting a hand on her shoulder. "You can do it. I know you can."

"And I'll keep trying your gran," Ethel said, patting the top pocket of her overalls, which was stuffed with feathers.

When Ivy turned to Seb, he hugged her so hard she almost fell over. "I'll see you at the table."

Ivy was shown into a room furnished with iron patio chairs and tables topped with teacups, saucers and pots of tea that smelled of honey and lavender.

The fifteen other contestants were already there. Some were sitting twiddling their thumbs, while others paced to and fro or chatted nervously with their opponents.

On a table in a corner stood an ornate bronze trophy. *The contest master's cup*—Ivy recognized it from the newspaper. A ribbon floated above it, writing again and again:

Contestants: you may collect your returned gloves.

Ivy pretended to be interested in a cup of tea. The contents of one pot smelled a bit like Raider's Tonic, so she poured herself a cup and sipped it slowly as she skirted the room, trying to stay out of people's way. She went to examine a notice board:

ORDER OF PLAY

TABLE 1: *Marcia Bow, Carson Crevitch, Ferdinand La Garde, Hui Hang*
TABLE 2: *Emiliano Agustin, Claudia-Rose Winters, François Filigree, Sid Irons*

TABLE 3: *Alexander Brewster, Bruno Cartwright,*
Lei Chang, Jorgen Valentine
TABLE 4: *Lady Margaret Crammington, Ivy Sparrow,*
Colin Mint, Captain Macintosh
FINAL TABLE: *winner of table 1, winner of table 2,*
winner of table 3, winner of table 4

Ivy did a double take as she read through the names.
Alexander Brewster . . . ?
But—after the fire at the alehouse, why would Alexander want to be involved in the contest? Another name caught her eye too.
François Filigree.
She spotted his strange white mask as he spoke to two women in satin ball gowns, and it set her worrying. François Filigree was the only other person who had seen her glove being damaged; he could have been involved in the plot to enter Ivy's name in the contest. She needed to be wary of him.

She scanned the room and saw Alexander sitting on his own. His apron was missing; instead he was wearing a smart gray suit with rubber boots. His scruffy red hair had been combed and flattened against his head with what looked like cooking grease.

Ivy took the seat next to him. "Hey," she said. "I didn't know you'd be playing."

Dark circles ringed Alexander's eyes. "My pa entered me," he groaned. "He taught me how to play when I was little. He said we could use the publicity . . . even if it was dangerous."

Drummond Brewster was so cruel, Ivy thought. Did he not care about his son at all? She hesitated before saying, "It was *you* who really invented Dragon's Breath Ale. . . . I don't know why your dad kept it secret; I think it's amazing."

Alexander's shoulders slumped.

Ivy bit her lip, searching for something less awkward to talk about. "Er—how's the alehouse?"

"I'm in charge of the cleanup. It's taking ages. Pa's been selling Dragon's Breath Ale from a temporary stall out front, but the customers aren't interested in buying anything from us now. They keep saying he's a fraud."

A man with freckled apricot skin and floppy black hair entered the room and cleared his throat. He was dressed in a burgundy and yellow uniform with sponsorship logos plastered all over it.

"Who's that?" Ivy asked.

"The contest master," Alexander told her. "Nix Wolf. He's a nine-time American Grivens champion. Oh, and a ghoul."

"All right, ladies and gents, time to head into the arena," Nix Wolf said in a smooth Texan drawl. "Those of you who have spotters—it's forbidden for you to look around or talk to them after we leave this room."

Ivy followed Alexander and the other contestants into the stadium. She blinked in the glare of the harsh uncommon lights as the *thud* of a thousand snow globes filled her ears. The tiered seating climbed the walls of the glass house, screening out anything happening in the undermart outside. The noise from the spectators was deafening.

In the center of the arena stood four high tables, spaced sixty or so feet apart. Each had a chalk circle drawn around it and a varnished wooden chopping board sitting on top.

Ivy steeled herself as Nix Wolf directed contestants to their respective tables. She took her place at table four, her hands sweating inside her gloves. As her opponents gathered around her, she felt a growing sense of unease. It was fairly straightforward to match each of the faces at her table with the names on the notice board.

On her right, a neatly dressed gray-haired gentleman in a red bow tie was, she guessed, Colin Mint—but only because the man on her left—who had blond dreadlocks and an eye patch—was surely Captain Macintosh. Lady Crammington, opposite, was a bejeweled woman with a pinched face and wearing a peacock-feather hat.

A small fanfare sounded, and then a woman carrying a flag decorated with Grivens pieces appeared on the arena floor. Behind her followed a line of excited uncommoners who were jumping up and down and waving to the audience. Only one of them looked unhappy to be there: Seb.

When the spotters reached the Grivens tables, they took their places. Captain Macintosh was the only other player on table four to have a spotter, so Ivy knew he must be alive. She stretched an arm out behind her to see whether Seb was within touching distance, but felt nothing. Assessing the positions of the other spotters, she gathered that he was standing more than an arm's length away. . . .

But not so far that she couldn't hear him.

"You're gonna be fine," he murmured. "Just try to think clearly. You're good at that."

Easier said than done when you're in this stadium, Ivy thought.

"See the second row of the stand in front of you?" he added quickly.

Ivy scanned the seating and picked out Judy and Mr.

Littlefair. They had made a banner from a strip of uncommon wallpaper, which kept folding itself into different messages: YOU CAN DO IT, IVY SPARROW! WE BELIEVE IN YOU!

She gave a glum smile. She was either about to prove them right or come to a decidedly messy end playing the world's most dangerous board game.

"Valian's in the stand on our right," Seb said. "Third row back in the middle. Next to a woman with a yellow hat."

Ivy searched and found Valian sitting hunched over with his hands in his pockets, scowling. The woman beside him kept waving toward the arena, shaking the feathers of her yellow bonnet in his face.

"I can't see Mr. Punch," Seb added flatly. "I'll keep searching."

When all competitors had taken their seats, Nix Wolf picked up a conch shell and announced the opening of the contest. There was a huge round of applause and everyone stamped their feet. Ivy's legs shuddered as the vibrations worked their way up through the floor. Her heart was racing.

The spectators hushed as four frilly tablecloths flopped down from the conservatory roof and hovered in midair. Everyone turned toward them as images appeared on their surface. *Materializers.* Ivy glimpsed herself in HD and resisted the temptation to cover her face with her hands. Her eyes were puffy and her messy curls were sticking to her pale forehead; it looked as if she had a fever. She wouldn't have blamed the audience for assuming she was a race of the dead, if she hadn't had a spotter with her.

She lowered her gaze to the chopping board and ran over what Ethel and Johnny Hands had told her. Nix Wolf passed by each table with a box of approved Grivens pieces. When it was Ivy's turn to choose, she shakily pushed her gloved hand inside and wiggled it around. It was easy to tell which piece was which: suitcases had sharp corners, bells were round and gloves had fingers. The stadium was nearly silent now. Ivy could feel the eyes of a hundred thousand uncommoners on her as she made her decision. Hoping that luck was on her side, she removed one of each piece and placed all three on the black area of the chopping board.

She started when she realized what she'd chosen. The glove piece was ornate, carved from a glassy purple stone a bit like amethyst. The bell had been turned from pale wood and the suitcase appeared to be made of stiff lightweight cardboard.

She studied her opponents' pieces as each placed them on the board. Some were fairly plain, while others were covered in gold leaf or studded with gems. Each time a piece was laid down, an "Oooh" rang out around the stadium and a close-up appeared on the materializers.

Nix Wolf cleared his throat. "Players, choose your first piece."

Ivy steadied her nerves and tried to ignore Colin Mint, who was flexing his fingers while sizing up his pieces—before finally choosing his suitcase. The other opponents made their decisions without hesitating, each pushing a piece forward. Lady Crammington chose an ebony glove while Captain Macintosh picked a wicker suitcase. A chorus of gasps and boos filled the stadium. Ivy hastily nudged her bell forward.

Nix Wolf grinned as, still standing outside the chalk circle, he used a long stick to spin the chopping board. Ivy tried to catch a glimpse of Seb on a materializer before she entered the

Krigvelt, but all too soon the stadium, with its bright lights and roaring stands, vanished.

The air shifted.

Ivy found herself in a large glass tank, somewhere underwater. Outside, she could see shoals of fish flitting through the glittering depths, but beyond them everything faded into shadow. The Grivens table and chopping board were bolted to the floor, the chalk outline smeared on the outside of the glass. The muffled echoes of the ocean filled her ears, while a salty tang permeated her nostrils.

She gripped the Grivens table for support. Her head felt woozy, as if she might faint at any moment, but her opponents showed no sign of discomfort.

The Grivens pieces wobbled—and then there was a disturbingly loud *crack,* and seawater began trickling through fractures in the glass onto the floor.

Ivy's chest constricted. She knew she wasn't the strongest swimmer; if the room filled up, they'd have to do combat in water.

Before she had time to really panic, the two suitcase pieces on the chopping board unfolded like origami boxes, reminding Ivy of the matchbox archive at the *Barrow Post.*

A miniature gleaming metal sword appeared in Colin Mint's suitcase, while a burning branch rose out of Captain Macintosh's. The items flickered like images on a TV and disappeared before reappearing full-sized in the hands of Colin Mint and Captain Macintosh. Both players' faces were set as they swung the objects defensively to and fro between Ivy and Lady Crammington.

Ivy leaned away as heat from the burning branch swept past

her cheek. She splashed her way toward the chalk line, but when her foot came into contact with it, she felt herself being pushed back and went sliding over the wet floor. Johnny Hands had warned her about this. She wouldn't be able to leave the circle, even if someone *was* wielding a burning branch. Seb was the only one who could pull her out.

Come on, little bell, she thought, glancing at her Grivens piece. *Please do something awesome.*

Opposite, Lady Crammington's ebony glove flexed its fingers. It wiggled them in the direction of Captain Macintosh, and a jet of water shot toward him, dousing the burning branch. As the flames were extinguished, the jet grew stronger. Captain Macintosh gasped for air and staggered backward, arms flailing.

There was a loud *pop,* and then he disappeared. As there was no trace of him in the Krigvelt, Ivy reasoned that his spotter must have pulled him out.

She looked at her feet. The seawater was up to her knees now, the icy cold making her toes numb.

Ignoring Ivy, Colin Mint turned his long sword on Lady Crammington. As he lunged forward, her glove piece made a "stop" sign and the sword simply *froze.* Colin Mint tugged on the handle, desperately trying to move the blade, but it was as if it had become lodged in the air.

Lady Crammington grinned maliciously and slammed her fist down on the chopping board, her glove piece mimicking her. Colin Mint stumbled back through the rising water as from out of nowhere a swinging blade appeared in front of him, cutting forcefully through the air and disturbing the water below.

Ivy turned her head away just before the blade hit home. She expected some sort of gruesome noise to follow, but instead there was another loud *pop*.

When she looked around again, Colin Mint had vanished and Lady Crammington was glowering at Ivy—the last player standing between her and the final.

Ivy stared at her bell piece, willing it to do something. The water was almost at her waist now and she was freezing. She wasn't sure she'd even be able to move, let alone swim. Lady Crammington made a punching action with her fist and the glove piece copied her, aiming for Ivy's bell.

Ivy thought of Seb before squeezing her eyes shut and preparing for the impact.

Where is he?

CHAPTER TWENTY-SEVEN

The force hit Ivy's bell and then crashed into her, leaving her winded. She bent over, holding her stomach, the pain spreading to her chest.

"Stop!" she called, hoping Lady Crammington might pause and at least give her time to think. The water was so cold; the surface bubbled as more water rushed in through the cracks in the glass tank. The stench of the sea was beginning to make Ivy feel sick.

She reached for the edge of the Grivens table and heaved herself upright. Her bell was still swaying with the force of the blow. . . .

And then it started to sing. There were no words as such, just sounds. The bell had an operatic voice that filled the air, making the water tremble. As the vibrations traveled through Ivy's body, the cold she'd felt faded away. The sound energized her tired muscles, sharpening her mind and relaxing her. She didn't know what it was doing exactly, but it felt amazing.

Opposite her, she saw that the bell's voice was having a very different effect on Lady Crammington, who looked as if she was battling to stay awake. Her glove piece drooped and then lay flat on the Grivens board. Lady Crammington yawned and slipped down into the water. As it began lapping at the chopping board, just under Ivy's armpits, Lady Crammington faded away like smoke.

Ivy tilted her head back as the water reached her throat. *"Seb?!"*

Everything went dark—and then the Grivens stadium took shape around her. The spectators roared. Ivy gasped with relief as the water disappeared.

"In the first round, winner of table four, using a bell to disarm her opponents," Nix Wolf shouted, "Ivy Sparrow!"

Ivy's head pounded. Her tunic and cargo trousers were soaking wet. Her damp face appeared in close-up on one of the materializers as the crowd began chanting, "Ivy! Ivy! Ivy!"

Her cheeks glowed. She wasn't used to uncommoners shouting her name in a *good* way.

"Yes!" Seb cheered, behind her.

She could see him on the materializers, punching the air and jumping up and down. "I *knew* that bell of yours would do something! Valian said it was bells you had to look out for."

Ivy's knees almost buckled with shock. All right—she'd survived that game, but only by luck.

There was no longer anyone at her Grivens table, so she searched for her three opponents. Captain Macintosh was being propped up by his spotter; he was coughing up water as if he'd nearly drowned. Colin Mint was being bandaged by a team of medics, while Lady Crammington was lying snoring on the stadium floor.

Ivy checked the other Grivens tables. Not all players had been so fortunate; two contestants from table two were being carried out of the stadium on stretchers, their spotters pale-faced and trembling.

Nix Wolf announced the winners of the three other tables. Their games had all lasted at least two rounds; only Ivy's had been over after the first. She was surprised but delighted to find that Alexander Brewster had beaten his opponents on table three. Their eyes met as his face was projected onto a materializer, and he smiled with relief. Carson Crevitch was the winner of table one and, with a sinking feeling, Ivy saw that François Filigree was table two's champion.

As the winners took their places around the final table, an eerie silence came over the stadium. Ivy combed the stands, searching for Mr. Punch. He should be back by now. She spotted Selena Grimes sitting in a VIP area, surrounded by other traders wearing elaborate Hobsmatch. The Jar of Shadows wasn't with her; Ivy wondered where she was hiding it.

Focusing on the game again, she smiled glumly at Alexander Brewster opposite. She couldn't believe that he had no spotter. Using her whispering, she checked to see if he was alive. The silence confirmed it.

Without a spotter, Alexander was putting himself in great danger. He gazed into the audience, his arms trembling. Ivy assumed he was looking for his father.

François Filigree stood on tiptoe, trying to see over the

table. Ivy wished she had X-ray vision so she could see the expression behind his Noh mask.

Nix Wolf cleared his throat into the uncommon conch shell. "Let the final game COMMENCE!"

Goose pimples rippled across Ivy's skin; she shifted her weight from one foot to the other.

As Nix Wolf offered Alexander the first choice of Grivens pieces, Ivy studied Carson Crevitch. He had no spotter, so she checked with her whispering: he was one of the dead.

Nix Wolf handed the box of Grivens pieces to Filigree. Ivy concentrated hard, trying to block out the noise from the stadium. Filigree selected a glove, a suitcase and a bell carved from dark red wood and placed them on the chopping board. The spectators oohed and aahed, but Ivy didn't hear them.

What she heard was a very different sound: a hushed voice. It didn't drift around like the whispers of the dead; it sounded muffled, trapped. Ivy scanned the Grivens table. The only uncommon object on it was meant to be the chopping board, but this garbled voice originated somewhere else.

Filigree's bell—she was sure of it; she'd practiced enough with her abilities to pinpoint where it was coming from. *It's uncommon.*

From what Johnny Hands had told her, she knew that Filigree must be cheating. Perhaps he'd planted the uncommon bell in the box before the contest. She already suspected him of being up to no good; he could be working for Selena Grimes. With a sickening jolt, Ivy considered the possibility that Selena had ordered Filigree to kill her during the game. . . .

A cold feeling washed over her. There was no way Seb could know that Filigree's bell was uncommon. Ivy could only hope that he had the sense to pull her out of the chalk circle before things got really bad.

"Ahem." Nix Wolf coughed, holding out the box of Grivens pieces toward Ivy.

She shook her head and put her hand inside. Her fingers curled around three pieces. She pulled them out and placed them on the Grivens board. She'd chosen a bell and glove carved from red marble, and a small white polystyrene suitcase.

While Carson Crevitch made his choice, Ivy weighed her options, trying to work out the best way to deal with Filigree's uncommon bell piece.

Without a spotter, there was a real risk that Alexander would be killed when Filigree played that bell. Perhaps if she could warn him somehow, the two of them could work together. She tried to attract Alexander's attention with a cough, but he was focused on his Grivens pieces.

The light in the stadium dimmed and a spotlight fell across the board. Ivy imagined the uncommoners watching the game all around the world, engrossed in her every move. Through the glass roof she could see that it was pitch-black outside in Lundinor. Inside the stadium, technicians whizzed around on uncommon rugs, directing lemon squeezers toward the action.

Fans leaped to their feet, waving. Ivy heard a ripple of shouts of "Ivy Sparrow!" *Uncommoners I've never even met before, willing me to do well.* She used their voices to steady her nerves as she turned back to the chopping board.

Nix Wolf's voice whipped around the stadium like a gust of wind. "Let the first round begin!"

Ivy had no idea which piece to play. If Valian was in her

shoes right now, he would probably pick the bell, whereas Seb would go for something more likely to attack—the glove. Instead, Ivy pushed the suitcase forward. Her opponents had already made their decisions: Alexander his glove, Crevitch a bell, and Filigree, of course, his uncommon bell.

Nix Wolf spun the board.

Learning from the last game, Ivy grabbed the edge of the Grivens table to stabilize herself. The dark stadium swirled out of focus and she saw a rich orange sunset against a purple sky. Blue sand dunes appeared—along with a fearsome howling wind. Ivy found herself on a small wooden platform at the top of a shady dune. . . .

In a desert.

She took stock of her opponents. Carson Crevitch was standing with legs apart and arms outstretched, ready to leap into combat. Alexander had a steely glint in his eye, though his thin frame was shaking. Filigree's mask revealed nothing.

The Grivens pieces lay still. Then, with an unimpressive flutter, Ivy's polystyrene suitcase flapped open and a rusty metal shield appeared in her arms.

She slumped with disappointment. She didn't know what she'd been hoping for exactly; she just knew that a medieval knight's shield wasn't it. Still, she adjusted the leather strap over her arm and aimed it toward the other three players, preparing herself.

Alexander's glove flexed its fingers, made a fist and then slammed down onto the chopping board with a loud *bang!*

Three giant cracks appeared in the wooden platform under the table, each snaking toward one of Alexander's opponents. Ivy steadied herself as the ground rumbled. The wind over the dunes picked up, the platform trembling beneath her feet. The crevasses were deep; she guessed that if she fell in, it would be the end of her game. She clutched her shield tightly, bracing herself as the fissure reached her toes.

Her shield wobbled, but the fault line came to a stop. She gave a crooked smile. Maybe the rusty piece of metal on her arm wasn't so useless after all.

Filigree managed to outjump his crevice on unnaturally springy legs, though it left him stranded on a wooden island a few yards from the table. Judging from Carson Crevitch's darting eyes, he hadn't formulated a plan to avoid Alexander's attack—when his bell piece rang out and the wood stopped splintering.

Crevitch smiled wickedly as an imperious voice emerged from the bell, talking in a language Ivy didn't understand. Outside the chalk circle, a mass of skinny black-and-yellow snakes wriggled out of the sand, their tongues tasting the air.

Ivy turned her back on the Grivens table and directed her shield toward the snakes, though she didn't know what good it would do. She looked over her shoulder at her opponents: Alexander had managed to hop onto a snake-free island, but Filigree wasn't reacting at all. Instead, his legs jerked; it looked as if there was something trapped under his jacket.

As the snakes crossed over into the chalk circle, Ivy flattened herself against the Grivens table, her shield trembling on her arm. Alexander was shouting. Only Filigree's uncommon bell was left to play. Ivy doubted that her shield would be powerful enough to protect her from it; Alexander was already defenseless; and Carson Crevitch's snakes might not help him at all.

She thought of calling for Seb to pull her out, but she knew that he would only be able to save *her*—not Alexander or Crevitch.

There was time to attempt one last thing: Ivy stretched out with her whispering toward Filigree's bell piece. The murmured voice coming from inside the bell clanged around furiously, as if it was trying to escape. Ivy tried something new: she reduced her field of awareness to concentrate her senses *inside* the bell. Immediately the voice became clearer.

Strike. Defeat. Destroy . . .

She could hear words! She'd never been able to distinguish what the voices inside uncommon objects were actually saying before.

Just then, Filigree leaped for the table and made a grab for his bell. A piercing scream shot out of it—full of rage and pain. Ivy put her hands over her ears, the sounds reverberating through her mind. She felt a wave of heat as a wall of black-and-purple flames rose around the chalk circle. *Blackfire.*

Filigree was laughing behind his mask, his small gloved hands stroking his wobbling belly. The dark flames seemed to lick off him, causing no damage whatsoever. Ivy could see that something was still wriggling under his jacket, struggling to be free.

The snakes thrashed around and buried themselves in the cold sand. Heat singed Ivy's clothes, but they were so wet from the previous round, they didn't catch fire. She hid her face behind her shield, gasping for air. Smoke was seeping into her lungs, stinging the back of her throat.

And the flames were getting stronger.

"Seb!" she cried. "Seb!"

She heard a loud *pop,* and an unmistakable silhouette appeared behind the blackfire.

"Seb!" she wheezed.

He was floundering on the other side of the flames, waving his arms and jumping up and down. Ivy wasn't sure what was going on, but it looked as if he couldn't get through.

Cowering behind her shield, she realized that Filigree's uncommon bell piece must have had something to do with it. Maybe this had been Filigree's plan all along—to prevent Ivy's spotter from saving her.

She knew that if there was no way for her to be rescued, she only had one option left.

I've got to stop that bell.

Her body was weak; she needed oxygen. She summoned all her energy and reached out with her senses till she found the bell's voice amidst the roar of the flames. She'd never heard anything so angry, so intent on destruction.

Strike them down. Defeat all. Destroy . . .

As a last resort she decided to try to reason with it, though she'd never communicated with the trapped soul inside an object before. Gasping for air, she managed to project words at the bell, but it didn't seem to understand her. Then she tried soothing thoughts, memories of soft music and still water, a clear blue sky, a peaceful ocean—all the things that made her feel calm.

Strike. Defeat . . . Tired . . . Desperate . . .

Slowly the voice grew tranquil. Ivy heard it mumbling in exhausted tones and sighing. She heaved cold air into her lungs as she peered out from behind her shield. The flames were subsiding.

"WHAT IS THIS?!" Filigree shouted. Ivy lowered her shield slightly and saw that he was hitting the Grivens bell, attempting to make the flames return.

"No!" Ivy yelled. She concentrated on the bell with all her might, trying to comfort the soul trapped within it. She could feel it growing angrier—not at her and the other two competitors, but at the person who was hitting it.

All at once blackfire shot up behind Filigree. He cursed the bell and started to bat the flames away with his fire-retardant gloves. Alexander and Carson Crevitch shuffled to the edge of the chalk circle, not sure what was going on—but scarcely able to believe their luck. Ivy studied Filigree closely. His white mask had started to melt in the heat, and a face was emerging beneath it. . . .

A very *green* face.

Six spindly legs burst free of Filigree's stomach, and the spiky, mantis-like body of Jack-in-the-Green sprang out of the torn overcoat. What was left of the furniture trader's Japanese Noh mask dripped like milk over the assassin's smooth green features.

Ivy stumbled back. François Filigree had been *Jack-in-the-Green* all along! But why had he used a costume to disguise himself, rather than shape-shifting? A large blue vase appeared behind Jack-in-the-Green's spindly legs—the same size and shape to have been smuggled in under Filigree's clothes.

Ivy recognized it immediately: *the Jar of Shadows*.

She had to get hold of it somehow. Jack-in-the-Green growled and lunged at her with his barbed pincers, but a barricade of black-and-purple flames rose up between the two of them, stopping him just in time.

Ivy knew she needed to act before he could open the jar. She reached out with her senses to the Grivens bell. Its voice was confused and frantic, intent on destroying Jack-in-the-Green. Before she had time to do anything about it, the fire gave one last roar, drowning out all other sounds—and then Jack-in-the-Green was engulfed in flames. . . .

Immediately her surroundings changed. The smoky purple desert vanished and the spitting of flames was silenced. Instead, raucous applause and angry shouts spread through the air. They were back in the stadium.

People were pointing and jeering. An underguard troop ran onto the stadium floor toward Jack-in-the-Green, who was shouting angrily, his skin charred and smoking. The Jar of Shadows was still standing on the other side of the Grivens table, unharmed.

Nix Wolf came forward and announced, "Our champion is . . ." He hesitated.

Ivy saw her face appear on a materializer and was surprised that she didn't look worse. Her skin was sooty, her hair frazzled and singed, but she didn't have a scratch on her. That ancient shield must have protected her better than she'd expected. The materializers then showed a wheezing Alexander and Carson Crevitch, who both had blistered cheeks.

"Ivy Sparrow!" Nix Wolf decided finally.

Ivy started. *She* was the winner?

The crowd roared with delight, whistling and stamping their feet. There were a few loud boos, but Ivy was too overwhelmed to be bothered by them.

She'd won; she'd actually *won*.

Her skin tingled with shock. She caught Alexander's eye

as he and Carson Crevitch were led away by medical staff. He smiled at her weakly, obviously relieved that it was all over. Nobody had approached the Jar of Shadows yet; in all the chaos, it seemed to have escaped everyone's notice.

Ivy stepped carefully out of the chalk circle, still feeling wobbly, and began edging her way around the table toward the jar. She'd forgotten that Seb was behind her until he hugged her tightly. "Well done," he said, his voice breaking.

With what strength Ivy had left, she shook him off. "Seb— the jar." She swatted away a cloud of floating snow-globe cameras as they zoomed closer. "People will see it—we have to get it out of here." She looked over to where Selena Grimes had been sitting. Her chair was empty.

Seb stepped inside the chalk circle and ran over to the jar. He bent down and put his arms around it. "It's too heavy!"

"Don't try to lift it," Ivy cried. "If you drop it, you'll release what's inside." As she searched for a solution, she heard another roar from the spectators. She turned and saw that they were rushing onto the floor. Sprinting at the front of the pack was Valian, carrying Seb's rucksack over one shoulder, with Ivy's satchel slung across the other.

He surveyed the scene, and then, without a word of explanation, dragged Ivy back inside the chalk circle and spun the Grivens board.

The stadium vanished. Ivy gasped as a canopy of dark leaves appeared above her head and the crumbling ochre ruins of some ancient temple rose from the earth around her. The light faded and the air was filled with a hundred birdcalls and the smell of the jungle.

Valian ran over the forest floor to where Seb was struggling

265

with the jar. "We've only got minutes before someone in the stadium connects a snow globe to the Krigvelt and can see us again," he said, tugging the Sack of Stars out of his jacket.

"Where are we going to send it?" Seb asked.

"I know," Ivy said, hurrying over and whispering something into the lining. "I'll explain when we get there."

As she lowered her head into the sack, the jungle disappeared behind her.

CHAPTER TWENTY-EIGHT

"Come on, come on." Ivy stared at the dark opening of the Sack of Stars, willing Seb and the Jar of Shadows to come out in one piece. "What's taking him so long?"

Valian fiddled with his gloves. "I don't know."

Ivy's pulse was racing, but her body felt numb and heavy, as if the Grivens contest had sapped all her energy. She took a great lungful of air, trying to stay calm.

It was quiet in her dad's office. The lights were off but moonlight crept in through the large bay window that looked out onto the street.

There was a scratchy rustle and the Jar of Shadows rolled out of the Sack of Stars onto the soft carpet. Ivy watched curiously as it enlarged from bag size to normal size. . . . It gave her an idea.

Seb sighed. "That was the most nerve-racking bag journey

of my life. We so didn't think it through. The jar could have smashed at any point."

"But it didn't," Valian said, giving him a hand up. Between the three of them they managed to right the jar.

Seb took a feather out of his rucksack. "I'm gonna send a message to Judy—let her and the others know we're OK."

"All right, but . . ." Valian scanned the piles of books, cardboard boxes and dusty microscopes in the room. "What are we doing here?"

"I thought of a way to protect the jar," Ivy said. "It might be crazy, but I was thinking we could hide it in the museum."

"*Here?*" Valian exclaimed. "But—the Dirge could easily breach the security in this building. It wouldn't be safe."

"But they'll never know it's here," Ivy argued. "There are hundreds of jars just like it in the museum's collection—I've seen them." She turned to Seb. "Do you still have the tape measure that Granma Sylvie gave you?"

Seb stuffed a hand in his rucksack and rummaged around. "I think so, yeah. . . ."

Ivy thought of the jar traveling in the Sack of Stars. "What if we shrink the jar so that it can't be recognized?"

Valian rubbed his chin. "Go on . . ."

She went over to a large cardboard box that was sitting open on a desk. "Objects are added to the museum's collection all the time," she explained. "One of the things our dad does is date and classify everything before it's put on display." She peered inside. "All we need to do is stuff the small Jar of Shadows in some bubble wrap and put it in here. Dad will assume it's been sent with all these other artifacts."

She turned and examined the porcelain jar properly for the

first time, running her fingers around the top. It didn't have a lid. It was like a money box—the only way to open it would be to smash it. "It'll be taken care of in here," Ivy said. "They'll think it's priceless."

"Technically it is," Seb pointed out. "If Dad tries to date it, he'll realize it's thousands of years old. You know what—this is just crazy enough that it might actually work."

Valian looked from one of them to the other and nodded. "All right, let's do it."

Ivy stood guard by the door while Seb and Valian resized the jar using the uncommon tape measure. It was quiet in the corridor that led into the museum when Ivy heard a scraping sound growing louder. She tensed as a shadow appeared behind the glass, and she stumbled back as the door opened. . . .

"I came as soon as I got your message," Judy said, skating inside. She stopped to catch her breath. "I hadn't even left the Grivens stadium." She caught sight of Seb, wrapping the miniature Jar of Shadows in bubble wrap. "Are you all OK?"

"Just about," Ivy told her, smiling. "Thanks for coming."

A line appeared on Valian's forehead. "You came from the stadium? How did you travel here so quickly? You couldn't have used a bag."

"Er—no, obviously not." Judy shook her head but didn't volunteer an explanation.

"You must have snuck in really quietly too," Ivy remarked. "There are security guards everywhere."

Judy shrugged. "I guess I'm too fast on my skates. They didn't seem to notice me."

Ivy had heard the loud thrum of Judy's roller skates out in the corridor; the security guards would surely have heard them too. Something didn't make sense.

She ran through the different ways in which uncommoners got around and remembered being startled when Johnny Hands had arrived almost immediately after she'd called him using his business card.

But Judy couldn't be dead, surely. . . .

Ivy relaxed her senses and allowed her whispering to spread out to the walls of the room. She could hear the Jar of Shadows and several uncommon objects mumbling incoherently, but there was another voice present in the air, something energetic and warm.

Ivy's jaw dropped. "You're one of the dead, aren't you? I can sense it with my whispering."

Judy went very still. "What?" She tucked a strand of shiny hair behind her ear, her eyes flicking to Seb.

"*That's* how you read Dead Man's Code," Valian said softly. "All the dead know how to read it."

Seb coughed. "Sorry—*dead*?" The expression on his face was disbelieving. "No, you . . . you can't be."

Judy examined her tutu, her voice wobbling. "I was going to tell you, but I thought you wouldn't trust me anymore."

Ivy's skin tingled with shock. She thought back to the times she'd been near Judy, trying to understand why she hadn't sensed that she was dead. There were broken souls everywhere in Lundinor; perhaps Judy's had got lost in the din.

Judy sniffed, trying to keep her emotions in check. "Look—the reason I came here was to warn you. At the end of the contest Selena was nowhere to be seen, and if the Dirge have been hunting for the Jar of Shadows this long, she's going to do everything she can to get it back."

"She can't follow us here—she doesn't know where we've escaped to," Valian pointed out.

"That's why I think she'll do something to bring you to her," Judy said. "Like use someone you love as bait, someone she can trace easily."

"*Granma Sylvie,*" Ivy said, tensing. "Has she been in contact?"

Judy shook her head. "Ethel was trying to get a feather-light to her when I left the stadium. Your granma still has no idea that you were entered in the Grivens contest."

Seb stopped glaring at Judy to refocus. "She must still be at the mansion. We have to go and check on her."

Valian picked up the Sack of Stars. "There's no time to waste."

As he pulled the bag over his head, Seb scowled at Judy. "You can stay put. We don't want liars coming with us."

The lights were on in the hallway of the Wrench Mansion. The place held bad memories from Ivy's last visit—of escaping from Selena's grim-wolf and fighting a host of vile dead creatures in the basement. Her senses were still on edge after the Grivens contest, and the mansion was a dangerous place. She stuffed the Sack of Stars into her satchel and brought out her yo-yo.

With the weapon clutched in her hand, she took a few steps forward over the thick carpet. "Granma?" she called uncertainly. "It's Ivy and Seb!"

"And Valian," Seb added, slipping his drumsticks out of his inside pockets.

The house was full of cobwebs and shadows. Portraits of hard-eyed faces covered the walls—Ivy's distant relatives.

She heard a rustle at the top of the grand staircase and began to climb. "Granma?"

There was a clatter, and then a door on the landing swung open. Silvery light came flooding out. Ivy almost tripped on the stairs. Seb and Valian stopped behind her.

"*Ivy?*" Granma Sylvie's silhouette appeared in the doorway. Her voice was shaky.

The three of them hurried up the last few steps but approached Granma Sylvie with caution.

As the light fell across her face, Ivy realized that something serious had happened. Granma Sylvie's eyes were red, as if she'd been crying. "What time is it?" she asked, rubbing her forehead. There was an unfamiliar edge to her voice.

"Before midnight," Ivy answered. She wasn't sure of the exact time; she only knew that the Grivens contest had started at eight. "Are you OK? Has something happened? You haven't been in touch all day."

Granma Sylvie sighed before two words slipped out of her mouth and everything changed.

"I remember."

CHAPTER TWENTY-NINE

In contrast to the rest of the gloomy Wrench Mansion, Granma Sylvie's teenage bedroom shone with the spirit of rebellion. Set into the roof beams—just like Ivy's own attic room—it had wallpaper of a shimmering sky blue, and linen curtains soft as clouds hung at the windows. Floating in the middle of the ceiling, an uncommon milk jug spilled pale light across every possible surface, illuminating the toys, books and odd knickknacks Granma Sylvie had collected during her childhood.

Ivy could see the moon outside despite the rain pattering against the glass. A London skyline spread out below; the mansion was temporarily residing in her home city.

"What happened?" she asked. She could see that Granma Sylvie had been rummaging through her things for a while—books and soft toys lay strewn across the floor, the wardrobe doors were open and there were clean patches in the dust on the shelves where things had been moved around. "Did it all come back to you at once?"

Granma Sylvie took a seat on the bed. "It was all to do with this room. I was so scared of setting foot in here, I'd persuaded the underguard to explore the mansion bottom-up; that way, I wouldn't have to face my bedroom—and all the secrets it might contain—till the very end."

Ivy came to sit next to her, placing her satchel on the floor.

"After the underguard left I eventually plucked up the courage to come in," Granma Sylvie told them. "I was surprised by how familiar everything was. Each time I picked up an object or opened a drawer, a memory returned. That's why I've been here so long." She laid a hand on her bed, stroking the dusty fabric. "I used to sit here and read with my mother, and we'd plan our Hobsmatch together in that mirror on the dressing table."

"It's like your own fears were preventing your memories from returning," Seb said. "You had to overcome them."

Granma Sylvie tucked a strand of hair behind Ivy's ear and tensed when she saw that it was scorched. "What on earth's happened to you? Are you all right?"

Ivy told her about the Grivens contest and Selena Grimes's failed attempt to open the Jar of Shadows—excluding any mention of her and Seb's involvement.

Granma Sylvie shook her head. "Selena Grimes and I were friends once. I knew what she did . . . what she became." A look of regret crossed her face. "I was never involved in her schemes, or my father's. My mother and I fought the Dirge in secret."

"We all knew you weren't one of the bad guys," Seb said.

Ivy smiled. At least now Granma Sylvie knew it for certain.

Valian looked out of the window. "The reason we're here is because we think that Selena might come after you."

Granma Sylvie scowled and pulled Ivy's satchel onto her lap. "Earlier I remembered about the postcard—Amos sent it. The photo on the front was taken when he and I first became friends." As she searched for the postcard, she came across the leather-bound journal. "This was Amos's most treasured possession." Her face glowed, as if something had been ignited deep inside.

"What do you know about Amos?" Ivy asked hurriedly. For the first time ever, she could ask her granma about something uncommon-related. It felt fantastic.

"He was invited to join the Rasavatum when we were just kids," Granma Sylvie told her, tapping the journal as the information flooded back to her. "He told me, because he knew I was fighting the Dirge too. During the last three years I spent in Lundinor I helped him to develop a tracer serum, which he was planning to use to track down several of the Great Uncommon Good. That's how he found the Jar of Shadows."

"*He* found the Jar of Shadows?" Valian said.

Granma Sylvie stroked the black leather cover of the journal. She frowned and then opened it up, flipping through the empty pages. She seemed to be counting, and after exactly forty-two pages she stopped.

"We need a liquid mixed with love," she muttered. "It's the only thing that activates the ink."

Uncommon ink . . . So that was what Ivy had been sensing

all this time. She thought carefully. "Valian, do you still have that Raider's Tonic that Miss H and Miss W gave you?"

Valian reached into his inside pocket and brought out a small pewter flask. "Never leave my room without it."

Ivy unscrewed the cap and poured a few drops onto the pages of the journal.

As the liquid sank into the paper, she shuffled closer to see what was happening. There was a rustling sound, and an odorless gray smoke rose from the spine of the notebook. Granma Sylvie closed it gently and laid it on her lap as the smoke continued to seep out.

Ivy's mind began to whir. *The smoke . . . The black cover . . .*

She shuddered. "No way! Granma, *that's* what you were seeing in your memory! It was never a black door with a smoking hourglass on it. It was *this journal*."

"That's right," Granma Sylvie said, sounding unsurprised. "My memories of what Amos was working on in his journal were trying to return; I just misinterpreted them."

When the gray smoke had stopped leaking out of the journal, Granma Sylvie opened it up again and fanned through. Neat black handwriting filled every page, along with sketches, diagrams and complex algebra—in a range of languages, from hieroglyphics to Chinese.

Ivy couldn't believe it had been hidden there all along. "What does it say?"

Granma Sylvie flicked to a point three-quarters of the way through the book, where the writing finished and the pages were blank. "Amos chronicled his hunt for the Great Uncommon Good, along with everything he'd learned about the Dirge's plans—including things about Selena. All his most important discoveries are in these pages. He protected his secrets by submerging the paper in a special uncommon solution he'd mixed. It meant that the words would only appear if a liquid mixed with love touched the paper. He believed it would prevent anyone with a cold heart from reading it."

Ivy wondered how Jack-in-the-Green had managed it; perhaps he'd used the help of someone else. She thought of Selena's desperate visit to the Dirge back in 1967. "Do you know what happened to Selena?"

Granma Sylvie's face was grave. "Yes, but perhaps Amos can explain it better than me." She flicked through and pointed to the top of a page dated October 20, 1967.

Two months before Selena died. Ivy began to read aloud so that Seb and Valian could hear:

"I am being followed. A quick-footed gentleman, possibly dead. Using a tracing serum (batch 2, formula 7.3), I tracked him to a cellar door on Lightning Bolt Lane, where he disappeared. I suspect he is working for the Dirge.

"Selena has noticed me looking over my shoulder. I'm wary of telling her the truth about my investigations into the Great Uncommon Good. I know she loves me, but it is too dangerous to let her share my secrets. I cannot put her at risk too—"

"Wait. Amos and Selena were in love?" Ivy said.

"They were engaged to be married," Granma Sylvie explained, "but Amos was afraid to announce it publicly in case the Dirge used Selena to get to him. She wasn't Wolfsbane back then. That postcard you found—she and I were friends at that time, but we grew apart as we got older." She nodded back to the journal, encouraging Ivy to read on.

"The twenty-fifth of October 1967

"A crooked sixpence was found at the scene of another murder today. The streets are empty; people are too scared to trade. With every innocent life that is lost, I become more determined to destroy the Dirge and their evil.

"Tonight I plan to go through the cellar door on Lightning Bolt Lane. Maybe my follower knows a thing or two. . . ."

The writing finished there. Ivy turned the page. "Wait—that's it?"

"That was the night Amos died," Granma Sylvie said quietly with a frown. "He was murdered on the other side of that cellar door, no doubt. His body was found the next morning in the street outside."

Ivy shivered and laid a hand on Granma Sylvie's arm. "He was your friend; I'm sorry."

She shrugged. "He became a ghoul for a few years before he Departed. I had some good times with him, but the experience had changed him. He was never the same."

Ivy flicked through a few blank pages before the entries appeared again, only this time with subtle differences. The ink was now a pale, ghostly shade of blue and the handwriting was wobbly. Amos must have used the rest of the book to chart what happened to him after he died.

"Selena came to me, devastated, after Amos was killed," Granma Sylvie explained. "Her grief was so overwhelming she decided she could no longer bear it; she wanted to become a ghoul too, so that she could be with Amos forever."

"That's why she sought out the Dirge in 1967," Ivy said. "She wanted them to turn her into a ghoul. That was why she died that night—they killed her and she asked them to!"

Granma Sylvie bobbed her head. "Except that her plan

279

failed, of course. The Dirge successfully turned her into a ghoul, but when she met Amos again, he was so disgusted that she'd made a bargain with the Dirge—the very people he'd spent his life fighting—that he told her he never wanted to see her again." She sighed. "I tried to reason with Selena afterward, but she was too heartbroken to listen. Consumed by grief and at her weakest, she sought sanctuary with the Dirge. . . ." She hesitated. "After that, I can only guess what happened. The previous Wolfsbane must have Departed—and then Selena was invited to take their place. The Selena I had known was gone. Selena today may have the same face as the girl I knew, but she is infinitely more cruel and dangerous."

A clatter sounded downstairs. Ivy felt the floorboards creak. "What's that? Is there anyone else here?"

Granma Sylvie stiffened. "There shouldn't be."

Using her whispering, Ivy searched past the walls of the bedroom and out into the mansion. One of the dead was approaching from below.

Before she could shout out a warning, a figure rose *through* the floor. A long dark braid, pale skin and thin red lips: *Selena Grimes*. Her stone-gray dress shifted around her body like a shadow and her face was frozen in an expression of disgust. She glowered at Ivy and Granma Sylvie, brandishing an ebony walking cane in her hand.

It sliced through the air like a scythe. "*That* journal belongs to me!" She lunged toward them, cane aloft. *Crack!* Several thorny creepers shot from the end of it, flying straight for Ivy's face.

She ducked out of the way just in time. The brambles ripped into Granma Sylvie's bed, tearing open the pillows.

Selena laughed. "You can-
not hope to escape this time.
I'm going to kill you all,
as I should have done
a long time ago." She
whirled the uncommon
cane above her head and
a forest of thorns ripped
through the floorboards,
shredding anything in
their path. "Give me that!"
she screeched, lunging for
the journal in Granma
Sylvie's hands. "How
dare you touch it!"

Granma Sylvie spun away, causing Selena to trip over a
pile of books and end up on her hands and knees, hovering
eerily above the floor. Smacking his drumsticks at Granma
Sylvie's old wardrobe, Seb sent it toppling over onto Selena
with a loud *bang*.

"You three, get to the stairs," Granma Sylvie ordered, grabbing Ivy's satchel and tugging out the Sack of Stars. "There's a
car in the drive; I'll meet you there. Go—now!"

Her voice spurred Ivy into action and she ran over to the
door. Selena was stirring, her body appearing through the
wardrobe. Ivy dodged several leaping brambles before escaping onto the landing, Seb and Valian right behind her.

"What about Granma?" Seb called, looking back into the
bedroom. Granma Sylvie was by the window, tossing Amos's
notebook into the Sack of Stars.

"It sounds like she has a plan. Do what she says," Valian urged. "Selena's trying to kill us. More of the Dirge could be on their way. We need to run—*now*."

Ivy tore down the stairs ahead of Seb and Valian, shooting through the front door and out into the night. The house was surrounded by a neat lawn and a trimmed box hedge; a vintage Volkswagen Beetle was parked in the drive. Ivy heard a scratchy thud on the lawn and saw Granma Sylvie touching down, lowering an uncommon belt to her waist. Ivy had used one before—they enabled you to fly.

"Kept one in my room for emergencies," Granma Sylvie called, shaking out the belt. "Get in the car! I've trapped Selena with an uncommon paper clip, but she'll break free at any moment."

The doors were unlocked. Seb took the front passenger seat while Valian and Ivy squeezed into the back. Ivy was all fingers and thumbs as she struggled to get her seat belt on. It was strange being in a common mode of transport again. Granma Sylvie got the engine running and pulled away.

"Where are we going?" Seb asked, still panting.

Ivy looked through the rear window as vines burst through the first-floor windows of the mansion and spread out across the front garden. Selena was nowhere to be seen.

"To the gardens," Granma Sylvie said. "We have to get back to Lundinor and find Ethel and the others. If Selena's risking using that cane on common land, it can mean only one thing."

"What?" Ivy asked, impressed by how much Granma Sylvie now understood.

"The underguard must be busy dealing with some[thing] else," she said. "Something very bad."

There was no underguard from Special Branch in the potting shed to escort them down the uncommon hose, so the four of them helped themselves to a garden sack each and took turns clambering inside. "Why couldn't we use the Sack of Stars to get there?" Ivy asked before pushing off.

"I've sent something else through it," Granma Sylvie said. "You can't use bags for two different journeys at the same time."

As Ivy twisted around and around the helter skelter into the main arrivals chamber, a scent began to fill her nostrils— charcoal and sulfur, like the smell of fireworks. By the time she touched down at the bottom and stood up, she was coughing.

On the opposite side of the chamber the Great Gates stood open, but their intricate design featuring orange and lemon trees had been altered to show something else:

The smoking hourglass.

CHAPTER THIRTY

"Stay close to me," Granma Sylvie said, leading the way through the Great Gates onto the Gauntlet. "Selena can't be far behind."

Ivy scanned the area. "Where *is* everyone?" The wide gravel road was deserted, and the only sound came from the wind rustling through the empty fields on either side. The thatched cottages had their blinds drawn and windows shut. Ivy knew it was late, but she had expected the place to be teeming with supporters leaving the Grivens contest.

Valian cast wary glances up and down the street. "I've never seen Lundinor like this."

They continued along the Gauntlet, searching for clues.

"Over there." Seb pointed to a blackened spot by the road-side: a small muddy hole surrounded by a ring of singed grass.

"What is it?" Ivy asked.

Valian bent down to inspect it. "A drain hole. Lundinor might seem different every season, but the core structure—the air filters, the sewage system, the road layout—is always the same. The drain network runs through all four quarters."

"They've overflowed." Granma Sylvie took out a pen, poked it into the sludge and held it under her nose. Ivy grimaced.

"This isn't drain water," Granma Sylvie said. "There's something uncommon going on here. You smell . . ."

Ivy screwed up her face, giving the pen a sniff. The mud smelled smoky and sweet, just like . . . "Dragon's Breath Ale," Ivy exclaimed.

"*Ale?* Interesting." Granma Sylvie wiped her pen on the grass and straightened up. "We'd better keep walking."

More scorched drains appeared as they continued. As the House of Bells came into sight, Granma Sylvie gasped. The thatched roof was smoking and half the wooden porch had collapsed, blocking the door. Chunks of splintered masonry lay scattered across the street. "Ethel!" she cried, hurrying closer. "Ethel, are you in there?"

Ivy shot Seb and Valian a look of concern as they followed her.

There was silence at first, and then a muffled voice called out, *"Sylvie?"* Ethel appeared at a broken downstairs window, her face sweating and pale behind the jagged pieces of glass. "What are you doing out there? Get inside; they'll smell you."

"*Smell* us?" Seb repeated. "What are you talking about?"

Before Ethel could answer, Granma Sylvie turned and stared into the distance, going very still. Ivy followed her gaze. Smoke was rising over a far-off hill, forming into a huge cloud that loomed under the cave ceiling.

"Ivy," Granma Sylvie said in a tight voice. "That cloud—what does your whispering tell you about it?"

Ivy concentrated hard, focusing on the distant patch of smoke. There were lots of broken souls there, with angry voices talking at the same time. "It's made of dead creatures," she said. "I think they're coming toward us." Suddenly she caught a sound on the air—a rumbling, crackling noise like a giant bonfire.

"*Pyroaches,*" Granma Sylvie growled. "They shouldn't be here; there isn't any fire."

Ivy recalled Mr. Littlefair's chilling warning about the creatures during the fire at Brewster's Alehouse. "Dragon's Breath Ale allows people to temporarily breathe fire. Could the flooded drains have something to do with it?"

Valian scuffed his foot on the blackened grass. "If the ale is in the sewers, any number of pyroaches could have drunk it. It would allow them to create fire themselves—to move around freely."

In the distance the dark swarm was getting bigger. Granma Sylvie's face was white with horror. "They'll be here in minutes. We need to get inside *now*!"

"Over here," Seb called, scrambling across the porch and lifting aside a plank of wood. "There's a hole in the wall we can fit through."

Ivy could hear the crackling noise getting louder. "Hurry—I think I can see them." A gigantic ball of fire turned onto the Gauntlet. Inside the flames was a mass of long dark bodies flying in warplane formation. Thatched cottages on either side burst alight as they passed.

Without a second to spare, Ivy, Seb, Valian and Granma Sylvie scrambled through the splintered hole into the House of Bells. Seb speedily covered it up with wood from the other side.

The cottage walls trembled.

"Get down!" Ethel whispered, kneeling on the floor.

They all crawled toward a window and peered over the ledge. The timbers rattled as the swarm of pyroaches shot past. With every glimpse, Ivy was able to build a more complete picture of the creatures, and it made her skin crawl. Each pyroach was the size of a small dog, with long wings the color of molten lava and a body that scraped and crunched as it flew. Its head was disturbingly human, but four black legs hung from the segment between its neck and chest.

Ivy tucked herself down under the window frame; she was shaking. The pyroaches' wings thudded through the air, making the walls of the House of Bells rattle.

After a minute or so the crackling noises began to fade.

"The pyroaches were waiting outside the Grivens stadium," Ethel said. "I managed to escape on a mop, but most of the audience fled to Mr. Punch's big top. Violet sent me featherlights to explain what was going on. Mr. Punch 'as protected everyone in the tent, but 'ow long 'e can hold out, I don't know. No one 'as any weapons to defend themselves."

Ivy thought of Judy—she must have left the stadium before anyone had discovered the pyroaches waiting outside. "Perhaps the sewers were flooded with Dragon's Breath Ale while the contest was going on."

Ethel blinked. "*Ale?* No one at the big top knows anything about that."

"Where's the underguard?" Valian asked as Ethel headed for the door at the back of the shop.

"A second swarm of pyroaches are besieging the station," she replied over her shoulder. "A few officers may 'ave escaped using body bags, but if they've tried to reenter Lundinor through the Great Gates, they'll 'ave just been driven inside."

The others followed Ethel into the storeroom.

"We've got to rescue them," Ivy said, curling her hands into fists. "We could evacuate people using the Sack of Stars."

Granma Sylvie reached into her handbag and pulled it out. Ethel cast the burlap sack a startled look.

"We can't," Valian said. "You remember what Mr. Punch told us: it's our responsibility to keep the bag hidden, no matter what. If the Dirge found it—"

"Evacuation wouldn't work anyway," Granma Sylvie cut in. "The pyroaches would overwhelm Mr. Punch before everyone was able to escape. It's him we need to help, only we'll need some more equipment." She patted Ethel's shoulder. "We can't fight pyroaches without putting out fires."

Ethel frowned at Granma Sylvie's hand. "You sound strangely sure of that, Sylv. . . . 'Ave you remembered something?"

Granma Sylvie's lips twitched into a smile. "It's *all* come back, old friend," she said, tapping her temple. "Everything."

Ethel started. *"What?"* She took a few steps closer. "Are you certain?"

Granma Sylvie exhaled. "Oh, will you just come here?" She threw her arms around Ethel, squeezing tightly.

The shrill grate of pyroach wings suddenly made the shop walls tremble. Ethel's face fell. "Better catch up later."

Granma Sylvie turned to Ivy, Seb and Valian. "You three go through the bag first. As soon as you reach the big top, go and find Mr. Littlefair and Violet, and *stay* with them until this is over. Ethel and I will see what we can do to aid Mr. Punch."

While Granma Sylvie went to help Ethel find an uncommon watering can, Valian lowered his voice. "Keep a lookout for Selena. The pyroaches won't bother her—they only feed on living flesh."

Ivy took her yo-yo out of her satchel and stuffed it in her trouser pocket, ready to use. She listened in as Granma Sylvie and Ethel discussed their plans.

"Pyroaches can smell you and see you, but they 'ave poor hearing," Ethel was saying.

Granma Sylvie tucked a plastic spade—just like the ones the castleguards had used to fight the fire at the alehouse—into her belt. "Agreed. Staying quiet and hidden is our best line of defense."

Ivy took note of their advice. With Selena on their tail, she didn't know when it might come in handy.

Granma Sylvie fixed her long hair into a ponytail and smoothed down her blouse. "Ready?" She laid the Sack of Stars on the floor in front of them. "Good luck, everyone."

The air in the big top was humid and filled with panicked conversation. As Ivy got to her feet, she searched for Mr. Littlefair and Violet. The majority of the uncommoners sat huddled in the center of the sandy floor; some were busy constructing a barricade at the entrance using the heaviest of Mr. Punch's chests. Pyroaches still circled the tent, the roar making Ivy shudder.

As she scanned the injured, her spirits fell. Casualties ranged from singed hair and minor burns to serious wounds. Young children were sobbing, hiding in the folds of their parents' Hobsmatch.

Ivy had never seen the traders of Lundinor look so vulnerable and helpless before. Her throat tightened as she glimpsed each anxious face. They were trapped, not only in the tent but in Lundinor itself—a gigantic cave now plagued by flesh-eating monsters.

At the edge of the tent she spotted Alexander Brewster, his face scratched and bleeding. Violet and Mr. Littlefair stood close by in a group of other Gauntlet traders.

"There they are," Seb said. The Sack of Stars rustled on the floor behind them as Ethel scrambled out. "Let's go."

They made their way across the tent toward Alexander.

"Ivy?" His eyes were watery. "My pa is outside—trapped in a building on the opposite side of the green. He's got nothing to defend himself with."

Seb winced. "Isn't there someone out there who can help?"

"Everyone's hiding." Alexander's voice sounded resigned. "Here—I'll show you."

They wove their way through to a small section of tent

wall that was dotted with golf-ball-sized holes. "They're big enough to see through but too small to let a pyroach in," Alexander explained briefly.

Ivy pushed her face against the purple canvas and peeked through the gap.

Outside, the place looked like a deserted movie set. The dark streets were empty and the only flicker of movement came from an orange light that flashed across the ground as the pyroaches patrolled overhead.

"Mr. Punch is outside the main entrance," Alexander said. "My pa is on the right, in the hotel with the stained-glass windows. We've been staying there while the alehouse is being repaired." He paused. "He didn't want to watch me in the Grivens contest; I think he's still angry about the fire and that business with the photo frame."

Ivy spied Mr. Punch in his red and black ringmaster's coat, standing alone on the grass. In his hand was a closed black umbrella, dripping with water. Above his curly orange beard, his face was stiff. A cloud of pyroaches plunged toward him, but Mr. Punch merely pointed his umbrella at them and opened it up. A barrage of icicles and raindrops shot out, slicing through the air and spearing pyroaches. The water droplets doused their fire and, weakened, they disappeared down the nearest drain.

Drummond Brewster was more difficult to spot, but Ivy eventually glimpsed his red face and barrel chest in the window of a three-story cottage across the green.

"There must be some way to get to him," she said, drawing back. "Maybe we can distract the pyroaches. . . ."

As Alexander peered through the hole again, Seb lowered

his voice. "Ivy, there are too many of them, and we're their *food*."

"Yes, but pyroaches have bad hearing," she argued. "Perhaps if we're quiet, we can sneak over without being noticed."

Valian chewed the suggestion over. "We'd have a better chance if we split up. Seb and I could create a diversion while you and Alexander fetch his dad."

After sharing their makeshift plan with Alexander, they found a spot behind a wall of cabinets where no one could see them, and Seb used his drumsticks to blast a hole in the soil under the tent. "I'll fill it in once we've crawled through," he said. "We don't want the pyroaches getting in."

Outside, the roar of the pyroach swarm was ferocious. The four of them dashed over the scorched grass and ducked down behind a smoking tree stump, staying as quiet as they could.

"The pyroaches are just rounding the tent," Valian said, pointing. "Seb and I will try to lure them down there, away from the big top. That should give you enough time to reach your dad."

Alexander nodded. Seb's knuckles were white as he clutched his drumsticks. "Wait here till you're sure the pyroaches have seen us, Ivy. You don't want to set off too soon."

Ivy hugged him. "Be careful." She watched as he and Valian raced out from behind the tree stump, sprinting toward a half-melted line of sky stop lockers.

Ivy turned her attention back to the big top, trying not to think about the danger Valian and Seb were putting themselves in. She tensed when she saw Mr. Punch. His face was weary and his appearance flicked between the red-haired ringmaster and the crooked-toothed old man.

Other uncommoners wouldn't be able to see the changes, but she understood exactly what it meant: he was getting weaker. If Mr. Punch's umbrella was anything like Ivy's yo-yo or Seb's drumsticks, you needed energy and focus to operate it, and Mr. Punch's were rapidly draining away. She didn't know how long he'd be able to keep it up.

"Mr. Punch's strength is faltering," she told Alexander. She thought of the families trapped inside the big top. "We have to help him."

Alexander blinked. "What about my pa?"

"We'll rescue him afterward," Ivy promised, "but there are too many lives at risk in that tent. Mr. Punch needs us."

"No!" Alexander grabbed her arm. "We have to save my pa now. The pyroaches will soon run out of ale and get desperate."

Ivy was about to suggest they split up, when something tugged at the back of her memory: Ethel had mentioned that no one inside the big top knew about the Dragon's Breath Ale. "How do you know about the ale?" she asked.

Alexander's face twitched. "It doesn't matter. We need to focus on my pa."

Ivy shook his hand off, overcome by an unsettling thought. "Alexander . . . did you have something to do with this?"

His voice was bitter. "It wasn't meant to happen this way. The vats were set to flood the sewers while I was in the stadium. I thought my pa would be in the East End, not here."

Ivy swayed on her feet as she absorbed his complete lack of guilt. "*You* released the pyroaches?"

"My plans have never gone wrong before!" he said defensively. "I make sure I take into account every eventuality—it's what mixologists do. My pa was never in danger on the other occasions."

The other occasions . . . ?

Ivy went cold as she realized what he meant.

"The smoking hourglass—it was *you*, wasn't it? *You* started the fire at the alehouse. *You* killed those underguards at the memorial!" She couldn't believe he had fooled her into feeling sorry for him. *"Why?"* she cried. "Why would you do that?"

Alexander squeezed his hands into fists. "I only did what I had to do to prove myself worthy! Being invited into the Rasavatum is the greatest accolade a mixologist can receive. I had to prove I was good enough."

The Rasavatum . . . That was why Alexander had used the smoking hourglass—to attract their attention and win their favor.

"I did it for my pa," he continued, gritting his teeth. "It's the only way he'll ever notice me." For a moment Ivy felt sorry for him, but then he added, "If people have to die, then so what? You have to make sacrifices to become great. I thought Mr. Punch would know that and invite me in." He scowled. "I guess he isn't the man I thought he was."

Ivy stiffened, wondering how Alexander had discovered that Mr. Punch was in the Rasavatum. "Alexander, listen to me," she pleaded. "You can stop this before it gets any worse." She checked on Mr. Punch, who was still floundering. "Help me fight the pyroaches."

"*Fight* them?" Alexander jerked his head. "Why would I want to fight them?" He took something out of his apron—a small plastic wand, the kind you used to blow bubbles—and stepped out from behind the tree stump.

Ivy shot to her feet. "No—wait!" She spied the glow of the pyroach swarm as it skirted the big top, heading toward them.

But she needn't have worried. Alexander ran toward the flaming mass holding the bubble wand to his mouth. As the creatures dived toward him, he formed a tiny O with his lips and puffed out his cheeks, blowing.

A blast of fire shot from the wand, directing the pyroaches away from him. Ivy remained frozen with shock as Alexander leaped onto a smoking tree stump at the mouth of the Gauntlet, opposite Mr. Punch. He had a confident look that Ivy had never seen before.

"What do you think of my show?" he asked, arms outstretched. "Is it not good enough for the Rasavatum?"

Ivy couldn't believe it—the gentle, meek boy she had first met . . . it had all been a façade. *This* was the real Alexander.

Mr. Punch looked horror-struck. "You have got it *all* wrong, Alexander," he cried. "The Rasavatum brew remedies that rebuild lives; they don't destroy them like this. You must stop this madness!"

"Madness?" Alexander snorted. "Do you know how many pyroaches there are, surviving in the fiery places on Earth? Hundreds of thousands! More than there are uncommoners in this whole stinking undermart; and they are free now because of ME! And the Rasavatum think that is madness?"

"Alexander, *listen!*" Mr. Punch boomed, his patience clearly at an end. "The Rasavatum will never accept you. It's *over!*"

Alexander snarled in fury. He raised the bubble wand to his mouth, and this time an orb of fire the size of a double-decker bus emerged and shot toward the big top.

"No!" Ivy shouted, running out into the open. If that

fireball hit, it would burn a hole right through the big top, letting the pyroaches in.

His expression grim, Mr. Punch took hold of his umbrella in both hands and swung it toward the fire like a tennis racket. "Gah!" he cried, his face straining. The gigantic fireball was repelled in a flash of steam. It jetted off toward the cave ceiling, where it soon fizzled away.

As Mr. Punch dropped to his knees, the pyroaches came thundering into sight over his shoulder. Ivy gripped her trusty yo-yo, wondering if she could use it to somehow trap them.

"Hey, bug-brains!" Valian shouted. "Over here!"

Ivy turned to see him and Seb zooming about on uncommon mops, trying to lure the pyroaches toward the other side of the green. Ivy assumed they'd scavenged the mops from the damaged sky stop. She couldn't believe Seb had found the courage to ride one on his own.

"Tasty human flesh snack!" he yelled. "Ready to eat!"

The pyroaches clocked them instantly, and the whole horde turned.

Ivy sprinted forward, reaching out with her whispering as she headed for Valian and her brother. She could sense the pyroaches approaching fast. "Seb!" she shouted. He did an about-face and caught her eye. "I'm going to try and trap them. Use your drumsticks to keep them contained."

Seb saw her yo-yo and nodded, steering his mop down toward the ground, while Valian remained in the air.

Ivy threw her hand down, charging her yo-yo with power. After a few revolutions she shot it over her shoulder, using her whispering to help find her target. A huge tornado exploded out of it, advancing on the pyroach swarm.

"Stop it!" Alexander shouted. "You're ruining every-thing!" He jumped off his tree stump and marched in Ivy's direction, bringing his bubble wand to his lips. Behind him, Ivy caught sight of Mr. Punch struggling to his knees.

Alexander took aim at Seb and Valian and blew a stream of orange fire toward them. Valian sent his mop into a nosedive, dodging clear of the flames, but on the ground Seb wasn't fast enough to outrun them.

Ivy screamed. "Seb!"

The fire was seconds away from engulfing him when a dark-haired figure wearing a pale pink tutu materialized out of thin air at Seb's back.

Judy . . . ?

She threw herself over Seb as if she was a fire-retardant blanket, forcing him to the ground. The flames coursed around them and then dissipated a hundred yards away, crackling in the grass.

Ivy ran toward them as Valian landed on his mop. A huge black scorch mark surrounded Judy's body. Slowly she peeled herself away from Seb. Ivy's eyes watered with relief to see her brother stirring. Judy's tutu had been burned to shreds and her roller skates were smoking.

There was no time for conversation. As Ivy skidded to a halt beside Valian, she sensed the pyroaches approaching and turned just as they collided with her tornado. The impact sent shockwaves through the air. Ivy was driven back across the grass so hard that she left marks in the mud.

The tornado whirled faster, dragging every pyroach inside it. It spun so rapidly that the creatures lost control and hurtled through the flames, crashing into one another.

Seb stumbled dazedly to his feet. He caught sight of Judy and then the tornado, and managed to slide his drumsticks free. Steadying himself, he aimed a few beats at the maelstrom, pushing back any pyroach that managed to gather enough momentum to pull free.

With the creatures temporarily contained, a flurry of people started dashing between buildings, trying to find better shelter. Ivy noticed a shiny-faced Drummond Brewster leave his hiding place and run out onto the green toward Alexander.

However, Alexander's attention was elsewhere. Glaring at Ivy, his face flushed with rage and he lifted his bubble wand to his lips.

Ivy floundered around, looking for an escape. She couldn't outrun a fireball.

As Alexander forced air through the wand, Mr. Punch charged him from behind. Too late, a flaming sphere the size of a small truck erupted from the wand and headed not in Ivy's direction but toward *Drummond Brewster.*

Alexander jumped up and down, waving madly. "No! Pa! Run!"

But there was nothing Drummond Brewster could do.

Ivy looked away as the flames hit. When she turned back, Alexander was running toward a blackened heap on the scorched grass.

A small group of people spilled out of the big top. Ethel hurried toward Mr. Punch, while Granma Sylvie came running up to Ivy and the others.

"The cyclone is dying," she cried, waving her hands. "Get back inside the tent, all of you. The pyroaches won't be contained for much longer!"

Ivy glimpsed the Sack of Stars in her hand and had an idea. "Granma, the bag—we can send the pyroaches through it."

Granma Sylvie's eyes gleamed. She hesitated for a moment, then brought the bag to her lips and whispered something into the opening. She sprinted toward the pyroaches, lifting an arm above her head, and flung the bag into the center of the flames.

With a great roar, the tornado imploded, gathering in on itself like a dying star. All the pyroaches were dragged inside the bag—but, as they disappeared, the burlap caught fire and was reduced to cinders.

Ivy sucked in a deep breath as the shock tingled through her. The Sack of Stars was gone.

CHAPTER THIRTY-ONE

Granma Sylvie trod on the patch of soot where the bag had once been. "Well, that's ruined one of Amos's theories. The Great Uncommon Good *can* be destroyed, obviously." She sighed and pulled Ivy and Seb toward her in a hug. "Are you two OK?"

"Some of the other traders 'ave gone to free the underguards," Ethel said, approaching them.

Ivy saw a stream of uncommoners cautiously leaving the tent, still clutching one another tightly and glancing around.

Ethel ruffled a hand through Ivy's hair. "Well done, kid. That move with the yo-yo really got those beasts disorientated. Shame about the bag."

Ivy couldn't believe it. One of the Great Uncommon Good—gone forever. There were only four left now.

From over by the big top they heard a cry. Alexander was

being wrestled away from Mr. Punch. His uncommon bubble wand had been taken off him.

"I'm sorry about your father, Alexander," Mr. Punch said sincerely. As he bowed his head, Ivy noticed that he was switching between the red-bearded ringmaster and the bespectacled, gray-haired shop assistant.

"Get off me!" Alexander roared, struggling to break free. "This is all your fault!" Then he pointed to Ivy and Seb. "And yours. You did this. *All* of you. You killed my pa!"

There was so much pain in his voice. After everything he'd done, Ivy still felt sorry for him.

Valian and Judy came running across the grass. The crowd emerging from the big top fell silent. Ivy noticed it parting, and into the gap strode . . .

"*Selena.*" A chill went down Ivy's spine.

"Stay close," Granma Sylvie said. "This isn't over yet."

"Traders of Lundinor!" Selena called, her voice as majestic as always. "I'm afraid I have some troubling news." She turned in a circle, catching the gaze of every trader. Her gray dress rippled like water. "This boy is not the true criminal among us, nor the true mastermind behind the pyroach attack." She swept toward Alexander and laid a hand on his shoulder. The burly gentleman who had been restraining him simply let go.

Alexander looked as if he didn't know whether he should make a run for it or wait to see if Selena revealed any more. He hesitated. . . .

"No need to fear, Alexander," Selena told him softly. "Just cooperate and I can reveal who is really behind this."

Ivy studied her closely. There was a stiffness to her movements, as if she was trying very hard to remain calm.

"Many of you may have noticed that I left the stadium earlier than planned," Selena continued, raising her voice. "This was because, shortly before the Grivens contest began, I received new evidence relating to a theft that I suffered many years ago. A powerful uncommon object was stolen from me, an item that would be dangerous in the wrong hands."

Amos's journal, Ivy thought. That was what Selena was referring to. She considered the information it contained— all the secrets Amos had discovered about the Dirge and Selena's involvement with them. Perhaps it wasn't Amos Stirling whom Selena wanted destroyed in those archive photos; perhaps it was his *journal.*

"I tracked down the object," Selena continued, "and found the thief." Her head snapped around and she pointed a bony gloved finger at Ivy. "It was none other than your Grivens champion, Ivy Sparrow!"

People started murmuring. Ivy saw frowning faces and shaking heads. A few were counting on fingers, trying to work out if Ivy was even old enough to be Selena's thief. Alexander gave a smug smile but remained silent.

Ivy folded her arms. Seb shifted his weight beside her, about to step to her defense. . . .

But someone much more unexpected got there first.

"Lady Grimes!" a voice called—so cold and sharp it sliced through the air. The throng parted for Inspector Smokehart. His uniform was shredded and scorched, and ash dusted his slick black hair. "Is this the item you're referring to?" In his gloved hand he was shaking Amos's journal.

Ivy nudged Granma Sylvie. "*That's* where you sent it in the Sack of Stars? To Smokehart?"

A wicked smile crept onto Granma Sylvie's lips.

"Inspector—that's it!" Selena cried, marching toward him. She reached for the journal, but Smokehart quickly withdrew it.

"I've just conducted a very interesting interview with Jack-in-the-Green," he said. "He told us that he is an employee of yours."

Smokehart must have been questioning Jack-in-the-Green since his arrest at the Grivens contest. Their arrangement can't have been that solid if he was willing to expose Selena.

She laughed. "Jack-in-the-Green? Have you quite lost your senses, Inspector?"

Smokehart rapped his fingers on the journal. "And then there was this notebook that appeared in my hands. We have a resident forensic mixologist expert at the station. He only managed to decipher a few pages, but that was all I needed."

Selena's face twitched. She reached for the journal again. This time Smokehart grabbed her wrist with his free hand and tugged off her glove.

The crowd gasped. The skin on Selena's hand was yellow with pus and writhing with maggots.

"All. These. Years," Smokehart growled, his dark glasses fixed on her rotting fingers. "Every order you gave me, every decision you made . . . You were never working for the uncommoners of Lundinor, were you? You were never working on the side of the law."

All the traders fell utterly silent. Ivy beamed at Granma Sylvie. She must have known that sending Smokehart the journal would have been enough to put Selena's true allegiance in doubt.

Selena dragged her glove back on. "Inspector," she cried, "are you quite well? You're not making sense." Selena looked over his shoulder at the troop of underguards. "Guards! Escort the inspector to the infirmary immediately; I fear he may be suffering from the pyroach attack."

She made another dive for Amos's journal, but Smokehart threw the notebook to the nearest officer, who neatly caught it and stood there waiting. None of the other underguards moved. Smokehart drew his toilet brush from beneath his cloak. "Lady Selena Grimes, I'm arresting you for being a member of a banned guild, and for perpetrating murder, corruption and the betrayal of your fellow uncommoners in the service of that guild. You do not have to say anything, but anything you do say may be used against you in a court of GUT law."

Selena leaped back, her body tensed, as if she was about

to pounce. She slid her ebony cane out of the folds of her silk dress and jabbed it in Smokehart's direction, sending thorns splaying through the air toward him. He parried the strike with his toilet brush, frying the plants with charged blasts.

Amidst the commotion, Ivy spotted Alexander slipping away.

"He's escaping!" she shouted, but the fight between Selena and Smokehart had everyone rapt, and no one listened.

Seb went up on tiptoe to peer over people's hats. "That way . . ." He grabbed the sleeve of Ivy's tunic and pulled her through the crowd onto the Gauntlet. Alexander had disappeared behind a hedgerow, along with someone in a long black cloak. Ivy and Seb crept after them and stopped at the corner of a cottage. Alexander and the stranger were talking.

"You have proved beyond any doubt that you are capable of great things," the stranger said in a hoarse voice. "The Rasavatum are fools not to accept you."

There was a sigh before Alexander replied, "Who *are* you?"

"The Rasavatum are quite brilliant," the stranger replied. "But they will never be *great*. There is only *one* truly great guild." The back of Ivy's neck prickled; that hoarse voice sounded strangely familiar.

"You're from . . . the *Dirge*?" Alexander asked.

Amos's lightprint. That's where Ivy had heard the voice before. The speaker was the same Monkshood she'd listened to in 1967.

"A boy like you could easily win a place with us someday," Monkshood said. "You have already demonstrated rare talents, and now, I believe, you have something that could prove even more valuable."

"The journal," Alexander said gruffly. "You want me to tell you what I read inside it, don't you?"

Ivy covered her mouth. Alexander hadn't hidden Amos's journal to protect her at all—he'd taken it to read what was inside. His curiosity had probably been pricked when he saw the smoking hourglass.

A loud *boom* shook the air. Ivy saw a flash of blue light over by the big top. "Granma Sylvie and Valian . . ." She turned to leave, but then listened for Alexander and Monkshood again; they had disappeared. "Let's go," she said urgently.

Seb hesitated for only a moment before sprinting back through the crowd and skidding to a halt on the other side.

Selena was holding Valian around the chest, her uncommon cane pointing at his neck. Its thorny brambles tightened around his throat. "Stay back," she spat, her voice full of venom. "Let me through." As she edged toward the Gauntlet, people hurried out of her path.

Ivy tried to catch Valian's eye, but there were too many people around.

Smokehart, his uncommon toilet brush sparking in his hands, stepped toward Selena carefully. "There is nowhere to go, Lady Grimes. No walls to walk through here. It's just a one-way ticket to a ghoul hole for you."

"Never!" Selena screamed, jerking the cane.

Valian tensed. Ivy could see blood dripping down his neck.

Mr. Punch stepped forward. "There is another solution to this, Inspector," he said wearily, inching toward Selena. "One where no one gets hurt . . ." His blue-green eyes picked out Ivy; she wondered what he was going to do. From under his ringmaster's coat he brought out a chestnut-brown violin. Ivy could sense it was uncommon.

She listened closely. The voice inside the violin was screaming and sobbing in alternate beats—just like the voice that floated inside Selena. They sounded as if they were crying out to each other, as if they desperately wanted to be reunited, like two halves of the same coin.

It was *the* violin—the one Selena had given Monkshood in 1967. It contained the other half of her soul.

Mr. Punch took a deep sigh. "Be at peace, Selena Grimes." He gently tossed the violin at her; it tumbled through the air, then suddenly sped toward her like an arrow. Both she and the violin exploded in a burst of light.

As Ivy shielded her eyes from the blast, she sensed a voice dancing at the edge of her hearing. She couldn't be sure, but she felt—just for a second—that the voice belonged to Selena, a *complete* Selena.

CHAPTER THIRTY-TWO

The steps of the Great Cavern Memorial were covered with bunches of daffodils. Ivy saw uncommon ribbons writing messages of condolence through the blooms. Some of them spoke of the tragic loss of Drummond Brewster or the casualties of the pyroach attack, while others commemorated past victims of the Dirge.

Ivy shivered. Up until a few days ago she'd never seen anyone die. Now she'd witnessed not only Drummond Brewster's passing but also the Departure of Selena Grimes.

"They got the graffiti off, then," Seb said, staring at the empty space, which had only recently been covered in garish purple paint.

Ivy assumed Mr. Punch had had something to do with it. If anyone was able to undo Alexander Brewster's handiwork, it would be a member of the Rasavatum.

Valian scanned the shell-shocked faces of the traders. People were muttering, their arms around each other's shoulders. "Everyone feels guilty that they didn't realize who Selena Grimes really was, that they let her control them for so long."

Ivy sighed in understanding. She still couldn't believe the scale of Alexander's deception; she was angry with herself for not seeing through it earlier. "What do you think everyone will do now?"

"After the cleanup I suppose they'll elect a new quartermaster for the Dead End," Valian said, "and things will return to normal."

"But the rest of the Dirge are still out there," Seb pointed out. "We've thwarted their plans twice now—they're gonna be angrier and more dangerous than ever."

Ivy had a sinking feeling Seb was right, though she wasn't sure what the three of them could do about it. With the Sack of Stars destroyed, they had no way to spy on the Dirge, and she and Seb were due back to school next week anyway.

"I don't think their numbers have reduced as much as we think they have," Valian said. "It was in all the papers this morning: a crooked sixpence appeared at Drummond Brewster's funeral. I think Alexander's joined the Dirge."

With Selena Departed, Ivy supposed there was an opening in the Fallen Guild for a new Wolfsbane. "I think we'll see him again before this is all over," she warned.

On the other side of the memorial a tall gray-haired gentleman came strolling toward them. His swirly blue-green eyes were familiar. Ivy elbowed the boys. "That's Mr. Punch."

He came to stand beside them and nodded at the memorial. "Remembering the past is not enough, of course. We must learn from it too."

"What happened to Selena . . . ," Ivy said quietly. "That's going to change things now, isn't it? The dead will know that in order to become one of the Departed, they must unite with the uncommon object that contains the other part of their soul." She remembered what Johnny Hands had said about accepting his existence for what it was. This new information would change all that; it was going to stir things up in every undermart around the world.

Mr. Punch straightened. "It is a powerful revelation—of that there is no doubt. The Dirge kept it to themselves in order to manipulate others. I hid it to prevent chaos. I see now that it was never my secret to keep."

Ivy could hear the regret in his voice and considered how many other tough decisions he'd had to make over the years. How strong he was to admit his mistake, she thought.

He smiled fondly down at the three of them. "Can I expect to see you back in Lundinor next season?"

Ivy shared a nervous look with Seb and Valian. *If we survive that long.* They knew that the Dirge would have the three of them in their sights; they'd want revenge.

As if reading her mind, Mr. Punch added, "You know, it isn't just the underguard that have been monitoring you over the past few months; a few friends of mine have been keeping an eye on you too. I will ask them to stay close this summer to make sure you're safe. Also, I have something for each of you." He brought three objects out of his jacket pockets: a small package wrapped in black cotton, which he gave to

Seb; a gold envelope, which he passed to Valian; and a heavy rectangular parcel covered in brown paper, which he deposited in Ivy's hands.

"For us?" Ivy wasn't expecting a gift.

"You have proved to me that each of these is rightfully yours," Mr. Punch told them, bowing his head. "Farewell, and good luck."

Seb unwrapped his black package. "They're gloves," he said. "Drummer's gloves. Cool." He tried one of them on, spreading out his fingers.

Valian and Ivy smirked at each other. "They're a bit more than that, though, aren't they?" Valian remarked.

"They're from a quartermaster," Ivy added, hinting.

"Wait, you mean . . . I've just taken the glove? I can trade now?"

Ivy smiled. "It's like Mr. Punch said—you've proved that they're rightfully yours." She was so proud of Seb. She recalled him riding that flying mop during the pyroach attack, facing his fears to save everyone in the big top. If anyone had earned the right to take the glove and become a proper uncommoner, it was him.

Valian opened the gold envelope and pulled out a card. "OK . . . weird." He flashed the front of the card to Ivy and Seb. It had a gold foil border and was embossed with the words:

Dear Sir,
  You are duly invited to
  Forward & Rife's Grand Globe-Trotting Auction
of Uncommon Treasures
  Nubrook
  Thanksgiving

Seb read it twice. "I don't get it. Why has Mr. Punch given you that?"

Valian frowned. "I . . . don't know. It's strange, though—I've seen that company name advertised before. Your phone has a map on it, right?"

"Yeah. Here . . ." Seb pulled it out of his pocket and tapped the screen a few times before handing it over. "What is it?"

Valian slid his finger across the screen. "Forward and Rife—their posters were up in every undermart the Sack of Stars took me to when I asked it to find my sister."

"So do you think Rosie has something to do with this auction?" Ivy asked.

"It's the only thing that connects each place." Valian studied the screen. "The undermarts I visited were here . . . here . . . here . . ." He went still. "You two were right—there's a pattern. They're moving from east to west along every main undermart."

"It's like the stops on a world tour," Seb mumbled.

"Or a Grand Globe-Trotting Auction," Ivy reread from the invitation. "That must be why the Sack of Stars took you to a different place each time—Rosie was traveling." Hope bloomed within her; after all these years, Valian might be on the verge of finding his sister.

His eyes went glassy. "That's where I have to go next," he

said, pointing to New York. "Nubrook undermart. It opens over Thanksgiving. That's where I'm gonna find Rosie."

Seb put a hand on Valian's shoulder. "That's great! American Thanksgiving is in November, right?"

Valian rubbed the back of his head. "Yeah, but I've been waiting over six years. What's six months more?"

Ivy hadn't yet opened her parcel from Mr. Punch. She tore off the brown paper. "*Amos's journal?* But why has Mr. Punch given me this?"

"Maybe he wants you to read it," Valian suggested, passing her what was left of his flask of Raider's Tonic. "Here—use this."

Ivy counted along to page forty-two and trickled the drink down the paper; a thick white vapor began seeping out. After the fumes had dissipated she flicked through the journal, glancing at the text on every page. There was too much information to take in at one sitting. She'd have to examine the journal properly to learn what Amos knew. Perhaps that was why Mr. Punch had given it to her—so she could find out more about his work.

She stopped abruptly when she spotted a short list, underlined and numbered.

"It's a list of the Great Uncommon Good!" Seb and Valian peered over her shoulder to read it:

1. THE STONE OF DREAMS—LUNDINOR
2. THE SACK OF STARS—UNKNOWN
3. THE SANDS OF CHANGE—NUBROOK
4. THE JAR OF SHADOWS—UNKNOWN
5. THE SWORD OF WILLS—MONTROQUER

Valian scowled. "The Sword of Wills and the Sands of Change are still out there, and you can bet five grade that the Dirge will be looking for them."

Seb stretched out his fingers in his new gloves. "Maybe if we can get hold of the objects first, we might be able to hide them from the Dirge, like we did with the Jar of Shadows?"

"The Sands of Change are in Nubrook," Ivy read again, "the same undermart where Forward and Rife's auction is taking place." She examined Seb's phone, which was still in Valian's hand. The map had zoomed in on a long, rectangular-shaped island . . . Manhattan. Ivy had never been to New York; she suspected that before the year was out, that would all change.

The Cabbage Moon was quiet. Most of the other guests had gone home early after the shock of what had happened at the big top.

"It feels so long ago that I was stuffing my suitcase with clothes to *come* here," Ivy said, cramming her pajamas inside.

Seb jumped down from the top bunk, his rucksack over his shoulder. "Tell me about it. These last couple of days have felt like an age."

There was a knock at the door and Judy's shiny dark bob appeared. "Hey." She flashed them both an awkward smile. "Thought I'd come and say goodbye before you left."

Seb's face froze.

Judy rolled in on her skates, head down. "I bet you're desperate to get home, aren't you? Had enough of the freak show for a bit."

Ivy shut her suitcase and stepped closer. "I don't know about that." She was eager to see her mum and dad again, but she was going to miss her uncommon friends and the extraordinary sights of Lundinor.

Judy gave a smile, but it didn't reach her eyes.

Ivy hesitated slightly before stepping forward and putting her arms around Judy. "Thanks for everything you've done to help us."

When they separated, Judy's eyes were shining. "You're welcome . . . of course."

"Even for saving Seb's life," Ivy added. "Which I don't regret—yet."

Seb shuffled his feet, and Ivy and Judy turned toward him. He ran a hand through his hair. "Does it make me any less of an idiot if I say that I'm sorry—and that I was a total idiot?"

Ivy could see the relief on Judy's face. "Sounds like a riddle from the Well at the World's End."

They both laughed. Seb gave Judy a hug, which made her blush.

"All ready to go?" a voice called from the hallway. Granma Sylvie poked her head around the door. She was carrying a beautiful Persian rug, which she dragged inside.

"We're not flying on one of those again," Seb moaned. "Are we?"

Granma Sylvie rubbed her hands together. "What are you talking about? This carpet is top of the range—storm-resistant, temperature-controlled. It's even got autopilot and a pop-up air freshener."

Judy stared at it. "Wow. That can't have been cheap."

"Well"—Granma Sylvie winked at Ivy—"ten thousand grade of uncommon objects does buy the best."

Ivy grinned. She'd given half her Grivens winnings to Granma Sylvie to spend, with the understanding that Ivy and Seb were given a generous allowance every season. The other half she'd used to pay Valian back . . . with interest.

"What are your plans after we get home?" Ivy asked. She assumed that Granma Sylvie wouldn't be returning to her old life, not now that her memory had returned.

She took a breath. "Ethel and I are going to do what we always intended to when we were younger—an undermart world tour." She nudged the rug. "That's why I got this. At my age, I plan to travel in luxury."

Ivy scooped Scratch up from her pillow.

"Excited home to go, Scratch is," he said, vibrating in her hand. "Seb promised with the Yoda."

Seb's shoulders slumped. "I promised I'd let him watch *Star Wars*—I'll be taking a bell with no eyes to the cinema when we get back. Life as an uncommoner, eh?"

"*Star Wars?*" Granma Sylvie chuckled.

"What?" Seb said, incredulous. "It's a great movie!"

"No, it's not that. It's just that it reminds me where I sent those pyroaches through the Sack of Stars."

"Where *did* you send them?" Ivy asked.

"To the farthest place I could think of where they'd be able to survive . . . ," Granma Sylvie said. "Jupiter."

EPILOGUE

Dr. Emmet Sparrow took another sip of coffee and put his mug down on the KEEP CALM AND WORK IN A MUSEUM coaster on his desk. He stretched and yawned. It was getting late and he needed to be home on time today—he'd promised his daughter, Ivy, that they'd finish their game of chess from the other night. She'd recently discovered a fascination with board games.

He adjusted his glasses and began to remove the bubble wrap from the last object in the box. It was a piece of pottery—a vessel small enough to sit in the palm of his hand. Greek. Hellenistic period, probably.

He couldn't remember seeing it before, but then this latest donation was so large.

The vessel was painted pale blue, with white figures dancing around it. The design was unusual; it was shaped like a pithos jar—with a small disk-shaped base and handles—but, of course, pithos jars were huge and used for carrying grain or liquids. This one had no opening at all and was a *lot* smaller.

He took a small plastic box from a stack on the floor beside him. Gently he stuffed some shredded paper inside and placed the mystery pot on top. It was probably from around 150 BC, but he'd ask another expert, just to be sure.

He scribbled his notes down in pencil on the label:

ITEM NO. 743, THE CARVALHO COLLECTION
POTTERY—150 BC?

It would probably be included in an exhibition somewhere down the line because it was so unusual, but that wouldn't be for months, maybe even years.

He stuck the label on the lid of the box and closed it tightly before grabbing his jacket and heading for the door. Ivy and that chess game were waiting.

ACKNOWLEDGMENTS

Writing *The Shadows of Doom* would have been an even bigger challenge without the support of so many generous and talented people.

I'd like to say a huge thank-you to my editors Phoebe Yeh, Mainga Bhima and Elizabeth Stranahan for helping me whip this story into shape; and also my UK publicist, Roz Hutchison, for all her great ideas and smiles when we have been out promoting the Uncommoners series together.

It has been a dream to work with the astonishingly brilliant folk at Crown. Massive thanks to everyone—in all departments—for working so hard, and to Katrina Damkoehler for designing such a beautiful cover.

To everyone at Rights People, my gratitude once again for helping to publish Ivy and Seb's adventures in many languages around the world. I'm very proud to be represented by you and the team at Greenhouse Literacy Agency. Sarah Davies, your wisdom and advice has been invaluable as always, and Polly Nolan, I wouldn't have achieved anything without you. You are my superhero. Thank you for coming to my rescue every time, no matter what the problem.

Karl James Mountford—sir, you are the finest and funniest illustrator a writer could ask for. Thank you for inspiring me with your incredible visions of Lundinor. I'm so thrilled that readers are able to see my characters brought to life through your extraordinary imagination.

My wonderful friends, you always manage to find time to help me. Alice, Frann, George, Charlotte and Sarah, thanks for listening to me go on and still being so enthusiastic. Peter, those last-minute solutions were a lifesaver. I hope I can pay you back one day.

This book wouldn't have been finished without the incredible understanding of Tereze, Kath, Tamara, Lucy, Jo and Leah from Tales on Moon Lane. I can't thank you enough for all you do to support me as a writer. Julia and Lottie, thank you for being early fans and for generously helping me to free up time to write.

Mum and Beth. We've lived it, haven't we? Thanks for laughing with me and letting me borrow your brilliant imaginations. I wouldn't have been brave enough to consider writing a book without your encouragement. Thank you for always telling me I could be whatever I wanted to be.

This book is dedicated to my dear friends Beks, Nichol and Tara because it's about friendship, and knowing them has taught me what that is all about. I'm so lucky to have such fun, compassionate, kind and loyal people in my life. Especially my Swiss Army knife best friend, who jumps into any role to help me—photographer, social media champion, editor, brainstorm partner. Thanks for sticking with me, Tara, no matter what.

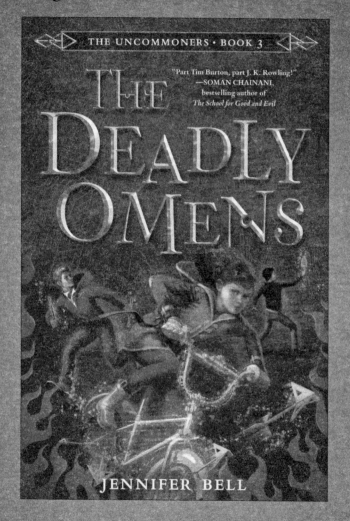

CHAPTER ONE

The new babysitter was a stout woman with a moss-green head scarf, long trench coat and round spectacles.

She was also *dead*.

"You must be Ivy," the babysitter said curtly, dropping her bag on the welcome mat by the front door. The corners of her mouth lifted clumsily, as if she was unaccustomed to smiling. "Your mum and dad have told me all about you. You can call me Curtis."

Ivy took a step back. Although she could sense the races of the dead, she'd never come across one on common land before. "My parents have just left to catch their train. . . . I'll get my brother." She dashed up the stairs two at a time and slammed her hand against his bedroom door. *"Seb!"*

Dressed in a warm hoodie, jeans and sneakers, Seb appeared slouched against the doorframe, scowling at Ivy from under his wavy blond hair. On any ordinary evening he would have answered the door in his pajamas, but at midnight tonight they had planned to sneak away. They were going to Nubrook, an uncommon market hidden under New York City, to help their friend Valian search for his missing sister. "You're interrupting my favorite Ripz video," Seb snapped. "What is it?"

"Our babysitter is *dead*," Ivy told him.

"What?" He straightened. "Are you sure?"

Ivy peered over the banister. Down in the hallway Curtis was hanging up her coat. A brooch in the shape of a forked arrow glittered on the lapel. Curtis might *seem* normal, but Ivy knew the tricky thing about most races of the dead was that you couldn't tell them apart from the living until they did something impossible—like float through a wall or transform into a giant stick bug.

"Positive," she replied. "I can feel it." As a whisperer, Ivy could detect the fragments of human souls trapped inside the dead. She widened her field of sense slowly, just as she'd practiced. The fleeting voice of Curtis's broken soul brushed at the edge of her hearing. "Her name's Curtis. If she's dead, then she must be an uncommoner. What's she doing here?"

A line appeared between Seb's thick brows. "Dad was complaining yesterday that all the local babysitters are fully booked because so many schools are closed for repairs, not just ours. Look——" He grabbed his TV remote and flicked through the channels until he found the one he wanted. A weather map on one half of the screen showed the isobars of a huge storm moving across the English Channel from Paris to London. The reporter was shouting at the camera, his coat flapping madly in the wind.

". . . *Meteorologists are still struggling to explain Storm Sarah's sudden appearance in Paris three days ago. The category two storm has caused widespread damage and disruption, with school and road closures throughout London and the Southeast. . . .*"

"I *tried* to convince Dad that we could look after ourselves," Seb continued, "and that we wouldn't need a babysitter for the few nights he and Mum are away at the wedding. But then Mum came home announcing she'd had a stroke of luck and had 'bumped into' an available sitter. . . . It must have been Curtis."

Ivy's skin prickled. It couldn't have been a coincidence. She snatched the TV remote and turned up the volume to mask the sound of their voices. "What if Curtis is working for the Dirge? They employ the dead all the time. She could have been planted here to spy on us—or worse." *The Dirge* . . . Ivy wished she didn't have to bring them up, but it was difficult to forget the organization that kept trying to kill them.

Seb stiffened. "I've been checking the uncommon newspapers that Valian sends us; the Dirge have been linked to all kinds of incidents since the spring. Surely they're too busy to bother with us?"

Ivy could tell by the tremor in his voice that he didn't believe that last bit, although he was right about one thing: the nefarious guild's activity *had* been prolific. Their calling card—a crooked sixpence—had been found at multiple scenes of crime around the uncommon world. In the Russian undermart, Mosvok, the Dirge had been connected to several cases of blackmail and kidnapping; in China, to widespread fraud. A series of shop raids in the Egyptian undermart of Cryp bore signs of their handiwork, as did the mysterious disappearances of key officials from Ausmark in Germany. Ivy was astonished that, with so much criminal activity linked to the guild, its six members still managed to keep their identities secret.

"Now that I think about it," Seb said, his pupils flicking, "I suppose Curtis turning up might be connected to a message Valian sent me earlier. He wanted to let us know that we can't use an uncommon bag to travel to Nubrook anymore—he didn't say why—but he's given us new instructions instead."

"He has? Why didn't you tell me before?"

"I couldn't risk it, not with Mum and Dad around. Don't worry; I'm sure it's nothing."

Ivy gritted her teeth. Her brother had a frustrating habit of taking everything at face value. "Seb," she said reproachfully, "Valian's been looking for Rosie on his own for seven years. . . . He's not used to asking for help. Something could have happened—" Ivy got a hollow feeling in the pit of her stomach when she thought of the repeated disappointments Valian had endured in his search for his little sister. She was determined to do everything she could to help him now. "This trip is his best chance yet to find her," she said, "so we've got to be there every step of the way."

Seb's cheeks flushed guiltily. "All right then, let's leave now for Nubrook. I don't fancy sticking around here to learn whether Zombie Poppins is planning to kill us or not." He dragged his prepacked backpack out from under his bed and switched off the TV. Ivy collected her things from her bedroom, stuffing an extra sweater into her satchel. A thick, leather-bound book poked out the top. The front cover was embossed with a symbol: a smoking hourglass. Seb glanced at it warily.

"You're bringing Amos Stirling's journal?" he asked. Ivy understood his concern. The journal was a notebook containing many dangerous secrets about the Great Uncommon Good—the five most powerful uncommon objects in history—and it attracted all kinds of trouble.

"I've only been able to translate a bit of it," she told him. "Amos wrote in languages not even Google understands. He'd discovered all sorts of things about the Great Uncommon Good, and he was trying to prevent the Dirge from getting hold of them. If I leave the book here and Curtis finds it . . ."

". . . the Dirge will learn all Amos's secrets," Seb finished. "I get it." He led her into the bathroom, shutting the door behind them. Ivy closed the blinds at the window.

"Did Valian tell you there was a secret entrance to Nubrook hidden somewhere in *here*?" she asked, thinking of the time she and Seb had entered Lundinor via a shed in a garden. There were many different ways of accessing London's undermart; perhaps entering Nubrook was the same.

"No," Seb replied, "his instructions were weirder than that." He plugged the sink and ran the taps. " 'Wash your hands and find the man in red.' That's what he wrote."

Ivy wondered why Valian had been so obscure. She tapped her satchel. "Scratch, are you listening to this? Do you have any idea what Valian means?"

The bag vibrated against her hip. She unfastened it and pulled out a damaged steel bicycle bell. Like all uncommon objects, the bell felt strangely warm against her skin, as if it had been resting in the sun.

"Finally goings!" exclaimed a childlike voice coming from the bell. "Never journeys to Nubrook has Scratch before." Ivy could hear the fragment of soul whispering inside Scratch—the very thing that made him uncommon. "Hmm. Unsure Valian why wantings hands clean," he added.

Ivy's shoulders slumped. Even with Scratch's back-to-front way of speaking, she understood his meaning.

A door slammed shut downstairs: Curtis was moving around.

With renewed urgency, Ivy steadied Scratch on the edge of the basin, pumped some liquid soap into her palm and lathered it up. Perhaps everything would become clear if she followed Valian's advice exactly. As she rinsed her hands she became aware of a broken soul somewhere nearby. She could tell by the clanging sound of its voice that it was trapped inside an uncommon object—

But this one wasn't coming from inside Scratch. Ivy opened the cabinet above the sink and saw, sitting on one of the shelves, a silver soap dish with two dolphin-shaped handles. "Seb," she said, "*this* is uncommon."

"Is it?" He eyed the soap dish nervously as Ivy removed it from the cabinet. "I've never seen it before. What's it doing here?"

Ivy turned the dish over to examine it from all sides. "Maybe Valian sent it? That could be why he told us to wash our hands—because he wanted us to find it. What do you think it does?" She deliberated the possibilities. Every object gained a special ability when it turned uncommon.

"Experimentings should Ivy," Scratch suggested helpfully, knocking against the taps. "Good way of discoverings uncommon uses."

Taking his advice, Ivy tried floating the soap dish on the surface of the water. A strange green froth appeared, churning around the dish and quickly swallowing it under. Before Ivy had time to decide whether that was a good thing or not, a shout erupted up the stairs.

"Do you need me to COME UP?" Curtis boomed. There was an unmistakable edge of suspicion in her voice.

"We won't be a moment!" Ivy called back, trying to sound as casual as possible.

Seb rattled the door, checking it was locked. "We need to be quick," he hissed. "Curtis might already have an inkling that we're planning to leave. She must have noticed you look more prepared for mountain-climbing than bed."

Ivy studied her reflection in the bathroom mirror. Her messy auburn curls contrasted sharply with the navy blue of her duffle coat. In her thick cargo trousers and clean hiking boots, she was dressed exactly as Valian had advised: she was ready for anything.

"We'd better try something else," Seb said, combing his fingers through the soapy water to locate the dish.

There was a sharp grating sound—

—and then Seb disappeared.

"Seb!" Ivy leaned over the basin, still careful not to make contact with the water. The soap dish had vanished along with Seb.

A distinct *creak* sounded in the hallway: Curtis was climbing the stairs. Ivy projected her thoughts inside Scratch: *Help! Do you know what's happened to Seb? Should I touch the water?*

Thinkings is Scratch, she heard him reply in her head. *Ivy must being carefuls.*

The ability to communicate with him like this was a recent development. To begin with, Ivy had only been able to hear vague murmurings coming from the fragment of soul inside Scratch, but now she could distinguish full sentences and send her own conversation back. She was learning that the more she used her whispering, the stronger her talents became.

The landing groaned.

Curtis outside! Scratch warned her.

With no other option, Ivy quickly shoved the bell back into her satchel. She splashed her hand in the basin, just as Seb had done, causing tickly bubbles to immediately rush up her nose. "Ah-*choo!*" she sneezed. In the split second her eyelids were shut, she heard another sound, shrill and scraping—

And the next moment she was standing in the shaky hull of an underwater vessel. Seb stood beside her, his nose scrunched up, as if flies had just flown up both his nostrils.

"What just happened?" he asked, rubbing his face. "Where are we?"

The metal craft was the size of a tugboat; it was round at both ends with a transparent hood of bubbles that sealed it off on all sides like a wobbly sunroof. Beyond it, the craggy forms of rocks were just visible in the murky water, and, closer to the vessel, Ivy spotted the elegant curves of a silvery dolphin.

"We're *in* the soap dish!" Ivy realized. Judging by the strong current, they were submerged in a stream or river. The air reeked of chlorine mixed with perfumed soap, like the changing rooms at the swimming pool.

"*Welcome aboard this aqua-transport vessel number 2895,*" said a machine-like voice. Ivy didn't know where it was coming

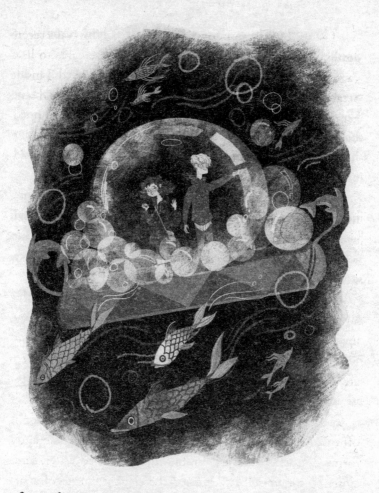

from; there were no speakers or controls visible inside. *"What is your desired destination?"*

"Nubrook," Ivy said.

The grating sound came again, like metal grinding over stone. The soap dish began rocking, knocking them to their knees. Seb clutched his stomach. *"Ugh* . . . I feel sick. . . ."

"We'd better stay down until it's over," Ivy advised. She

didn't know how long it was going to last or how turbulent it would be.

Then the dolphin at the rear of the craft flicked its tail, sending them speeding forward. Ivy held on to the sides for support. Their surroundings were full-sized, so she presumed the dish had enlarged after moving to its present location; but she still wasn't sure how she and Seb had been transported inside.

They swept through tendrils of muddy pondweed before moving into clearer water and diving deeper. As they zoomed along, Ivy gazed through the swirling rainbows in the hood at slow-swimming fish and barnacle-encrusted pipes. They were soon skimming over a dark and sandy plateau. *The seabed.*

In no time at all, the dish began to ascend. It rose to the surface of the water and, with a heavy shunt, beached itself on a platform. The bubble hood burst, and Ivy jolted as a wall of noise hit her in the chest.

"Welcome to Nubrook," declared a jolly voice, "the deepest undermart in the world!"

Go back to the beginning and start
a richly uncommon adventure.

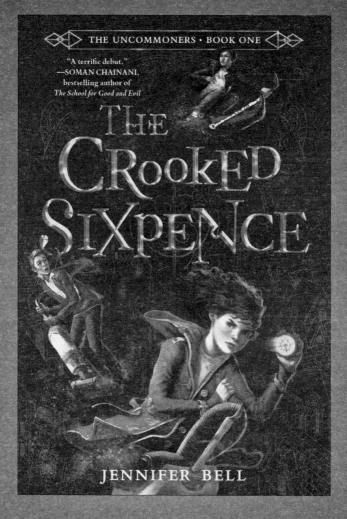

AVAILABLE NOW!

CHAPTER ONE

Ivy rocked forward as the ambulance turned a corner. Everything inside rattled.

"OK then," the paramedic said, looking up from his clipboard. He was a bald man with faded tattoos all the way up his
forearms. "What's your full name?"

"Ivy Elizabeth Sparrow," she fired off, tapping her yellow
Wellingtons on the floor. It was so stuffy; she needed fresh air.
She looked over the paramedic's shoulder and wondered if she
could ask him to open one of those blacked-out windows. She
could see her frizzy brown curls bobbing in the glass, even
more out of control than usual.

The paramedic made a note with his pen and turned
toward the rear of the vehicle. "What about you?"

At the other end of the bench, leaning forward, legs apart,
sat a boy in a gray hoodie bearing the logo of the band the

Ripz. His wiry blond hair had fallen in front of his eyes, but Ivy knew he was glaring at her.

"It's Seb," the boy replied drily. "I'm her brother."

The paramedic smiled as he jotted down the name. Ivy tried to push Seb out of her mind. This was all his fault.

She leaned over to the stretcher and took Granma Sylvie's hand. It felt softer than usual. There were Velcro straps across her granma's chest, a brace supporting her neck and a misted oxygen mask covering her nose and mouth. Ivy had never seen her look so fragile before.

"And how old are you both?" the paramedic continued.

"Eleven," Ivy replied, shuffling ever so slightly closer to Granma Sylvie.

"I'm sixteen," Seb said in a deep voice.

Ivy frowned and glanced sideways at him. He had only turned fourteen last month.

"OK, good." The paramedic's face softened. "Now, I understand that you're both very concerned at the moment—but trust me, the best thing you can do to help your gran is to stay calm. When we get to the hospital, we'll take her to the emergency room so the doctor can have a good look at her, and then she may need an operation, so she'll be in for a while."

Ivy grimaced. She knew of only one other occasion when Granma Sylvie had stayed overnight in the hospital—everyone knew about *that*—but it had happened before Ivy's parents were even born. "Do you know what's wrong?" she asked.

The paramedic frowned. "I think she may have broken her hip, and possibly her wrist as well, but we won't know till we see an X-ray."

While he scribbled down some notes, Ivy stroked Granma Sylvie's hand and wondered if she'd suffered broken bones *that* time as well. Probably. She'd had a car crash during a freak snowstorm and had been unconscious for days; when she woke up, she couldn't remember what had happened during the accident, or anything before it. The police only knew her name because she was wearing a necklace with SYLVIE engraved on it. Retrograde amnesia, Ivy's mum called it. Ivy knew the exact date of the crash because the family discussed it so often: January 5, 1969. Twelfth Night.

"Before we get to the hospital," the paramedic said, "I need to confirm what happened." He checked his watch. "I make it eight-thirty a.m., so the fall must have happened at about seven-forty-five? And you said that your gran slipped in the kitchen while you were both in the other room . . . ?"

Ivy imagined Granma Sylvie losing her balance and tumbling onto her back, legs in the air like an upturned beetle. If only she'd been there to help.

Seb swallowed. "She was baking mince pies. We heard her shouting."

Over our *shouting,* Ivy remembered. She shot her brother a look of regret. They had been arguing about the stupid new Ripz poster he'd got for Christmas—Ivy had accidentally knocked her orange juice over it. If he hadn't been ranting at her, they might have got to Granma Sylvie sooner.

The paramedic flipped his paper around. "OK, that'll do. Are you able to get hold of your mum and dad?"

Ivy sighed. *If only.* More than anything, she wished her parents were there now.

"I've texted them, but there's been no reply," Seb said. "I'll try calling when we get to the hospital. Mum's working, but we might catch her before she starts her shift."

Ivy had said goodbye to her mum yesterday morning. If

she was there now, she would have clapped her hands together and taken charge of this whole mess in an instant. Ivy and Seb had done nothing except ring the ambulance.

"Our dad's in Paris," Ivy added in a quiet voice. "He's working too."

Their dad worked as a consultant for the famous Victoria and Albert Museum in London, which meant that he was an expert in everything old, and people from around the world were always asking for his advice.

The paramedic raised his eyebrows. "So that's why you're staying with your gran?"

"Mum and Dad were with us over Christmas," Ivy explained, feeling the need to defend them. "They just had to go back to work early."

It had never really bothered her—them staying in London and leaving her and Seb six hours away in Bletchy Scrubb with their granma—but then, this kind of emergency had never happened before.

The paramedic put down his clipboard and turned to Granma Sylvie, who despite the neck brace made an effort to smile. Ivy doubted she could even hear what was being said with that thing on; she hadn't corrected the paramedic about Seb's age.

"OK then, Mrs. Sparrow, I'm just going to check how you're doing." He untucked Granma Sylvie's blanket and rolled it away until her arm was exposed. There was a thin cotton sling around it, secured behind her neck. Delicately he loosened the knot and slid the material out from underneath. Granma Sylvie winced.

As the sling was taken away, Ivy caught her breath. Her

granma's entire arm was purple and bloated like a giant eggplant.

The paramedic took the damaged wrist carefully between his fingers. "Hmm, looks like that swelling is getting worse. It must be sore." He studied it from every angle. Ivy caught a flash of gold on her granma's skin. "I don't see any clasp on your bracelet. I think we might need to cut it off to make you feel more comfortable, Mrs. Sparrow. Is that OK?"

Ivy's chest tightened; she imagined Granma Sylvie's was probably doing the same. That solid gold bangle was one of the few items that remained of Granma Sylvie's life before her amnesia. She had been wearing it at the time of the accident, and Ivy couldn't remember her ever taking it off. The bracelet was special to her—everyone knew that.

Granma Sylvie squeezed her eyes closed. Ivy heard a rasping "Do it."

The paramedic found a pair of small silver pliers. Ivy shivered as two soft *snickt*s pierced the air and the halves of the bangle fell away.

"Ivy, my bag . . ." Granma Sylvie lifted her other hand, pointing shakily.

Ivy reached down for the handbag and held it open. Very carefully, the paramedic placed both pieces of the bangle inside.

"Will you look after it for me?" Granma Sylvie asked.

Ivy nodded, forcing a smile, and opened the bag to check that the bracelet was safely in the inside pocket.

"Be careful," the paramedic warned. "The ends are sharp."

Ivy made sure not to touch it as she zipped up the pocket.

"Here," Seb grunted, picking something up off the floor. "You just dropped this." He handed Ivy a black-and-white photo the size of a postcard. Ivy had seen it many times before because Granma Sylvie always kept it in her handbag. It was the only photo of her from *before*. The police had found it in the glove box of her car after the crash. "Weird," Seb said, shaking his head. "I haven't seen that since I was little."

We used to look at it all the time, Ivy thought. But she didn't say anything.

"Granma still doesn't know who the other woman is, does she?"

Ivy shook her head. The photo showed a woman standing beside Granma Sylvie. She was slight, with sharp dark eyes and unruly hair poking out from under a round black hat. She wore a thick tartan dress and studded cowboy boots. Granma Sylvie was dressed in washed denim dungarees with what looked like satin ballet shoes on her feet.

"What were they *wearing*?" Seb asked. "It's like really bad fancy dress."

Ivy shrugged. "Who's to say it wasn't the fashion?" She didn't really think it could have been; she just didn't want to agree with her brother.

"Keep that safe," croaked a voice. Ivy turned. Granma Sylvie was waving her good arm in their direction.

"Sorry." Ivy hastily tucked the photo back into the handbag and fastened it up.

Seb slid away from her before she had to push him.

CHAPTER TWO

"D ad?" Ivy squinted. The split-screen image on Seb's phone was distorted and moved in slow motion. She nudged Seb in the ribs. "I told you a video call was a stupid idea. Why didn't we just ring them?"

Seb grumbled something about reception and repositioned the phone higher on his knee. "If you owned a phone like most people, you'd know it's easier to three-way-call using video chat. But you don't. Because you're weird."

Ivy rolled her eyes. *Whatever.*

"Mum? *Dad?* Can you see us now?" The video flickered. Ivy shifted in her seat. Around her, the ER of Bletchy Scrubb Hospital was teeming with people: doctors in white coats with stethoscopes draped around their necks, solemn-faced relatives, nurses carrying clipboards, and hobbling patients clutching swollen limbs. Ivy ran her eyes over the linoleum floor and glossy white walls. There wasn't a trace of tinsel or glitter any-where. Three days after Boxing Day and Christmas had been forgotten, just like that. Granma Sylvie would hate it.

"*Ivy?* Are you there?"

"Dad!" *Finally.* The image sharpened. He was far too close to the camera, his pale freckled face taking over most of the left of the screen. On the right, Ivy's mum could be seen sit-ting at a table in her staff lounge. She was wearing a pale blue nurse's tunic with a silver pocket watch hanging from the top pocket.

Her mum tucked a stray wisp of brown hair behind her ear and leaned closer, frowning. "You're back now, but you keep going all fuzzy."

"I'm on the train to Paris," Ivy's dad called. "My recep-tion's bad. Can everyone see me?"

"We can see both of you now," Ivy said. "Did you under-stand what I just explained about Granma?"

Her dad frowned. "Yes, just about. I can't believe it. Is she all right? Are you two all right?"

Ivy shrugged. "We're OK."

"Seb," their mum said sternly, "are you looking after your sister?"

Seb was slouched in the hospital chair beside Ivy, his scuffed white sneakers on a plastic coffee table with the phone wedged between his knees. His headphones snaked into his lap.

"Yes," he muttered. "Don't worry."

Ivy thought for a moment. "Seb lied about his age; he told them he was sixteen."

Seb's eyes turned to slits as he looked at her. "If you're six-teen, you can be on your own. It's the law."

Ivy pulled a face at him.

"It doesn't matter about that now," their dad said. "As long as you stay together. How's Granma?"

Ivy gazed over at the blue cotton curtain fluttering a few feet behind Seb's shoulder. It concealed a small room, where Granma Sylvie was lying on her stretcher. Ivy paused before answering, trying not to get upset again. "She's asleep right now. We're in the ER, but the doctor said she's going for an X-ray later. What do you think we should do?"

Her dad hesitated. Ivy could hear the rattle of the train in the background.

"There's only one option, really," their mum said, pursing her lips. "You both return to Granma's house and sit tight till we get there. Even if I leave now, it'll be a good few hours before I get to Bletchy Scrubb."

Their dad started nodding. "Agreed. Seb, you can pay for the bus back to Granma's house out of that money I gave you yesterday."

Ivy's heart lifted. "So you're coming back? Both of you?"

Her mum swept a hand across her forehead. "Of course we are. You've done a great job so far, but don't worry. We'll sort everything out when we get there."

"I might not arrive till late this evening, but I'll be there," Ivy's dad said. "You'll be OK, won't you? Make sure you have something to eat—look after each other." He paused and lowered his voice. "Or at least *try* to."